praise for psychics of oracle bay

Not in the Cards

An Exciting Introduction: Amy's books immediately go to the top of my queue when they are released and they never disappoint. This was an exciting introduction to Oracle Bay and I'm looking forward to getting to know the rest of the inhabitants in future books.

Found Another Great Author! I didn't know what to expect when I went into this book. The premise of the book sounded like something I would enjoy. At first, as I started reading the book, I wasn't sure I was going to like it. However, after a few pages, I was drawn into the book and it never let me go. In fact, by the end of the book, I was so ready to find out what was going to happen next from all the hints that were given, I wanted the next book right then. This book was well-written, had a great plot (both romance and intrigue), and I loved the characters, even the villain who I loved to hate. Can't wait to read more and I highly recommend!

Fantastic: A well written story with great characters and the location of Oracle Bay was inspired. The heroine in this story is a tribute to enduring heartache and finding a new life and love.

First Hand Knowledge

The author does a bang up job of making this mythical place not only enchanting, but a place I'd want to go. To live, even if I were the only mundane in the lot. She also expands characters from her previous book 'Not in the Cards' and keeps the story arc alive and moving forward. There's something to be said for a series that continues with the lives of all the characters, even when the focus is on only two at a time.

Wing and a Prayer

I have this terrible problem with Amy Cissell's books. I get hooked within the first few sentences, and want to read the whole thing in one sitting. They're addictive, fun, clever stories about people you wish you knew.

* * * * * ★ ★ ★ ★ ★ * * * *

Belle of the Ball

This is the third book in the series, and I think this series is getting better each book. I love how silly, fun, and interesting this book is. Drew and Bill's romance was great, touching, and romantic. And, the mystery was great, too. Add to that, there were some revelations that were hilarious. There was a also point at the very end of the book that made me laugh out loud because when Drew couldn't see Bill, I thought he'd been turned into a toad. What really happened and why? You'll have to read this and find out. If you love a fun, cozy, romantic mystery, give this book and series a try; you'll love it! Highly recommend! I was provided a copy which I voluntarily reviewed.

Hell and High Water

I throughly enjoyed this book. It touches on so many possibilities of paranormal people. It has a good lead in, full rich characters with quirks and an unexpected ending.

Tempest in a Teapot

The ending got me! I have really enjoyed this series, and I was so darn excited to see another one in the series.I was extremely happy with this book as I couldn't figure out who the villain was. I had ideas, but the author was skillful at red herrings. Then the end hit...I was so darn angry! LOL! Highly recommend.

There are curses and bonds, mystery and mild romance, friends and family-both related and found. I do love Oracle Bay. I'm excited for the next story for Morgana

Psychics of Oracle Bay

Not in the Cards
First Hand Knowledge
Wing and a Prayer
Belle of the Ball
Hell and High Water
Tempest in a Teapot
Elements of Surprise
Dead Giveaway*
Bad to the Bones*
Shoot for the Stars*
Fun and Prophet*

Box Sets (ebook only)
Seeing is Believing in Oracle Bay (Books 1-4)

* forthcoming

elements of surprise

PSYCHICS OF ORACLE BAY
BOOK 7

AMY CISSELL

BROKEN
WORLD
PUBLISHING

ELEMENTS OF SURPRISE
Amy Cissell

A Broken World Publication
13820 NE Airport Way, Suite K395495
Portland, OR 97251-1158

Elements of Surprise
All Rights Reserved
Copyright © 2023 by Amy Cissell
ISBN 978-1-949410-89-1 (ebook);
ISBN 978-1-949410-90-7 (paperback)

Cover Design: Cissell Ink
Edited by: Suzanne Lahna & Christopher Barnes

This is a work of fiction. Names, characters, businesses, places, events, and incidents are either the products of the author's imagination or used in a fictitious manner. Any resemblance to actual persons, living or dead, or actual events is purely coincidental.

Portugal
You are the best I've ever had.
I can't wait for us to ditch this long-distance thing and get back together.
Forever.
xoxo

one

Morgana stared into the red wine and swirled her glass absentmindedly. The Pour House was crowded—tourist season was in full-swing—and it was strange to see so many people completely oblivious to not only the murders last month, but the events of the last few years.

Oracle Bay worked hard to protect itself, and part of that protection was encouraging people to forget what they couldn't understand. Even those mundane humans who were aware of the magic that permeated the town were hazy when it came to the details.

Morgana looked around the bar again, took a deep breath, then let it out slowly. She wasn't quite relaxed, but she was closer than she'd been in over a year. The last few months had been terrible—mentally, physically, and magically. She wasn't even going to think about the emotional wounds left by walking away from the first man she could have loved since her first lifetime.

The three days and nights in her sanctuary healed much of the damage that'd been done to her body and the garden that housed her magical repository, and three weeks resting and meditating started the journey towards healing her mind and soul, although that was another wound that would leave a jagged scar.

She'd been too late to save Violet and Joanna and the twenty-two women that'd been victims of the power-mad witch, and those deaths would always hang on the guilt scales in her mind. But they'd stopped the dark witch, Bridget had been remanded into custody, and no one else would die by her hand.

She pulled herself out of the regret and guilt that would take over if she let it and turned her attention to the spectacular show, visible through the wall of glass leading out to the expansive deck, captivating most of the bar's patrons. Vivid orange and red lit up the horizon as the sun slowly disappeared into the Pacific Ocean. It was just past nine p.m., and the light would linger another hour. The solstice was in four days, and it would present another boost of power, allowing Morgana to further heal her sanctuary and replace what she'd lost. Her power wasn't completely replenished, and it wouldn't be until Bridget was forced to release what she'd stolen—something that should happen any day now—but she was strong enough to stand against almost any magical attack.

It was comforting to be in company of the people she considered friends. Most had gone home, but Andy, Ceri, and Misty sat across from her, while Paska was at her side.

Morgana would never admit it, but she considered Andy to be almost as close a friend as she'd ever had. Part of it was the deep understanding of power he shared with her, as well as the weight of age that weighed on a person's mind. Her experience was minuscule compared to a nearly ageless, immortal fallen angel who'd recently risen from hell to take his place among mortals, but something about the attack she'd suffered, that the town had suffered, narrowed the gap between their cantankerous sniping and friendly teasing.

As if he sensed her thoughts, he turned towards her with silver eyebrows raised quizzically above his stormy grey eyes.

Morgana sighed deeply, shook her head, and mouthed, "Demon."

"Penny for your thoughts, witch," Andy said, his voice holding none of the mockery that usually accompanied it when he spoke to her.

"My thoughts are worth significantly more than that, demon," she replied. "I'm not sure you could afford them."

Andy shoved his hands into the pockets of his jeans and pulled out a crumpled five-dollar bill. He waved it at her face. "I'm willing to offer a bit more."

Morgana rolled her eyes, and the others at the table laughed along with Andy. She leaned back and watched Ceri and Misty tease Paska while Andy watched with a peaceful smile. For a moment, the world felt in balance.

There were still secrets separating her from true camaraderie, though. No one in Oracle Bay knew the truth about her connection to Paska, other than they'd known each other for a very long time and were older than they looked. Morgana looked like she was in her late thirties, and now that she'd been able to drop her suburban house-wife disguise, she was back to her long black hair and the pale skin that perfectly matched her Morticia Addams goth vibe. Today she was in leather pants, a tight wrap-around sweater, and lace-up leather boots—all black, of course.

Paska appeared to be in his early forties. He kept the build he'd had for more than a thousand years, toned without being muscle-bound, and had tanned white skin, salt and pepper hair, and eyes so dark there was no definition between the pupil and iris.

They looked nothing alike. They had once, but sixteen hundred years leaves marks on a person, even if they're not immediately apparent. But now, no one would ever guess they were related, much less siblings. And it needed to stay that way, although the reasons for that seemed less and less clear the closer she grew to this small community of psychics in Oracle Bay.

Morgana's cellphone beeped to announce a text message, and she pulled it out of her pocket. Paska straightened from his regularly affected indolent pose and stared at her.

She had a text from Donovan, and she tensed. There was only one sentence.

Bridget has escaped.

Morgana looked up from her phone.

Paska went from his public persona of an indolent, perpetually tipsy man to alert. For a moment, power thrummed through him, and the table vibrated. "What is it? What's happened?" He grabbed Morgana's cell phone, cursed loudly and creatively, then shoved Morgana's phone back to her.

Fear swirled through her body, and the edges of her vision greyed as she pushed back the panic threatening to rise. She was stronger than this, stronger than Bridget. She took a beat to form a reply to Donovan. *When? Do you know where she's going? Are you safe?*

Andy leaned forward. "I'm sure Paska will share with us eventually, but I've heard him swear before, and it will be awhile before he runs out of anatomically impossible, illegal, and highly unethical suggestions. What's going on?"

Morgana licked her lips and willed her heart to resume its normal pace. "I just received a text from Donovan. Bridget escaped the Scales." She held up her hand to forestall any questions. "I know nothing else. That was all the text said. As soon as I learn more, I will share with you."

"Will she come back here?" Misty asked, speaking over Paska's muttered curses. Her voice was an octave higher than her usual pitch, and her fingers drummed an irregular rhythm on the table. "If so, we need to be better prepared than we were last time."

"At least we'll know who it is," Ceri said. Her pale complexion could give Morgana's a run for its money, but where Morgana was dark-haired and eyed, Ceri was fair. She had strawberry blonde hair that gently curled around her slightly pointed ears, clear blue eyes, and a smattering of freckles across her elfin nose. She showed few signs of the near-death experience she'd had just months before. In fact, she was practically glowing with health. Ceri was the picture of summer innocence and looked nothing like a powerful seer who held the key to infinity in her mind.

"That will help," Morgana agreed. "We need to find out when this happened, see if there's a trail, and bring in everyone we can to defend Oracle Bay. I know it's not guaranteed that she'll return here —it would be monumentally stupid to do so since this is where she was defeated, *and* we'll obviously be expecting her—but I think the stolen power is rapidly destroying her mind."

Paska's curses had wound down. "You're not wrong about that. She was never meant to hold that much power—few people could, and even those with the ability and capacity would be hard-pressed to stay sane."

"You probably know that better than any of us," Morgana said sweetly. It was an old joke between them, although lately, Morgana had wondered if there was more truth than jest in it.

"Indeed, I would," Paska said. A dark thread was laced through his words, but the smile he turned on the rest of the table was cheerful. "We are the five most powerful beings in this town, and now we know the full breadth of the evil that rides that witch's soul. There is little doubt that she will be unable to gain a toehold in this town again if we can work together to keep it safe. We won't do anything rash, though." He glared at Morgana. "We *do* know who she is, and we can plan accordingly."

Ceri worried at her lower lip and stared at the beer in the glass in front of her without taking a drink. "I cannot tap most of the power I hold, so I'm not sure I deserve a seat at this table."

"Nonsense," Paska said. "You are at this table because even without what lies behind the curtain in your mind, you have centuries of experience and the ability to see into the future better than anyone else not at this table. And unless we're in danger of imminent apocalypse, there is no reason for you to reach for the power concealed in your mind, anyway. What's hidden away protects itself from people like Bridget, and it will protect you in case your angel isn't there to do it himself."

Andy growled lightly, and a tendril of smoke floated above him.

"No insult meant, Andras," Paska said. "But even you must admit that you cannot keep her glued to your side every minute of every day."

"Mostly because I'd kill you if you tried," Ceri muttered. "You might be a powerful immortal demon, but I have the key to everything in here"—she tapped her temple—"and I'm pretty sure that includes several ways to imprison and murder one's fallen angel boyfriend."

Andy smiled at her and wrapped an arm around her, pulling her close.

A pang of jealousy shot through Morgana, and she squashed it down immediately. She was not jealous of what they had. She'd always known that wasn't in the cards for her, and she wasn't about to get angry about it now, no matter how much the events of the past few weeks had driven home how truly alone she was.

Morgana's phone beeped again, and silence dropped over the table as they waited for her to read the message.

I'm ok. 7 dead. 10 more injured. 3-4 hrs. ago. No idea where she's going. Don't assume you're safe. I'll be there as soon as I get out of the hospital.

Morgana read the text while she typed her reply. *What is happening on the ground? What is the Scales doing to find her?*

The reply was instantaneous. *I don't know. I'm under guard, and no one is talking. I'll let you know as soon as I do. Drugs kicking in. I'll be asleep soon. Love you.*

"Let me see," Paska demanded, holding out his hand.

"No!" Morgana clenched the phone to her chest and took a deep breath, then read all but the last two words of the message.

"Where are they? Where'd she escape from?" Misty asked.

"London," Morgana said, not taking her eyes off the screen. "The Scales is headquartered there, and that's where they have their secure prison."

Misty was on her phone, pulling up a flight app. "The earliest she could be here is…" There was a long pause while Misty sorted various flights, made mental adjustments for time changes, and added in driving time. "Four hours ago was five o'clock here, so one tomorrow morning in the UK." Misty looked up, her green eyes wide with fear. "She could be on a flight by noon, in Seattle by three, and here by six tomorrow night."

"Okay," Morgana said more decisively than she felt. "We have twenty-one hours to prepare. That's better than none. At least there were survivors"—*at least Donovan survived*—"who could warn us. Let's come up with a plan tonight, then call everyone in tomorrow morning to go over it."

"I don't think we should have that conversation here," Ceri said with an apologetic look at Andy. "I know this bar is secure, but it's still a public house. I don't want to risk anyone overhearing us."

Paska nodded. "That is an excellent point. We will contact the others and gather at my home."

Morgana wasn't the only one staring at Paska in shock. In all the years they'd lived in Oracle Bay, he'd invited no one into his home except her. Ceri exchanged a look with Andy that Morgana couldn't read, but she saw the scryer's shoulders journey up towards her ears.

Misty was wide-eyed. The drumming on the table increased in tempo and erraticism. "Um, okay, that sounds perfect." Her voice radiated uncertainty threaded with fear. "Let's get some sleep tonight and do the group thing at Paska's in the morning."

It was a sign of the tension he held that Paska did not make an off-color joke at Misty's suggestion.

"I'll let Hazel and Brandy know they're closing tonight and meet you there," Andy said. He stood, dropped a kiss on Ceri's upturned lips, and strode out of the alcove.

Morgana let the others file out ahead of her, then turned her phone back over and quickly typed. *Glad you're okay. Please be careful. See you soon.*

Paska stopped near the door and turned around to stare at her, and she saw something she hadn't seen in over sixteen hundred years. Her brother was afraid.

two

Paska's living room was surprisingly clean. Last time Morgana had spent any time in his home that wasn't a quick visit in the kitchen, the room had been cluttered. Every surface had been nearly invisible under stacks of books and implements—some of which were magical, some modern and mundane, and all incomprehensible and often disturbing. His walls had been papered with maps of varying size, type, and age, from city maps of every major and several minor—including Oracle Bay—cities, what looked like original world maps dating back a thousand years, and some hand-drawn maps that looked like they'd been created by a particularly unskilled preschooler.

But now, every surface was not only bare, but aggressively clean. There wasn't a mote of dust in the air, the antique wooden furniture she hadn't known he owned practically glowed, and the scattering of chairs and loveseats looked like they'd never been sat on before. They may never have been sat on by anything but books, the odd and upsetting talking owl-like toys he'd been obsessed with a couple decades ago, and a map of Hecla, South Dakota.

"Is it up to your standards?" Paska growled from the doorway. He placed a tray of wine glasses on the sideboard next to three sweating ice buckets and an empty silver tray.

"I've never seen this room so habitable," Morgana replied. "There are places to sit. It's nice, but a little alarming. Have you finally gone mad? Are you ill?"

Paska walked out of the room without answering and returned with three bottles of sparkling wine and a large carafe of orange juice.

"It's nine o'clock in the morning," Morgana said, looking askance at the wine. "I'm not sure anyone will be drinking."

"They might not want a mimosa when they walk in, but we will run out of the sparkling wine by the end of the meeting," Paska said. He opened a door in the sideboard and removed a bottle of Midleton Dair Ghaelach Single Pot Still Irish whiskey and Glenfiddich 30-year-old Scotch and framed them with three rocks glasses.

Morgana shook her head and walked to the front door. "If you don't provide some food with your booze, the young ones will end up intoxicated."

Paska scoffed. "I know how to host a gathering."

Morgana pulled open the door before Drew could knock and ushered him, Ceri, and Sandy into the house.

"The demon stay behind?" Morgana asked.

Andy stomped up the front steps. "The demon wouldn't miss a chance to spend time with the witch," he said.

Morgana smiled at him. As long as they continued their long-standing insult exchange, she would not worry. It was an odd bar to set, but it reassured her, nonetheless.

"Paska, did you cook?" Ceri asked.

Morgana turned around and gaped. While she'd been answering the door, Paska had brought out cinnamon rolls, breakfast sandwiches, and a large basket of muffins.

"I can cook," Paska grumbled. "I just choose not to. I don't want people clamoring for my food once they realize they'll never have better."

Ceri picked up a cinnamon roll and shoved half of it into her mouth. While she chewed, a look of ecstasy dipped over her face.

"Hey, you're not supposed to look like that for anything besides me," Andy grumbled. "Especially not food from another man."

"You have to try this. I thought he was exaggerating, but this is amazing." Ceri picked up another cinnamon roll and handed it to Andy.

He took a bite, and his eyes rolled back into his head. "This is divine."

"Ha. Angel. Divine." Drew pulled one roll in half and took a small bite. "Okay, if you don't want me to tell Bill that he should hire you to help him bake, you're going to owe me big time."

Paska smiled enigmatically. "Bill would not enjoy me as an employee, and I would be delighted to work for him for a short time to prove it."

Car doors slammed, and Morgana walked to the door. Russell and Misty were getting out of her blue Miata convertible, and Jezebel was climbing out of a red Jaguar. Before Morgana could close the door behind them, Ezekiel rode up on a single-gear bicycle. He leaned it carefully against the house and walked up the stairs.

Morgana barely moved out of the way before Ezekiel strode by. Not much surprised Morgana, but Zeke's presence at this meeting did it. He was always invited, but seldom even responded to the invitations.

"Ezekiel. Thank you for coming," Paska said, striding forward and offering his hand to the prophet.

After looking down at Paska's hand for a moment with a furrowed brow, Zeke took it. "This fulfills my debt to you."

Paska laughed and shook his head. "A meeting? No. You owe me much more than your presence, but it's a start. Before the year is out, your debt will be paid in full."

Zeke smiled, and there was a hardness in his eyes Morgana had never seen. "Favors repaid can take many forms, and not all of them benefit the grantor."

Paska pulled Zeke in, slapped him amicably on the back, then let him go. "We'll see, prophet. Already, the wheel turns, and I think you're going to find your faith upside down before the end of June."

Zeke grunted and pulled his hand back. "I am not here to discuss theology with a Godless pagan."

"Godless?" Paska raised an eyebrow, sardonic amusement dancing across his face. "After everything you've seen, you should know better."

"Tell me where your gods were when they were called on to avert the apocalypse, and I'll revise my statement," Zeke countered.

Morgana stepped between the men. "No one is here to discuss theology, nor is it the time to question each other's gods and how and when they respond to requests. If you wish, we can compare notes some other time."

Zeke nodded stiffly and let Morgana draw him into the room.

"Drink?" Paska asked amiably, as if their exchange had been nothing but friendly.

Zeke's lip curled when he regarded the extensive collection of alcohol on the sideboard. "Coffee."

Ceri handed him a cup a second later. "Help yourself to food," she said. She grabbed a glass of orange juice and a second cinnamon roll, then curled up on a loveseat, setting her breakfast on the end table next to her.

Once everyone had selected their breakfast—no one touched the booze except Paska, who poured a generous glug of whiskey into his coffee—Morgana walked to the center of the room and turned, catching the eye of each of the seers.

"Did anyone invite Hazel?" Sandy asked. "She's one of us now, isn't she?"

Morgana closed her eyes and nodded. "She is, but I didn't think to extend an invitation." It was the exclusion of a magical resident of Oracle Bay that'd led directly to Joanna's death, a fault she'd sworn never to repeat. Yet here she was, only weeks later, making the same mistake.

"I invited her," Ceri said. "It was because of me Joanna was left out of our meetings. I'm responsible for her death, and I have a lot to atone for."

A smile ghosted across Morgana's face. She'd seldom met anyone in her fifteen hundred years who had the same combination of taking responsibility for everyone and grabbing all the guilt and self-recrimination for even the most minor infractions. She knew why Paska was drawn to the elfin redhead. He hadn't been joking, nor had he been trying to tweak Morgana—not much, anyway—by referring to Ceri as a sibling he'd never had.

"It's no one's fault," Misty said briskly. "Or else it's all of our faults. Ceri, did Hazel say she was coming?"

"She's working a couple mornings a week for Bill now and opened Caffiend Dreams this morning. She had to wait for the next barista to come on shift before she could come over." Ceri looked at her watch. "She should be here in about twenty minutes."

"She could've just asked Bill for the time off. He gets the need to respond to psychic emergencies, and he knows where I am this morning, even if I was a little sketchy on the why." Drew looked at Morgana, curiosity and concern creasing his brow.

Morgana sighed. "Misty, Ceri, Andy, and Paska were with me last night when I received a text message from Donovan."

Paska made a noise of disgust, drawing the rest of the psychics' eyes to him.

"You do not have to like the man, but you cannot deny the news he delivered concerns Oracle Bay and is more than enough to cause great distress to everyone here." Morgana fixed Paska with a stern look.

After a moment, he nodded and twirled his finger to indicate she should continue.

"Bridget escaped from the Scales prison in London yesterday. She killed seven and injured several others. Donovan is in the hospital, and no one knows where the blood witch is. Misty calculated that it was possible Bridget could be in Oracle Bay as early as six o'clock this evening, provided she was able to obtain a passport and catch the earliest flight to Seattle." Morgana looked down at her hands. They were clasped. She took a breath and unlaced them. It was a sign of distress, and she would not show her anxiety and fear to anyone, not even these people she considered friends.

"Why didn't you let us know last night?" Jezebel demanded. "I know you don't think I'd be a target because I don't have the same power levels as Hazel or Misty—or you—but have you really looked at me or Sandy recently? Things change, Morgana, and it's arrogant to believe you have all the answers."

It felt like she'd been struck by Jezebel's words. She hadn't looked at anyone recently. She'd tested them when they came to town to see if they were the real thing and had a place in this group, but that was the last time she'd concerned herself with any of the psychics' power levels. Donovan had looked at everyone but must have assumed she already knew how strong her friends were. "You're right, Jezebel. I was remiss, especially since I knew there was a blood witch looking for powerful women. If you don't mind, I would like to look now."

Jezebel nodded tightly. "After the big magic we did together to find the answers to Ceri's problem, you should've known better."

Morgana walked forward and placed her hand on Jezebel's shoulder. She could see the future, but she didn't have the ability to sense power the way Donovan did, and she needed physical contact unless the subject was in the process of wielding magic. Plus, an astrologer didn't wield power the same way a witch did.

She closed her eyes. It always took a minute to find where power was housed when it wasn't the same kind as hers.

Morgana's eyes flew open in less than a second. Jezebel's power wasn't hidden. It swirled through her entire being like a ribbon, twisting around, breaking apart like quicksilver, then finding itself again. How she'd never seen this before, she didn't know. She really had been negligent in the last year. "How? When?" She was at a loss for words, something that seldom happened. Today was a day for humbling surprises, apparently.

Jezebel smiled smugly. "Do you remember when I left town to 'find myself' and came back with the weird oracles who wanted to be called Pythia and Trophonius? I told you then, they'd taught me how to move past my ability to read a person's future with astrological charts, but to read the heavens? That requires more power than simple astrology."

Sandy walked forward and touched Morgana's arm. "You'll want to look at me, too. Whatever we did to help Ceri changed things for me."

Morgana touched Sandy's shoulder. Her power didn't hit Morgana as hard as Jezebel's had, but there was more than when the tarot card reader had arrived in Oracle Bay. She'd had enough genuine magic then to see into a person's soul and interpret the cards in a way that was always accurate, but nothing beyond that.

She dropped her hand; Sandy walked back to her chair.

"Why didn't you tell me?" Morgana asked. "This would have been excellent information to share, especially when we knew a blood witch was hunting Oracle Bay."

Jez shrugged. "I can't speak for Sandy, but I assumed you knew. You were linked to us when we combined our abilities last year. You said neither of us were in danger when Bridget showed up. I thought you knew what you were talking about. How was I to know you didn't? You give off an aura of being an all-seeing old woman. Forgive me if I took you at face value."

Old. Morgana did not like that word at all, no matter how true it might be. She pursed her lips and did not respond to Jezebel's jab.

Jez grinned, the tip of her tongue sticking out between her teeth. The woman was mocking her. It was well-deserved, but still it stung.

"Jez pretty much covered it," Sandy said. "What she didn't say, and maybe this isn't happening to her, is that when I'm doing a reading and sense my client needs more than insight, if I open myself fully to my abilities, it's way more than it was before, and it's not all coming from me."

Morgana had not been expecting this. "Are you drawing on the bonds we created when we tied ourselves together to find a way to keep hell from erupting in Oracle Bay? Are you pulling on the collective powers of everyone in this room?"

Sandy shook her head. "No. At least I don't think so. It's more like the town is giving me what I need. Never too much, although I kinda think it would give me more if I asked."

The bottom dropped out of Morgana's stomach. She'd known since meeting Misty that her powers were augmented by her family history and their tie to Oracle Bay the town but hadn't considered that would channel its vast power through anyone else.

"Do the rest of you feel this, too?" she asked, spinning in a slow circle.

Drew nodded slowly. "I hadn't put it all together, but yeah. There's a little bit more there when I need a little bit more. We can all tell when someone needs more than what we see for most people, and it's not only easier to do it now, it's better. Or maybe not better, but deeper?"

Sandy and Jezebel nodded.

"Yes, that's exactly it," Sandy said.

Misty shook her head. "I haven't noticed any changes, but I guess I wouldn't, would I? After all, the town has been augmenting my powers forever."

"What about the rest of you?" Morgana asked, looking between Ceri and Paska.

Paska shrugged. "Nothing for me."

"Me, neither," Ceri said. "But I don't take many clients anymore, and when I do, most of my energy is spent trying to keep the universe from flooding my mind and giving me information I don't need."

"I don't talk to the dead often enough to have noticed a difference," Russell said. "But when I was in Eden Valley last fall, it was easier to stop the zombies than I thought it would be. I chalked it up to the work I'd done with Aunt Sybil. I mean, you never know what's going to happen to you after spending time with her."

"Hashtag truth," Misty muttered. "That woman is a menace to society."

Russell leaned over and bumped his cousin with his shoulder. "If you ask her, we are blessed to not only be related to her, but to have the opportunity for her to impart her 'great wisdom' to us."

"And you, Ezekiel?" Morgana asked.

"Why would you ask me?" Zeke replied stiffly. "I was not present at your great working last spring, nor do I serve as Her prophet anymore. Even if She had something to impart, it is unlikely it would be of any interest to those in this town besides Andras. The powers of those in this room have as little in common with my God-given ability as the mountains have in common with the sea."

"Yet you are here now," Morgana said. "Why?"

Zeke didn't answer, just leaned back in the chair and took a drink of his coffee.

Before Morgana could question anyone further, a car door slammed outside. Hazel was here, and now they could get started.

three

Morgana sat in the recliner she'd claimed. She'd imparted what little she knew again and fielded too many questions for which she was forced to admit she didn't have answers.

"Can I make a suggestion?" Sandy asked hesitantly.

"Of course. Suggestions are why I brought you all together," Morgana said.

Sandy straightened her shoulders. "When we came together last year, we were not only more powerful, we were able to find the answers we needed. We're stronger together. I mean, I know you and Paska and Ceri are already super powerful and old—"

"Hey," Drew muttered. "I'm old and powerful, too."

Sandy graced him with a grin. "And Drew, of course. But there's a reason we needed to work as a team then, and it'd probably be good to do it again, right?"

Morgana was shaking her head before Sandy finished speaking. She couldn't risk the others—too many people had already died because of her, and she wouldn't put anyone else in danger. "That was a unique situation when the danger was from one of us. Oracle

Bay recognized Ceri as under its protection and knew that failure would destroy the town as well as Misty, who likely would have died if the source of her power was eliminated."

"Thanks for the heads up," Misty said.

Paska shrugged. "Would it have helped for you to know? Or would that knowledge have made things harder?"

Misty grimaced. "Fine, but you still should've told me."

"You're not incorrect. There are too many secrets in this town, and we keep too much from each other." Morgana shot a look at Sandy, then Jezebel.

Jez rolled her eyes. "You're one to talk. Trust me, when this is over, there will be more than one conversation about 'keeping secrets for the good of the order' and all that shit."

Sandy leaned forward in her chair and fixed Morgana with a stern glare, an expression Morgana had never seen on the young woman's face before. "Maybe this time *is* different because Oracle Bay isn't in danger of being sucked into hell, but aren't we all in danger? You were the one who was attacked last time, and you're just as much a part of this town as the rest of us."

Morgana tipped her head back and looked at the ceiling. She didn't want to dismiss Sandy's words without considering them, even though her first instinct was that combining their powers the way they had to help Ceri was not only a terrible idea, but wouldn't work. Finally, she turned her attention back to Sandy. "It is not a terrible idea," she said, then held up a hand when Sandy opened her mouth. "However, I do not believe it is the answer for this situation."

Sandy's lips made a tight line, and she headed to the drinks table to pour herself a mimosa.

"I suppose you have a reason?" Paska asked. He stood and refilled his coffee cup, although the ratio of coffee to whiskey reversed. "One more compelling than 'I'm a lone wolf, and I don't have a partner'?"

She ignored his second statement and focused on the first. She was perfectly capable of working with others. "If Bridget was able to escape the Scales' prison, which is warded against blood magic and guarded by powerful warlocks who are not easy targets, she likely figured out how to counter and absorb their power. This is not only unprecedented, it is nearly impossible. Warlocks are usually male, and their magic works differently than a witch's. Witches work with the elements, drawing our power from earth, air, fire, and water." Morgana took a breath. She wasn't used to explaining the way her magic worked, and it felt wrong to do so now. She'd adapted her language over the years to mirror common beliefs about the ways it worked, but sometimes it was still difficult to translate the magic she'd known for sixteen hundred years into popular culture terms.

"And spirit, to relate it to modern beliefs about witchcraft and magic," Paska added. "Most witches are strongly aligned with one element and can only pull power from the others with great effort, if at all. However, spirit, energy, the music of the spheres, or the force —whatever you want to call it—is what gives them the ability to draw the magic into themselves and store it."

"Can anyone draw on more than one?" Hazel asked, speaking for the first time since accepting a mimosa that was only about a quarter orange juice from Paska.

"Yes." Morgana hesitated, then added, carefully not looking at her brother, "I can. Earth and water are the ones with which I'm most strongly aligned. I can use air and fire, but it is easier if they are fed to me by someone who controls them naturally."

A pensive expression appeared on Hazel's face, but she didn't say anything. Morgana had obviously missed something else in this town. She would follow up with the young witch when this meeting ended, and a plan was developed.

"Witches are not always women—although in more modern times, the power, which is often inherited through generations, is harnessed better in women who are socialized to have a closer rela-tionship with their emotions and the natural world than men. Warlocks' power comes from blood and sacrifice, although many have some innate ability, just not enough to use effectively. That doesn't mean they are evil. It just means that they always need words and blood to use the power they build. They can, and most do, use a drop or two of their own blood. For larger spells, they may rely on the willing donation of the blood of another warlock. Anyone can learn to be a warlock, but for reasons unknown to me, most of their number are male."

Paska leaned forward. "They're male, and usually cisgender male, because that's who the more experienced warlocks look for as apprentices."

Morgana nodded, filing away that piece of information, and continued, "Most witches can't see a warlock's power, much less counter it. If Bridget was able to push past their defenses and drain their power—and since she killed several, that is likely what happened, considering they are all trained fighters, both magically and physically—then she has access to even more magic than she did when she was here before." Morgana held up a single finger, even though no one had opened their mouth to offer a retort. "She did nearly drain me before, which would have been disastrous, but she had an accomplice, unwilling as he was, who allowed her access to my garden where I have connected to earth and water to boost and store power against future needs. She will not take me by surprise again, nor will she be able to access my sanctuary or my power." Morgana didn't add that it was partially because she hadn't returned to full strength and hadn't yet been able to heal the earth in her garden, nor replenish the magic in the water.

"She's afraid of water," Hazel said. "Or fish, at least. That's how Morgana beat her before. She made a hurricane and sent the death beads back at her. Oracle Bay has a lot of water here. It made her uncomfortable. She complained about it a lot. A lot a lot."

"I still think working together would be better than letting her attack us individually," Sandy said stubbornly as she poured herself another drink.

"There is one more consideration," Morgana said. She hadn't wanted to make this argument, but Sandy's refusal to back down meant she had to deliver a harsh truth. "Bridget will be more powerful than last time she was here, and she will have access to magic none of us can counter, and most of us cannot even sense. She was already mad when she was here last time, and this influx of unfamiliar power will push her further into insanity. If we are joined, as we were when we joined to discover the best way to avert the destruction of this town, Bridget might be able to burn through the link, extinguishing each of our powers in turn before grabbing hold of the source of Oracle Bay's magic."

"Wouldn't that mean the town was in danger and would protect us to save itself?" Misty asked.

"It might not realize until it was too late," Morgana countered. "I won't risk any of you on that slim hope."

Sandy crossed her arms but didn't argue.

Drew leaned forward—he, too, had exchanged his coffee for an alcoholic beverage. "Then we have a backup plan. Or we make this the backup plan."

Paska opened three more bottles of sparkling wine in quick succession, interrupting Morgana's counterargument. Everyone in the room, with the exception of Zeke and Andy, jumped, then laughed nervously as Paska made the rounds, sans juice, refilling glasses.

Misty accepted Paska's offer, then propped her elbows on her denim-clad knees, folded her hands and rested her chin on them. "I'm not sure you get to make that decision for all of us. You can refuse, of course. But you can't stop the rest of us from pooling our powers in defense of this town and everyone in it."

Morgana took a deep breath. Arguing would do little good. Misty was correct that she had little control over what the rest of the seers chose to do. After ensuring that she would be able to speak with quiet calm, she said, "Of course you are free to do anything you'd like. I advise against it, though. I would not like to see any of you hurt, drained of power, or slain. I would prefer to come up with a different plan and welcome any suggestions."

"Do you though?" Jezebel asked. "Because you shot down

Sandy's suggestion, which was pretty good. My guess is you welcome any suggestions because you're trying to look like a team player, but in the end, you'll do your own thing, probably get yourself killed, and then leave the rest of us to fight Bridget on our own. Doesn't seem very responsible of you."

Zeke stood and pointed at Morgana. "You're an idiot and likely to get yourselves and me killed. There are more important things happening right now than one stupid witch on a killing spree. Hire a sniper and take her out the minute you see her."

"Why don't you ask your god to smite her?" Russell asked. "That'd be a lot less likely to attract notice than a lone gunman."

"Gunwoman," Jezebel muttered.

Drew nodded in her direction but didn't take his eyes off Zeke.

The look Zeke leveled at the necromancer was contemptuous. "Even if that was still a possibility, I would not ask Her to interfere with the petty problems of a bunch of heathens." He stalked out of the room and slammed the door.

"Why not just hire a hitman? Hitperson," Drew asked.

"We could do that," Morgana admitted. "And as a backup plan, it wouldn't be the worst idea. I'm sure Paska knows how to do something like that without attracting notice."

Paska bowed slightly in her direction.

"Last time she and I fought, she wasn't warded against physical attack. I prefer to address magical crime with magic—it's easier to escape notice from the authorities and not have loose ends that might demand explanations. And there is also this." Morgana held up a single finger. "If she has warded herself against physical attack, as she should have done after our last encounter, any such attack could rebound on the attacker. It's another life risked." Anger rose in Morgana's chest, and she pushed it down. She did not want to lose her temper. Control was necessary if she was going to convince the others she was correct, and that would be easier than walking out of this room in disagreement. "I welcome any suggestions, but do not feel the need to accept them if they would leave you vulnerable."

Paska leaned over and grabbed the bottle of whiskey, no longer even creating the illusion that he was drinking Irish coffee. "Why don't you tell us what you're going to do, Morgana. Don't keep us guessing and searching for answers you don't want."

Morgana lost a little of the control she prided herself on. "Don't you have anything to offer, old man?"

Paska held up the bottle. "You know me. I'm just here to drink the booze I found in Andy's cupboards and offer sarcastic retorts. You're the brains of this operation."

Morgana smiled tightly. She would not let him goad her. Those days were long gone. She turned her focus away from her brother. "I do have a suggestion, and it involves working together, although not in the way Sandy suggested. Bridget was unable to get past my shields without help, and only then because she'd claimed a human as a familiar. I do not have the power to put up a similar shield around the magical inhabitants of this town, but with my knowledge and all of your assistance, particularly Misty's, we can protect ourselves."

There was silence as the other psychics contemplated her words. Russell was the first to speak. "It's not a bad idea, but what about those who aren't magical? She could target anyone, right?"

"She killed Rowan," Hazel said. "She doesn't just go after power."

"She killed Rowan accidentally," Morgana said. "She was trying to kill you."

Hazel pursed her lips. Her expression of grief and anger preceded her next sentence. "Accident or not, it happened. And if she's as crazy as you claim, what's stopping her from mowing down the regular humans in this town on her way to us?"

It was a good question, and one Morgana didn't have a ready answer for. "I don't know," she replied. "I can't lie to you and say it isn't likely to happen; she is unpredictable. As far as we know, she hasn't deliberately killed anyone who didn't have power to steal, but we all know she will go to great lengths to get what she wants. I can teach you all to shield yourself against her, but I can't extend that out over the town. Some of you might have the ability to pull others within your shields, but that will require close proximity. Misty will be able to shield Joseph if they're in the same room, but I doubt it would work if they were apart."

"And what? That's the only solution you can offer? Teach us a defense that won't keep the ones we love safe?" Russell asked. "Working together, taking the offense, that's what we need to do if we're to get her out of town and take her down altogether. No more prisons or trials."

"You would kill her in cold blood?" Morgana asked. She didn't disagree. Bridget had crossed so many lines, it was impossible to believe she could be rehabilitated. But she'd found that younger people were much less likely to take the necessary steps to stop great evil. There were benefits to trials before judgment, and Morgana was not in favor of the death penalty for mundane crimes, no matter how egregious. But magical crimes were something different altogether.

Russell met her eyes. "Death is not so very different from life."

"You would know, necromancer," Morgana said with a smile. If anyone under the age of sixty was going to advocate for execution without trial, it would be the one who was just as at home with the dead as the living.

"It would have to be more than death. Even as a ghost, with that much power and crazy rattling around in her, she could be dangerous. We'd have to destroy her." Russell's words had a finality to them that was impressive.

"Can you do that?" Hazel asked.

"That's what happened to Felicity," Ceri said. When Hazel raised her eyebrows, she added, "She was the witch who stabbed me in the Pour House. I had a bunch of ghosts following me around, so Russell shoved them all into Felicity. She exploded, and her soul was fragmented. The ghosts were okay, though. That helped them move on to wherever ghosts go next."

Hazel nodded silently, her wide eyes saying everything she couldn't.

"I wouldn't need to use ghosts to do it this time," Russell said. "But I would need her to be subdued. And someone else would have to kill her."

"Squeamish?" Paska asked.

"Not in the least," Russell said. "But I don't want any of the dead who hang around constantly looking at me like I'm the kind of person who can make more ghosts for them. They're already demanding enough. If it got out that I'm willing to kill, I'd be in too high a demand, and I don't feel like trying to convince any ghosts that I'm not a contract killer/ghost creator."

Misty narrowed her eyes. "That's not the real reason."

Russell shrugged. "It's not, but it's the only one you'll get from me. If you want me to destroy her soul, someone else will have to help her take the first step."

"This is ridiculous!" Sandy exploded. "If we kill her in cold blood without a trial, we're just as bad as she is. Maybe worse because we can't even claim the insanity defense!"

Morgana watched carefully. Sandy was the same age as Hazel, but she was the newest to her power. Hazel may have done nothing with her magic except learn to glamour her way out of trouble, but she'd been aware that it existed since she was sixteen. And Sandy had never seen anyone murdered by blood magic.

There was a time to be slow and careful with someone, and a time to push them up against the hard wall of truth.

"What do you think we should do with her?" Morgana asked. "Arrest her? Send her to jail in Oracle Bay? Or should we send her back to the supernatural prison managed by the Scales?"

Sandy didn't answer right away, but the stubborn set of her lips signaled that she wasn't yet ready to walk back from this line. "Oracle Bay's jail wouldn't hold her, especially since we don't even have our supernatural police chief anymore," Sandy said.

"I'll find someone," Misty interjected. "It just takes a while."

"And she already broke out of the Scales' maximum-security prison, killing several of her guards," Morgana pointed out.

"I don't know the answer, but there has to be another choice," Sandy said, but with less conviction. "We can't just...stoop to her level. I won't be a murderer."

Morgana smiled at her. She'd grown up in a different time, and she'd never questioned the necessity of protecting the innocent by taking the lives of the guilty, but she understood Sandy's conflict. "It is not an easy thing to seal someone's fate when they're not here to answer for themselves, and it goes against everything you have learned your entire life about justice. I will not attempt to change your mind, but I will ask you to consider why it must be this way. Bridget has killed over two dozen people we know of, and she's shown herself to be unable to let a loss go. She didn't get what she wanted in Oracle Bay the first time, and I have no doubt she'll be back. But everyone has to be on board with how we'll deal with her, or they'll need to sit this one out."

Sandy nodded stiffly. "I'll think about it." Her chin tilted up slightly, and Morgana saw the stubborn look in her eyes. Sandy might think about it, but she'd be looking for a different way. And if she found one that was plausible, Morgana would be happy to consider it. She might be older and more pragmatic, but she didn't relish the thought of killing someone and destroying their chance to move on to another life, no matter how many lives they'd taken and futures they'd ruined.

"That is all I'm asking," Morgana said. "Thank you."

"Will you teach us how to shield ourselves against attack?" Drew asked. "Even if we decide to take a different tactic, that's still valuable knowledge. We don't know she's coming here, but if she is, she could be here in six hours. That's not a lot of time to mount a concerted offensive, so we might as well at least protect ourselves while we figure out what to do next. In the meantime, Paska can look for a magically inclined sniper."

No one argued, and Morgana heaved a sigh of relief. "Yes. Let's start with that."

Misty drummed her fingernails against the table in the alcove of the Pour House, just like she'd been doing for the last ten minutes.

Morgana gritted her teeth, took a long drink of the wine Andy had dropped off for her, and tried to breathe through her annoyance. It was a singularly irritating noise, but the tension that had been riding her body for the last five days—five days with zero signs of Bridget and no news from London other than they were sending Scales operatives to secure the town and provide the magical snipers Paska had asked for—was elevating her stress responses, and it wouldn't do anyone any good if she yelled at Misty.

"Would you please knock that the fuck off?" Russell said, breaking the silence that was weighing down the table.

Misty's hand stilled, and she tucked it into her lap. "Sorry," she said, sounding more irritated than apologetic.

"Every single one of us is on edge, waiting for Bridget to strike," Morgana said. "Tension is high and tempers are short. We'll have to extend each other as much grace as possible while we wait for Bridget to make herself known."

"I almost wish she would show up," Sandy said. "At least then, we'd know."

"It's given us time to prepare," Morgana pointed out. "Each of you can shield well enough to fend off an initial attack and buy time to get help. Five days to master this skill is impressive, even for those of you who were familiar with similar magics." She cast a glance at Ceri, who'd needed very little in the way of instruction. "It seems I really did underestimate you all."

Paska walked into the alcove and dropped into the vacant chair next to Morgana. "I can't see her. I don't know how she's hiding so completely, but if the Scales goons can't get a lock on her, and I can't even sense her on the magical plane, she's better than any of us gave her credit for."

Morgana heard his unspoken frustration. There were few things that could hide from Paska. She could do it if she wanted, although she seldom had. If she wanted to be left alone, it was just as easy to tell him to go away for a few decades.

"It's been almost a week," Jezebel said. Her voice was tight and higher than her usual pitch. She darted glances towards the door every couple minutes, and Morgana knew she was eager to leave and check on Natalie.

The other paired up psychics looked less nervous, but that was probably because Sandy's fiancé Vincent, Drew's fiancé Bill, and Misty's boyfriend Joseph were at a table within eyesight waiting for the Thursday night karaoke to start.

"Call her," Ceri said. "We all know you're dating—you even brought her to Misty's when we were hiding from Bridget the first time—and even if we didn't, there's nothing wrong with inviting a friend to karaoke. If it helps, I can text her and invite her."

Jezebel responded with a tight smile and sharp nod. "Please."

Morgana exhaled away some of the tension. She still believed that Bridget wouldn't target any mundane humans, but the witch knew how much Morgana valued her friends, and that might make them targets.

"Can I get anyone anything else to drink? Slips of paper to sign up for karaoke? Food?" Hazel popped into the alcove and smiled.

"I'll take another glass of wine," Morgana said, then looked around. "And a couple more pitchers of whatever those were."

"Pearly Gates Pale, coming right up." Hazel wrote the order down, then paused with her pen poised above her order pad.

"Can we get a couple baskets of tots, too?" Sandy asked.

"Regular or totchos?" Hazel asked.

"Totchos? I don't know what those are, but I definitely want some," Misty said.

"It's just tots with nacho cheese and sour cream," Hazel said. "Luis was feeling a bit experimental tonight."

"One hundred baskets of totchos," Misty said.

Hazel laughed. "You got it. Anyone need anything else?"

"Earplugs?" Paska muttered.

Hazel laughed, grabbed the empty pitchers, and took off back towards the bar.

"Don't be ridiculous, old man," Ceri said. "You don't have to get up and sing, although you and I both know it's inevitable, but there are very few people who are going to make your ears bleed."

Paska grumbled something under his breath, but his shoulders relaxed infinitesimally.

"Why don't you let me choose a song for you," Ceri coaxed. "It'll be fun."

Paska glared at her, pulled a bottle out of his pocket, and dumped the contents into one of the empty pint glasses on the table. He took a long drink, shuddered slightly, and smiled. Then, he pushed the glass across to Ceri.

She pushed it back. "Not today. If I drink any whiskey, I'll end up on stage trying to sing Celine Dion, and then you really would need earplugs."

A commotion near the front door drew Morgana's attention. She stood and slipped behind Paska. She knew it was ridiculous to hope it'd be Donovan. He was still in the hospital recovering from whatever had been done to him. He'd texted every day, but other than reporting that there was still no sign of Bridget, there was little other content to his messages. He hadn't told her he loved her again, and she tried not to let that bother her. He also hadn't told her what had happened to him, and she let that bother her a lot.

A group of men, identically dressed in black trousers, black, short-sleeved shirts, and black combat boots, stood in the doorway. They radiated enough menace that even the mundane humans were glancing warily in their direction. The Scales operatives were here, but Donovan was not one of them.

Morgana rolled her eyes. They could not have been less unobtrusive if they'd tried.

"I think the Scales personnel have arrived," Morgana said softly.

A glass tipped over, and water spilled out. Morgana turned around in time to see Paska throw a napkin over the rapidly spreading puddle and Drew pull Ceri into him, shielding her face.

"I won't go crazy if I look at the water puddle," Ceri said, her voice muffled by Drew's shoulder.

"Excuse us for caring," Misty said without rancor. "We all remember what happened last time you accidentally got a vision from some spilled water."

Drew let go of Ceri, and she laughed, albeit a little shakily. "That's a fair point. But unless one of you not only spilled the glass of water but also was ready to pull down the barrier protecting my mind from infinity, I'll be okay. Who spilled the water, though? I was drinking that."

No one confessed, but they didn't need to. Morgana fixed her brother with a look, and he glanced over at her and winked.

Ceri was terrified of witch hunters. She'd never talked about it, but Morgana could sense the red-headed psychic's fear whenever they were mentioned and knew Ceri had an excellent reason to be afraid. Paska's accident was a brilliant way to keep Ceri distracted and grounded.

"I will go talk to them and keep them away from the rest of you,"

Morgana said. "There is no need for anyone else to have to deal with a group of warlocks. They are either arrogant or stupid if they believe appearing in matching black uniforms will not catch more attention than if they'd merely walked in dressed in denim and flannel shirts. Perhaps they would be more successful at hunting down rogue magic users if they learned to fit in."

"It's okay," Ceri said, straightening her shoulders. "Andy will be here in a minute, and I want them to know what they'll be up against in case the witch hunters decide that any quarry is better than none."

Morgana looked out towards the Scales warlocks again. They'd stopped at the bar and were talking to Brandy. The bar manager was smiling at them, but even at this distance, Morgana could read the insincerity in her expression.

Andy walked up to Brandy, joined in the conversation for a moment, and directed the men to a table on the opposite side of the bar. Then he walked around the tables, stopping to chat with a few folks in his role as affable if a bit eccentric bar owner, and wound his way up to the front where the karaoke leader was setting up.

Andy grabbed a microphone.

"Is he going to sing?" Misty whispered.

Ceri clasped her hands in front of herself. "If he does, this will be the best night of my life, even with the witch hunters here."

"I've got my phone camera ready to record," Drew said, aiming it at the stage. "It will be perfect for social media."

"He'll kill you," Ceri said, but she pulled out her own phone and pointed it at her boyfriend.

"Hey folks!" Andy called.

Morgana did not bother to hide her amusement at the jocularity that colored his voice, so different from the grumpy personality he adopted around her.

A chorus of greetings answered him.

"We're about to get started with karaoke tonight, so hurry up and get your songs in! Remember to tip your KJ, tip your servers, and have some fun! Tonight, everyone who sings gets a free drink when they're done, so I expect to see all of you up there." Andy replaced the microphone, paused to speak with the KJ, and left the makeshift stage.

"Disappointed," Drew muttered.

Ceri scrunched up her face. "Me, too. He's such a tease."

It was another five minutes before he made it to their alcove. "They probably know who's back here, but I didn't want to make it easy for them," the fallen angel said without preamble. "They were asking Brandy where to find Morgana, and I wasn't sure if you wanted them back here, or if you were going to go to them."

"They might as well come back here," Morgana said. "We don't have enough chairs, so we can make them stand uncomfortably and watch us enjoy ourselves with the drinks we aren't offering them."

Andy grinned. "I'll help Hazel get you set up for another round, then let them know where to find you."

Morgana nodded. "Much appreciated, demon."

"I live to serve, witch." Andy bowed mockingly towards her, then exited the alcove.

"They might be wankers, but even warlocks have their uses," Paska said. "Cannon fodder is one of those."

Andy and Hazel reappeared with two heaping baskets of totchos and four pitchers of beer. Andy set a bottle of wine in front of Morgana and a bottle of whiskey next to Paska. Hazel took the only vacant chair, pulled over one of the water glasses, and took a long drink.

"I'm on break for the next thirty minutes," she said. "Andy thought it'd be better if we were all in one place for whatever these guys want."

"All of us but Zeke," Russell noted. "I haven't seen him since we met at Paska's."

"He comes to work, but he barely talks to anyone," Hazel said. "And he's switched to the morning shift. I think it's so there's less chance he'll run into any of you."

"What is going on with him?" Misty asked. "I mean, he's always been weird, but this is...extra."

"There are a lot of events happening outside Oracle Bay that are sending cosmic ripples through anyone sensitive to changes in the Christian heaven and hell," Ceri said. "Andy doesn't talk about what's going on very much, but he's spent a lot of time texting with Barachiel, so I think whatever's going on is in Eden Valley."

"Will it affect us?" Sandy asked. "I don't think I can handle one more thing."

"Not immediately," Paska said. "We'll have to deal with the ramifications eventually, but things will be more settled in heaven and hell before we have to think about it."

Sandy opened her mouth like she was going to ask another question, but before she could, the KJ started talking.

"Hi everyone, my name's Bryan, and I'll be your KJ tonight." Morgana leaned out of the alcove. Bryan was one of the brother-sister realtor team who ran Mind Your Manor. He was a giant—over six and a half feet tall and broadly muscular—Black man. Tonight, he was wearing a tight, red t-shirt that showed off his shoulders, and a pair of dark-wash blue jeans that molded to his thighs. Morgana let her gaze linger on him appreciatively for a moment. He was a beautiful man, and even though she had no intention of pursuing anything—and wouldn't be successful if she did as his taste leaned strongly towards men—she always took the time for some light, unobtrusive ogling.

"I'm not going to get you started tonight like I usually do. Instead, I have a Pour House karaoke debut. Vincent, come on up. Guys, gals, and non-binary pals, put your hands together for Vincent and his rendition of 'I'm Too Sexy.'"

"What?" Sandy squeaked. She climbed over Jezebel and pushed past Russell and Misty to join Morgana in the alcove doorway in time to watch Vincent stride to the stage. Sandy's fiancé was a handsome man with golden skin and dark brown hair. He was usually very serious whenever Morgana had occasion to speak with him, but his time with Bill and Joseph had visibly mellowed him a great deal, and he swayed a little on his feet when he accepted the microphone from Bryan.

Vincent waved at Sandy and blew her a kiss. "This one's for my best girl," he called out before breaking into song.

"Oh. My. God." Sandy covered her mouth with both hands, which did nothing to muffle the laughter shaking her body. "I have never heard him sing before. Never. He told me he hates it and would rather die than go to karaoke. I don't know what kind of magic Bill and Joseph weaved over him, but maybe they're the warlocks in the room and not the secret-ops cosplayers in the corner."

Morgana permitted herself a small grin, then backed up a little to give Sandy a better view of her fiancé, who was gyrating during the instrumental interlude.

As Vincent finished his song to thunderous applause, Morgana saw the Scales warlocks get up and make their way towards the alcove.

"They are walking over," she informed the psychics behind her. "Pour your drinks and look very happy to be here. I want them to feel as out-of-place as possible."

Morgana watched their progress through the bar. It was a lot more crowded than usual. Karaoke nights had proven to be a very popular event. Andy's bar manager Brandy was the best thing that had happened to the Pour House.

A wave of energy flooded the room, hitting Morgana like a tsunami. She was pushed back against the doorway, and her head hit the wall with an audible thunk.

"What's wrong?" Sandy said, darting forward to help Morgana steady herself.

"Attack," she said. Her lips hurt, and she tasted blood. "Shield." She pushed out her shields, trying to cover as many of the humans around her as she could, pushing through the ringing in her ears.

Sandy scrambled by her and skidded to a stop at the table where Bill, Joseph, and Vincent were sitting. She dropped onto Vincent's lap and thew her arms around him. As if they'd practiced a hundred times, Bill and Joseph slid in until the four of them were in contact.

An obsidian dart bounced off the space behind Bill's head, and Morgana gave silent thanks to the goddess for Sandy's instincts and her aptitude for shielding.

Misty and Drew pushed their way out of the alcove to join Sandy and push their shields over the humans between them and the stage.

Satisfied that the humans were safe, Morgana walked forward towards the source of the power burst. It'd come from the warlocks but hadn't felt like their magic.

She broke past the barrier of people between her and the Scales personnel and halted in her tracks.

Three of the five men were on the ground, obsidian darts matching the one that'd deflected off Sandy's shield lodged in their throats. Morgana knew if they removed the men's shirts, they'd see the same three Ogham runes that'd been found on every one of Bridget's victims. The remaining two were crouched on the ground next to their comrades, obsidian wands held discretely in their hands. They were not just warlocks, they were demon callers, and they were ready to use those powers that skirted the edge between the light and dark.

A smile ghosted across Morgana's face as she contemplated what would happen if they tried to summon a demon in Andy's bar. It would be a sight worth seeing.

Someone screamed, and Morgana turned towards the sound.

Brandy was standing at the end of the bar in her customary seat. There was a pile of mail in front of her, and it looked like she'd been opening it.

In her hands was a large manila envelope covered in swirling frost patterns and three small holes. Morgana watched the envelope slip out of Brandy's grasp, hit the floor, and shrivel into a puddle of wet paper. The outlines of the three Ogham runes that marked Bridget's death curses glowed red before disappearing into the remains of the envelope.

Three darts were lodged in Brandy's chest and one in her throat. Blood oozed around the puncture wounds.

Morgana ran forward, but she was already too late. Runes bloomed red through the sheer material of Brandy's t-shirt, and she toppled off her barstool.

The woman who'd been sitting next to Brandy kept screaming, and it was all Morgana could hear. Every other sound in the bar disappeared.

Morgana knelt next to Brandy, even though she knew there was nothing she could do. The woman was marked for death, and there was no one who could stop that from happening.

A wave of heat barreled towards her, and she ducked instinctively, shielding the shell that had once been Brandy Farris in her arms. When she turned around, the part of her that was still clinically observing the events and not choked with fear and guilt saw the two standing Scales operatives dragging their fallen comrades out of the bar without a backwards glance. She scowled after them. Cowards.

The stink of sulphur rode in on the heat's wake. Andy stalked towards her, Ceri beside him with one hand on his arm.

"Everyone out!" Andy yelled, and his power reverberated through the bar. Chairs were pushed back and tipped over as Pour House patrons rushed to the exits.

Russell beat Andy by two steps. He pulled Brandy out of Morgana's arms and into his. "No, no, no, no, no," he said over and over, rocking her back and forth. "Stay. You can't go now. Not without giving us a chance. You promised."

Morgana rocked back on her heels and stood. She backed up until she was no longer between Andy's fury and Russell's grief.

"Sorry," Brandy croaked. "I..."

"Shhh..." Russell put a hand over her mouth. "It'll be okay. Morgana can fix this. Or Andy."

"No," Brandy said. "Already dead. You know. You won't tell me, but I see you now. Too late." She convulsed in Russell's arms while Morgana looked on, her horror and anger growing.

The earth shook, rattling the barware and swinging the lighting.

"Stop, Morgana," Paska said. "Your anger will do nothing now but bring the ceiling down on the rest of us. Bridget already had a death sentence over her head, but if I find her before she finds us, I will visit upon her every horror she's perpetrated a thousand times over. You may be good at meting out punishment due, but I am good at making it last."

Russell's low wail cut through any answer Morgana would've given.

Brandy was dead.

Morgana dangled her feet in her backyard pond and let the warmth of the evening summer sun take the edge off the ocean breeze trying to raise goosebumps on her arms. She tried to find the detachment she'd prided herself on for centuries. People died; it was inevitable. She'd watched so many move from this life to the next, and although she'd mourned from time to time, she hadn't felt this level of soul-deep grief in over fifteen hundred years.

It didn't make sense. She'd known Brandy well enough, but they hadn't been close. They probably hadn't spoken more than a dozen words a week to each other. So why was this death hitting her so hard?

A raptor landed on a rock near the back fence, and Paska shimmered into existence. He walked over and sank cross-legged to the ground next to her.

Morgana leaned her head against his shoulder, and he wrapped his arm around her.

"You're taking this one hard," he said.

"It makes no sense," Morgana replied. "She wasn't my friend. If it had been Sandy or Mystic, the grief would be understandable. Even if it had been the demon, I would expect to feel this way. But Brandy? I did not know her well enough to mourn this much."

Paska tightened his arm around her, then dropped it to his side. "You feel responsible for her death."

Morgana shook her head. "It wasn't my fault. I know that."

"Your mind knows, but your heart does not. You always take on more guilt than you should. It's one of your many failings." The gentle smile he graced her with removed a bit of the sting from his words.

She did feel guilty. "I should have killed Bridget when I had the chance."

"You were in no condition to deliver her death sentence. I could have, though." Paska knitted his hands in front of him and stared into the water that was purpling as the sun sank behind the horizon.

"Guilt from you as well?" Morgana asked.

"Yes. I seldom hesitate to do what is necessary, but I was afraid that if I meted out the justice Bridget deserved, the power she'd stolen would push back to you in an uncontrollable wave and overwhelm your mind. You were already weakened from the theft, and I didn't know if you were strong enough to survive a violent return." Paska unlaced his boots and took them off. He slipped off his socks— brightly striped with lime green and flamingo pink—and slid his feet into the water next to hers.

"Is that why—" The question died on Morgana's lips. She wasn't sure she wanted to know.

But Paska answered anyway. "The Scales would have executed her immediately upon her arrival at their prison. They didn't care what would happen to her power on her death, nor were they interested in releasing it in a controlled fashion. That was irresponsible of them."

"How did you do it? Convince them to wait, I mean. The Scales has never been merciful to witches, whether they're serial killers or just potential victims. It's hard for me to believe they waited out of kindness."

Paska laid back and looked at the sky. "It was not kindness, as you well know. But there is not a person alive who could say no to me when I truly want something."

Morgana drew in a deep breath, then exhaled slowly, lowering herself to the ground beside her brother. The sky was purpling, and the first stars were popping into existence. "Did your interference make them complacent?"

Paska grunted but made no other answer.

They lay in silence until the sky turned from purple to indigo to black, and the Milky Way bloomed above them, lighting the backyard with help from the waning crescent moon. Frogs began their evening love songs, and the crickets chimed in, accompanied by the sleepy calls of the pair of mourning doves that usually overnighted in the lilac bushes against the back fence.

She hadn't heard from Donovan today, not even after she'd texted him about the events at the Pour House. Her mind pinged through a hundred possibilities, and none of them were good.

She'd know if he was dead, wouldn't she? They were bound. Maybe not as tightly as she and Paska were, but there were threads tying them together. She'd left her phone inside; she didn't like to violate her sanctuary with technology, but now she wished she'd brought it with her. In addition to waiting to hear from Donovan, she wanted to check on Russell and Andy.

Misty and Joseph had taken Russell home with them, and he was refusing to see or talk to anyone. Morgana could ask Paska how Andy was; he'd likely stopped by to talk to Ceri before coming to see her. But she wasn't sure she wanted to know how angry they were with her, how much they blamed her for making them vulnerable.

"I don't think so," Paska said. "It gave her time, though."

The break in the silence startled Morgana, and she jumped, splashing the water and interrupting the frogs. It took her a minute to wind her way back to the question Paska was answering.

"I should have let go of their minds weeks ago, but I didn't know if you were ready." Paska sighed loudly. "If I'd taken control of their worker bees rather than those making the decisions, I would have known as soon as Bridget escaped. Maybe I could have done something. I told myself it was too difficult to monitor the minds of so many from so far away, especially since they might have little ability to refuse a direct order, no matter how tightly I held them. I am more to blame than you."

"She must have had a store of the obsidian darts," Morgana said, shifting the subject away from Paska's self-recrimination. "She would not have been able to craft so many so quickly, even brimming with stolen power."

"I found another half dozen of her death-spelled letters in town. All of them were addressed to the businesses rather than an individual," Paska said.

Morgana rolled onto her side, then pushed herself up. "It makes sense that she'd send one to the Pour House knowing Hazel works there and we are there often, but there were no guarantees her spells would hit any of us. If she is no longer targeting only those with power, then she is even more unpredictable and deadly than before."

Paska shrugged, but the grim look on his face belied the casualness of the gesture. "You have to find her, and the only place I know to start is her last known whereabouts. That is where your search should begin."

"*My* search?" Morgana asked. "Will you not come with me?"

"You have to go after her. None of us are safe while she lives, and you will find her more easily than me." Paska pushed himself up and pulled his feet out of the water. "The death spells were easy enough to disarm since I knew what to look for, but even as powerful as our friends are, they won't be able to see the subtle markings of her curse until it's too late. I will not leave our friends, nor this town, undefended."

"I will not be able to keep the Scales out of my hunt," Morgana said.

"I know, but we can control who you'll work with." Paska stood and paced her mossy lawn.

"The way you controlled the Scales before?" Morgana asked, her voice sharper and more accusatory than she'd meant.

"That was an error on my part, and no mistake," he said. "I was overconfident, and my arrogance got Brandy killed, not to mention three Scales operatives."

Paska reached down and hauled her to her feet. "Do you feel better?" he asked.

"Not better, but less at sea. You are correct, I need to leave Oracle Bay. It will hopefully remove the target from this town, and the Scales have already proven they cannot hold her."

A pained look danced across Paska's face, and he turned away from her.

"Your compulsion was not responsible for her escape," Morgana pointed out.

"Not directly, but if I had let them go, she would already be dead, and your powers would have returned to you." Paska walked towards the fence and rolled his shoulders.

"You could leave my house on two feet and walk through the front door like a regular human," Morgana said.

Paska looked back at her. She couldn't make out his expression in the light of the stars, but there was no mistaking the weight of years and sadness infusing his voice. "You and I haven't been regular humans for centuries, sister. And it is time for us to stop pretending."

He shimmered and took the shape of the raptor that had given him his name.

Morgana watched him spiral into the sky and disappear into the darkness.

six

"Russell hasn't spoken to anyone since..." Misty's voice trailed off, and she shot a glance at Morgana. "He won't come out of the guest room, although he is eating and drinking—or at least the food we're leaving him on a tray is disappearing."

"It has only been three days," Paska pointed out. "It takes a person more than that to recover from heartbreak."

"I'm not asking for recovery," Misty shot back. "I'm asking for him to talk to me. We're all sad."

"He was in love with her," Ceri murmured. "They've been seeing each other since the apocalypse, but she refused to make it anything other than casual. Said he was hiding too many secrets from her for her to trust him enough to take the next step."

"How do you know that?" Misty demanded.

"I'm in the Pour House a lot," Ceri said. "And Brandy works there. I'm such a fixture that it's easy to forget I'm there. I overhear a lot of things."

"I didn't know," Andy said. A tendril of smoke curled up above him, filling the air with the scent of sulphur. "Shouldn't you have told me?"

Ceri put a hand on his knee, and the smoke disappeared. "It wasn't my secret to tell. I'm all about sharing with you, but that doesn't extend to other people's business, especially when it's something I found out by accident." She leaned back into the loveseat she shared with Andy and tucked her jeans-clad legs under herself before worming her way under his arm.

Morgana leaned back into the plushness of the soft overstuffed chair against the far wall of Misty and Joseph's living room. The room was designed with comfort in mind rather than any particular style. Soft, upholstered furniture of various styles and colors was scattered in a rough semi-circle facing a large fireplace. End tables were placed strategically so that everyone had a handy surface to rest a glass of wine or beer, and the walls were painted a shade of green that called forth the feel of the rainforest that sprawled across the Olympic peninsula to the north.

Joseph walked into the room, looking like he'd just come in from the barns. He had dark jeans with mud-stained cuffs and a dark green long-sleeved tee the same color as the walls. He was also carrying a couple of bottles of wine.

Drew followed him into the room with a handful of wine glasses held precariously and haphazardly by the thin stems. Joseph set the bottles down on the table closest to Misty, bent over to kiss her upturned lips, then waved to the room. "I'm going to shower off the creamery. When I come back, you're all going to tell me everything that's going on and what you're going to do about it." He stared down at Misty, reproach in his eyes.

She flushed slightly. "I didn't want to worry you. We had it handled."

"Uh-huh," Joseph replied. "From now on, no matter how 'handled' you have things, you need to share. Turns out you weren't the only one in danger this time." He walked out of the room.

Misty bit her lip, smearing her scarlet lipstick, then sighed. "I should've told him. I just didn't want him to worry, you know?" she said to no one in particular.

"It is difficult to decide what to share with those who are mundane," Morgana said, speaking for the first time since arriving at Misty's.

It'd been three days since Brandy had died. Three days without word from Donovan. And three days with no further contact from the Scales. Their surviving operatives had disappeared with the bodies of their fallen comrades before the police and coroner had arrived to take Brandy, and no one had seen them leave.

Morgana knew they were still out there, watching, but for some reason had decided against announcing their presence or contacting her. The Scales prided themselves on being the epitome of a secret society, and the amount of contact she'd had with them recently was nearly unprecedented. She knew as well that the witch hunt would be going in earnest, and that they would not keep her or the Silver Eye apprised of their lack of progress.

For that matter, the Eye wasn't keeping Morgana apprised of anything. Calls to them had gone unanswered, and the only contact she'd had from them since Brandy's death was left on her doorstep. The message was handwritten on a thick vellum and sealed with the mark of their order—an open eye with large, stylized eyelashes, a round iris, and the pinprick pupil—and coated in the kind of magic her order specialized in. Only Morgana would see the missive, and even if that failed, no one else could open and read it. The message was simple and to the point. "Find the blood witch and go alone. If you involve anyone else from Oracle Bay, they will be eliminated. This is your last chance." Was the Eye plotting against Morgana as well as Bridget? It was more likely they didn't want any more people than necessary involved and potentially finding out about the secret organization, but it was a possibility she couldn't afford to ignore.

Morgana had burned the note and let the wind take the ashes. There would be no further help coming from the Silver Eye, and no forthcoming information from the Scales.

Not sharing their progress nor asking for her help marked them foolish, though. Paska had been correct when he'd stated she was probably best equipped of anyone to find Bridget. Not only was Bridget in possession of her stolen power, Morgana had been tracking down rogue magic users for over two hundred years, first on her own as a way to keep her part of the world a little safer, then later for the Eye. It was easier in some ways to work for someone else. She had nearly as much autonomy as when she was on her own, and the targets were acquired for her.

"I recommend sharing everything," Drew said. "The good, the bad, and the scary. I spent too much time alone because I was keeping secrets from Bill, and I won't make that mistake again."

Misty hung her head a little, then looked up, eyes full of resolve. "You're right. Of course you're right, it's just that..."

"It's your first major relationship with someone, especially someone who knows about you and us," Ceri said gently.

Ceri was so good at saying the right things, and she was the one everyone came to for advice. Even when she'd been dying, she was sought out for answers she inherently had without needing to tap into her gift.

Morgana envied her a little. No one had ever come to her for comfort or advice. Most people were wary if not afraid of her, and even when she'd been undercover as an upper middle-class PTA president, she hadn't been able to project warmth the way Ceri did.

Misty sighed and grabbed the bottles of wine, following Drew around the room to fill the glasses he distributed. Morgana took a long drink of her wine and watched her friends. This scene was so familiar. They gathered once a week at someone's house to catch up on news, both mundane and supernatural, and to enjoy each other's company. It had been Drew's turn to host, but they'd switched to Misty's out of concern for Russell.

Footsteps pounded down the hall, and Joseph burst into the living room, dripping wet and with a towel around his waist. "He's gone!"

Morgana was on her feet in a moment, Paska right behind her. She ran out of the house and scanned the area. A figure was running down the driveway. Paska shot past her, and she didn't bother following on foot. He was a much faster runner, and although he was unshod, his propensity to only wear shoes when he was in public meant the soles of his feet were tougher than hers. There was also the fact that once he was out of sight of the house, he'd be able to take flight.

But before Russell disappeared around the bend in the driveway that led towards the county road, he vanished.

Paska skidded to a stop in a cloud of dust, and Morgana winced in sympathy. Her brother did a slow turn, then walked back to Morgana. The rest of the crew was gathering behind Morgana, but she doubted they'd seen what she and Paska had witnessed.

"He disappeared," Paska said, bewilderment evident in his voice. "You saw that, right?"

Morgana nodded. "I have seen something like that before, but it has been decades, maybe centuries."

"What do you mean he disappeared?" Misty demanded. "Where did he go?"

"I don't know," Paska said. The words sounded strange coming from him. "He vanished into thin air."

"He shouldn't be able to do that," Morgana said, feeling nearly as helpless as her brother sounded. "He is a necromancer, not a sorcerer. I've never met anyone but you who could make themselves invisible."

"Don't give away all my secrets," Paska growled. "But this wasn't invisibility. He didn't just vanish from sight—he could not have hidden from me. He was no longer there. I heard the moment he ceased to occupy the space in front of me, and the air rushed in to fill the void left behind. It reminded me of something, but I can't quite remember what."

"You can make yourself invisible?" Sandy asked.

Paska smiled at her. "Morgana is kidding. No one can make themselves invisible. She says ridiculous things when she's nervous, and she's always nervous when she doesn't know what's going on."

Morgana rolled her eyes at Paska, then turned to Misty. "Were you aware he could disappear at will like that?"

Misty shook her head. "I didn't. I had no idea. But why did he run away if he could just vanish like that?"

"Let's go back inside and figure out where he might've gone," Ceri said. "And then we need to talk about how we're going to find Bridget and take her out for good this time."

Morgana schooled her expression. She'd known this would be the main topic of conversation that evening. There was no way to avoid the subject, and now that she'd decided to do as Paska told her she should, there was no reason to draw things out.

Once everyone was seated again, Morgana looked at Misty. "I suspect Russell went home. He must be desperate to contact Brandy's spirit, and it's been three days. It's an auspicious number of days between life and death in many traditions. Today would be the best day to reach out before she's out of reach of anyone on this plane."

Misty nodded. "He doesn't need a Ouija board, but he prefers to use one. It helps him focus his gifts."

"We all have a focus like that," Morgana agreed. "One of us should go after him before he does something rash."

"He is nearly mad with grief; he'd have to be to disappear that way." Paska grimaced, then looked at Misty. "It took a moment for the memory to surface—it was a very long time ago. But I know what he did. To answer your earlier question, he walked away because that kind of travel is not only exhausting, it's dangerous. I am not a necromancer, but I am more familiar with the space between than most people. It is possible to walk the line between life and death, to step into the veil, as it were, and travel there, but it leaves a person open to meddling."

"What kind of meddling?" Misty demanded.

"Possession," Paska answered shortly. "But that isn't my main concern right now. Someone needs to get to his house now before he does something terrible."

Drew stood. "I'll go. Misty, you should come with me. He might listen to you where he wouldn't to me."

Paska nodded. "That is a good idea. I will follow along shortly in case more backup is needed."

Drew and Misty disappeared, Misty practically running out the door in her haste. Paska refilled a flask from a bottle of whiskey he pulled out of a large cabinet against the far wall, then leaned against the wall and downed the rest of the wine.

"I don't understand what the big deal is," Hazel said. "I mean, I get why traveling on the other side of the veil is bad, ghost possession isn't that great, but he's been possessed before, right? Didn't he do that when he was helping Ceri with her haunting? But what is he going to do with a Ouija board that's so bad? Why can't he talk to Brandy if he wants to?" She gulped her wine.

"It's not the talking that's worrying people," Jez said. "He's a necromancer."

"And?" Hazel wrinkled her nose. "Sorry, I just don't understand."

Jez leaned forward and planted her elbows on her knees. "Necromancers can talk to the dead, but then again, so can any medium. That's not what they're famous for, though, is it?"

Hazel's hand flew to her mouth. "Oh. Oh! You think he might try to...raise her from the dead? Make a zombie?"

"Probably not," Morgana said. "But it's better to make sure that doesn't happen. If he has the power to walk between life and death, he has the power to pull her soul back to this side and push it back into her body. Being re-ensouled would slow the natural decay of her body, but it cannot stop it completely. It is a longer, slower death, but the end result would be the same."

Andy stood and drained his glass, took the wine Ceri held up to him, and downed that, too. "I will let the others stop Russell, but I will not let you leave this town without me, Morgana."

"I don't know what you mean," Morgana said.

"Don't lie to me, witch," Andy growled. Silvery-grey wings pushed back behind him, brushing the wall and ruffling the curtains.

"You are going after that blood witch, and it's about fucking time. She has killed too many. She made my bar a murder scene, and she killed someone I deeply care for. I will have my revenge for Brandy's death."

The tips of his wings flared red for a moment, then blackened before returning to their usual grey.

"I am leaving," Morgana said. "That is one of the things I wanted to discuss tonight. I should have gone after her the minute I learned she escaped. It is because of my hesitation that Brandy was killed. But you cannot go with me, demon. You and Paska must protect the others in case she attacks here again before I find her."

Andy shook his head. "I'm not needed here, and you could use someone else with the ability to sniff out foul magic." He held up one finger when Morgana opened her mouth to argue. "There's also the fact that I cannot be killed, and if she tries to steal my power, she'll probably explode."

He made good arguments and wasn't wrong about anything. It would be a convenient way around the threat the Eye had made against anyone she chose to accompany her.

"You can't go," Ceri said, sliding an arm around his waist.

"*You're* not going," Andy said.

Ceri reached up and cupped his face with her hand, drawing his head down until he had no choice but to meet her clear, sapphire eyes with his stormy grey ones. "I will ignore the fact that you are trying to tell me what to do. I need you here with me."

"You've seen something," Jez said. "When you looked into your wine glass, you froze, then handed it to Andy."

Ceri laughed. "You see a lot, Jezebel."

"I spend a lot of time in the background watching, just like you." Jezebel sounded a little smug.

Morgana held back a scowl. The mood of the group was all over the place tonight. She knew lighthearted banter was often a foil for the deeper, darker feelings people felt, but it was something she'd never mastered.

"Will somebody tell me what the fuck is going on?" Andy said. "Tell me why I can't leave, or I will accuse you of making the same cavalier decisions about my life that you tell me I can't do."

"I'm pregnant," Ceri said simply.

Andy's jaw dropped. "How is that possible?"

"You're thousands of years old and don't even know how babies are made?" Paska tsked. "I knew you weren't good enough for Ceri, but I didn't realize you were stupid."

Andy tore his eyes off Ceri and glared at Paska. "You are such an ass."

Paska grinned. "I really am. It's what makes me delightful. And Ceri, I am so glad you finally found out. It's been a real trick making sure you think all the drinks I've given you are alcohol."

It was Ceri's turn to look astonished. "You knew? You knew I was pregnant and didn't tell me?"

Paska's grin was unrepentant. "I did. But I didn't know how you were going to feel about it and thought it better to keep my knowledge to myself."

"Is this good news?" Sandy asked hesitantly.

Ceri smiled. "It is. Good, but unexpected. Angels and demons are able to conceive with humans, but it's rare, and I'm not exactly young anymore. I believe this goes far beyond what's commonly called a 'geriatric' pregnancy."

Sandy stood and threw her arms around Ceri. "I am so happy for you!"

Andy looked over Ceri's head at Morgana. "I guess you're on your own, then."

"Thank you," Ceri said. "If you don't stay with me in Oracle Bay until after the baby is born, we'll die."

"But you won't if I'm here?" Andy asked. His wingtips were flashing between fiery red, sooty black, and ashy grey fast enough to make Morgana nauseated.

Ceri smiled up at him. "You know there are no guarantees in life, but the two futures I saw ended very differently. In the one I'd prefer, you were at my side holding our daughter, and in the other, you were at my side crying over my body."

"I'm leaving tomorrow," Morgana said.

"Where are you going first?" Hazel asked. "Do you want me to come with you?"

"London," Morgana said. "That's where the prison is, so that's where I'll start my search." She considered for a moment, then exhaled. She was going to break a century of silence—not to mention her vow to uphold the secrecy of the organization—but she had to if she was going to keep her friends safe. "And it has to be alone. I work for an organization that specializes in protecting witches. This—finding the blood witch responsible for the murders and power theft of so many witches—was to be my last job, and I have to see it through now, or my contract will not be broken. I received a message stating that anyone who accompanied me would be eliminated."

"Anyone who accompanied you, or anyone from Oracle Bay who accompanied you?" Paska asked.

Morgana narrowed her eyes. There was no way he could've seen the note. "Anyone from Oracle Bay," she replied.

"Couldn't Paska go, anyway?" Ceri asked, her arm wrapped tightly around Andy's waist. "Between Andy and the rest of us, we can protect the town. But you need someone to go with you; you won't make it if you're on your own. And Paska is almost as inde-structible as Andy."

"I cannot," Paska said. "I am the only one who may be able to stop Russell from completing his ill-conceived plan. There are other reasons, as well; they will become clear in time. The Eye will know how to kill her—they employ no one without having every failsafe in place—which means they will know how to eliminate me. But Morgana will not be alone."

"Also, you're afraid of flying," Ceri added.

Paska grinned but didn't deny it.

"Who—?" Morgana asked, then clamped her mouth closed.

She'd ask him later. She knew him well enough that if he intended to share the name of her soon-to-be companion, he would have.

"Please keep us updated," Ceri said, reaching out a hand to Morgana. "You're important to us. Don't sacrifice yourself needlessly. If you make the right choices and trust the right people, you'll be back in Oracle Bay in a month."

"Alive?" Morgana asked, although she didn't really want the answer.

"You'll come back to Oracle Bay alive," Ceri said. "But if you don't follow your heart instead of your mind, you might die here and take others with you." Her eyes darted towards Paska so quickly, Morgana thought she might have imagined it.

It should have been reassuring, but she couldn't follow her heart, either—not if she was going to keep the curse at bay. Another mystery and another wrinkle in an already creased plan.

Andy scooped Ceri into his arms. "If there's nothing further?"

Ceri rolled her eyes. "If he has anything to say about it, I won't be walking anywhere for the next seven and a half months."

"There's nothing else," Morgana said.

"Where are you flying out of?" Jezebel asked. "Portland or Seattle?"

"Portland. There were no first-class tickets left on the direct flight from Seattle," Morgana said.

"Perfect. I was heading to Portland the day after tomorrow, anyway. I'll go a day early and drive you."

"Very well," Morgana said. "I would appreciate the ride. Please pick me up at eight tomorrow morning." She walked out of the room, but not before she saw the look of surprise on Jezebel's face.

By the time she got to her car, the reality of what she was doing crashed down on her. She was afraid. It wasn't an emotion she felt often, but it wasn't completely alien. She'd been scared when Bridget had her magically pinned in her own garden, but that had been situational and sudden.

The fear she was experiencing now was closer to dread, and that was something she hadn't felt since watching her daughter running towards the cliff's edge, knowing what was about to happen, but hoping blindly she was wrong. Her power was slowly returning, and if she kept herself at capacity, she wouldn't be caught by surprise with only her natural magical levels intact. She'd have to drop all the shields she was holding over her house. She couldn't afford to maintain anything that would siphon power from her, not if she was going to be at her best when she found Bridget. There were ways to speed up the healing, although it would have long-term effects, both on her and on the elements she drew from. But those effects would be worth the price to meet Bridget at full strength.

Morgana closed the door and started her car with shaking hands. She stared at them until they stilled, then put the car in gear.

<h1 style="text-align:center">seven</h1>

The sun was barely above the horizon when Morgana knocked on Paska's door.

"I'm in the garden getting the fire started," he yelled.

Morgana grimaced. She should have known that not only would he have anticipated her arrival, he would know why she was there.

She walked around his house to the large, ivory-colored gate carved into the shape of two merlins in flight that formed the barrier between his front yard and his sanctuary. She sat on the bench by the gate and removed her shoes, slipped on the light sandals she kept there for this very purpose, then pushed it open and walked into Paska's space. The moment the gate closed behind her, the outside world disappeared, and wind chimes took over.

Morgana's back yard was full of plants and flowers. It was green and earthy and had herb gardens growing in spirals in the four corners and a large pond in the center. Anyone who knew about the witchcraft she practiced would recognize her affinity with earth and water.

Paska's yard was very different. An enormous fire pit took up most of the space. An eight-foot high, elaborately carved white fence ran the perimeter of his yard. It was beautiful, and few would recognize it for what it was—bone. Gaily colored ribbons danced in the breeze that was omnipresent when Paska was here, and wind chimes and lanterns, currently unlit, hung from poles placed at regular intervals near the fence.

The fire in the pit had just caught, and it burned brightly as Paska fed it small sticks, urging it to grow. Beside him was a four-by-four basalt box with the lid propped open, revealing a jawbone sitting on top of a pile of smaller bones.

"Is that Vortigern?" Morgana asked. She braced herself against the impotent rage she usually felt when she thought about the man responsible for the death of her daughter. It didn't come. Instead, cold settled in her heart, and she shivered.

"Yes. I've been saving him for something important." Paska's words had an undercurrent of bitter mockery. He fed the fire, coaxing the flames higher, then took the larger pieces of wood and placed them around the ones already in place, reaching through the flames to ensure everything was just as he wanted. When he withdrew his hands, the breeze in the backyard kicked up a notch, sending the wind chimes into a cacophony of sound and pulling the fire higher.

"What do you want to know?" he asked, picking up the jawbone and staring into the fire.

Morgana thought. The way she asked was important if she wanted the answer that would be the most informative. Questions swirled through her head. She wanted to know if the curse was already in effect, if Bridget would be the instrument of the curse, if Paska had to die, where Bridget was hiding, if Ceri and Andy's baby would survive the birth and grow into adulthood, and if Donovan would ever forgive her for pushing him away.

"How do I kill Bridget and release the powers she's stolen in a controlled manner to those who should've inherited them?" Morgana asked, eyes focused on Vortigern's jawbone.

Paska's mouth formed a hard line, and his dark brown eyes took on a coldness that mirrored what Morgana felt. He nodded once, a sharp jerk of his chin, then gripped the jawbone. He pulled the bone across his right hand with his left, then handed it to Morgana.

Blood dripped from Paska's hand and stained the few teeth left on the bone. Morgana pulled it across her left hand in a motion that echoed her brother's, mingling her blood with his and smearing it across the bone that would give her the answers she needed.

She glanced at Paska. He thrust his chin towards the fire.

Morgana tossed the jawbone into the flames and stood back. Paska walked forward, closer than anyone could stand to a fire without the heat stealing their breath and becoming unbearably uncomfortable.

She knew it would take a while before the answers formed in the cracks in the bone and the dance of the flames. She sank to the ground, crossed her leather-clad legs in front of her, and waited.

"Why should I answer you?"

Morgana jumped, then scrambled to her feet. That voice, that sneer, was too familiar, even after a millennium and a half.

"You'll answer because I command it," Paska said coolly.

Morgana couldn't tell if Paska had expected this, or if he was just as startled as she was. She'd been present for countless fires Paska built to seek answers from beyond the veil and in the realm of knowing past and future, and never once had the bones spoken aloud.

Morgana squirmed with impatience at the long silence.

"Now!" Paska's voice cracked across the yard, and the chimes jangled nervously. Wind whipped the dust up, and the fire burned higher and hotter. The jawbone turned incandescent, then hairline fissures appeared running the length and width of the bone.

"Noooooooo!" the voice howled.

"I don't need my answer anymore," Morgana said. "Tell me how to break the curse."

Shrieking laughter filled Paska's backyard. "You'll never figure it out in time. Already I can see your end."

Paska reached into the fire and picked up the jawbone, clenching it in his hands. "Tell us."

The laughter continued, getting louder and louder until Morgana clapped her hands over her ears to drown out the sound. It didn't help. It continued reverberating through her body and exacerbating her nausea.

Paska growled, and the jawbone cracked.

Vortigern stopped laughing, and the sudden silence that followed was almost as violent as the laughter had been. "The answer isn't here."

"So, there is an answer," Morgana said.

"There's always an answer, and it usually comes at the beginning and not the end." Vortigern's voice trailed into a whisper as more fissures appeared on the bone.

Paska grunted in disgust and flung the jawbone back into the fire. The flames claimed it again, and the cracks deepened. Pieces started to break off.

The fire died down, and a gentle wind lifted the ash from the fire, swirled it around, and scattered it into the air.

Morgana inhaled sharply, then started coughing.

"Careful," Paska said, handing her a bottle of water. "You don't want to end up with a lungful of Vortigern."

"Too late," Morgana croaked. She took a long drink of water, then cleared her throat before speaking again. "Do you know what he meant? Do you know how to break the curse?"

Paska shook his head. "Not yet. I've been looking for a way to end this curse off and on for centuries. There is always a way, although death curses are harder to break than anything else."

"For anything else, you can just kill the one who cast it," Morgana muttered. "Hard to kill someone who's already dead."

"Huh," Paska said, tapping his left index finger against his chin. "You might be on to something there."

Morgana shook her head. She was well used to being three steps behind her brother when it came to the arcane, but that didn't mean she liked it any better now than she had when they were children and she chased him around, trying to get him to pay attention to her.

"Don't worry, little sister," Paska said gently. "Worry instead about how you're going to defeat Bridget when you find her, since that was the answer you were supposed to seek instead."

Morgana twisted her mouth in consternation. "It was, and it would have been a lot more useful than finding out that he couldn't be compelled to answer the other."

Paska shrugged. He gestured towards the fire, and it died in a puff of smoke. "I know more than I did before, but nothing of any substance. It's there, floating ephemerally, but the connections aren't made yet." His eyes unfocused, and Morgana held her breath, afraid to disturb him and scare away the threads that would tie everything together and bring it to the forefront of his mind.

"Do you remember the exact words he uttered?" Paska asked.

Morgana bit her lip and searched her memory. "He said, 'I curse you and Gwenddydd to be bound to one another, undying, until...'" Her memory faded. "Until love comes between us, right? I don't remember the exact words."

After a moment, Paska's eyes refocused, and she shook his head. "I cannot recall, either. It's almost there, though." He sighed, and his expression changed from frustration to something more pleasant. "Before we go inside and have a cup of tea, there are two more things you need to do. Take off your sandals."

Morgana did, and when her bare feet touched the earth of his sanctuary, power rushed up into her, filling her with magic until she nearly overflowed with it. She gasped in pleasure, then delved deep within herself to make the power her own and store it. In moments, she was completely replenished—more than replenished. She was replete.

"Thank you," she whispered. "This is a gift. How long have you had this?" She waved towards the earth.

He grinned widely at her. "I've been developing it for years and filling it since Bridget nearly killed you. I knew you'd need it and that you wouldn't think to ask. It isn't as easy for me as it is for you, but I can do it with a little magical help to guide me."

"Who?"

Paska clapped his hands and shook his head. "In a bit. Now for the second thing you must do!"

Morgana eyed him warily. She was never quite sure what to expect from Paska, and the glee with which he spoke made her suspect that whatever it was, she wouldn't like it as much as she'd appreciated his first requirement. "What is it?"

"Talk to me," Ceri said from the doorway into his house.

Morgana's eyes widened, and she looked between Ceri and Paska. "How long have you been standing there?" she asked.

"I thought you were going to wait inside," Paska said.

"You told me to wait inside. I wanted to see you work on more than just filling the earthen well for Morgana. It's only fair, right? You've seen me do my thing more times than I can count. And since we're such good friends, now, I didn't think you'd mind." Ceri smiled at Paska and batted her eyes rapidly.

Morgana tensed, waiting for Paska to explode. He didn't lose his temper often—he had a long fuse that seldom stayed lit for any length of time—but he guarded his privacy fiercely.

"Did you see the whole thing?" he asked, his voice infused with curiosity rather than anger.

"And heard it," Ceri confirmed. "I put the kettle on. Come inside. I saw more last night than I revealed. Partly because I was a bit overwhelmed with the other news." One of her hands dipped down and rested briefly on her low abdomen. "Three hundred and fifty years of sex and I never got pregnant. I kinda thought my fertility ship sailed a couple centuries ago."

Morgana glanced at her brother again, looking for the tell-tale signs that he was furious. There were none. Instead, there was a twinkle in his eyes and a fond smile on his face.

"Paska is an excellent name," he said.

"I'm not going to name her Paska," Ceri replied, rolling her eyes.

She held the door open and waved him and Morgana through. "I don't know why you chose it, but it is utterly ridiculous."

"It's not ridiculous," Paska protested. "And it would be nice if my godchild shared my name."

"Your godchild?" Ceri exclaimed. "Awfully presumptuous, aren't you?"

Paska threw an arm around her shoulders and pulled her in for a hug. "Lass, you know there are no better choices in this town. Who else would you ask to be the godfather of the most precious thing to arrive in Oracle Bay since me?"

Ceri laughed and pulled away from him. "I don't know, old man. I was thinking Barachiel would be an excellent choice."

Paska gasped in mock surprise. "That idiot angel? You would choose him before me?"

Ceri smiled sweetly and grabbed the kettle, pouring the boiling water into the teapot. "You love him. I've seen you two talking."

Morgana laughed. Ceri wasn't the only one who'd noticed the odd friendship between Paska and the angel who was not nearly as capricious as he pretended.

Paska huffed and slumped into a chair. "Fine. I won't protest anymore, no matter how hurt my feelings are."

Morgana looked between them, watching the banter like a game of badminton. She'd known they were friends, that Paska cared more for Ceri than he had for anyone in a long time, but to see him this free and easy with anyone who wasn't her was…astonishing.

"Name her Elaine," Paska said suddenly and with deadly seriousness.

"Elaine?" Ceri asked, looking at Morgana. "That's a beautiful name. Was it yours?"

Morgana shook her head, and the rage she'd expected when seeing Vortigern's bones earlier surged forward. She didn't know what Ceri saw in her eyes, but the younger woman leaned back and flinched as though Morgana had slapped her.

"If you don't want me to name my daughter Elaine, I won't, no matter who suggests it. I don't want to give offense." Ceri held her hands out in front of her.

"No," Morgana replied, her voice thick with unshed tears. "It is a beautiful name, and I would be honored beyond measure if it is the one you chose." She paused and took a deep breath, not sure if she wanted to share anything else. But Paska trusted this woman, and he trusted so seldomly, she had to believe Ceri was worth it. "Elaine was *my* daughter's name. She died almost sixteen hundred years ago. She was so beautiful and full of joy and magic. You couldn't help but smile when you saw her."

"She sounds like a gift," Ceri said. She picked up the teapot and poured three cups of tea.

"She was," Paska said. "There was no one she couldn't see the best in, and ultimately, that's what led her to her death."

Ceri bit her lip, and Morgana knew she wanted to ask more questions.

"I cannot talk about that now. Please don't ask." Morgana took a sip of her tea.

"Of course," Ceri replied. "Instead, let me tell you why I'm here, in your *brother's* home."

Morgana winced. "You know that is secret, right? You cannot tell anyone, not even your demon."

"Obviously, I know it's a secret," Ceri scoffed. "If it wasn't, everyone would already know because you would've told us ages ago."

A smile crept onto Morgana's face. Ceri really was a delightful person. "Of course. Now, please tell me what else you've seen. I'll take any help I can get."

Ceri leaned forward again and pulled Morgana in with her gaze. "You cannot take her on alone. You will need every asset you can find to take her down. I told you last night to follow your heart and not your head, but I know you won't listen. At least not right away. I know you don't care about yourself and would even find it noble to sacrifice yourself to save others, but it will not work. I will tell you again—if you try to take her out without someone at your side, not only will you die, but you will give her everything. Take the help that will be offered to you in London, or Bridget will not only have the power she'll drain from you, she'll have the means to follow the cords of your love to Paska and take his as well. Do not let her do that, because if you do, we are all going to die."

eight

Morgana settled into her first-class seat and accepted a glass of champagne from the flight attendant. Her phone pinged with the notification of an incoming text message, and she turned it off without looking. Perhaps driving herself to the airport without notifying Jezebel of the change of plans was impolite, but she'd needed time to think. After a second, she picked up the phone. It probably was Jezebel, but she couldn't ignore the possibility that it was someone else.

I'm okay. See you soon.

Relief whooshed out of her in one long breath. Donovan was okay.

The seat next to her shifted as someone settled into it. She glanced over and saw long legs stretched out and clad in denim so tight they outlined every muscle.

She sucked in a breath and her heart beat a little faster. She let her gaze travel up his legs, past his abdomen, pausing on his chest and shoulders—her weaknesses—and up to his face.

Disappointment deflated her, and she barely registered the stranger's smirk.

It wasn't a repeat of her last international flight; this man might be nicely built, but he wasn't Donovan.

It's for the best, Morgana told herself. No matter how much she yearned for him, she wasn't sure she could walk away a second time.

"Like what you see?" the man asked, amusement and cockiness dancing in his light brown eyes.

"Sorry," Morgana muttered. "I thought you were someone else." She pulled a paperback from her carryon, shoved the bag under the seat in front of her, settled her noise canceling headphones over her ears, and opened the book.

The man made a couple more attempts at conversation but gave up when Morgana didn't so much look at him.

Morgana refused all the meals but accepted Champagne every time it was offered. She knew she shouldn't. Even with her enhanced ability to metabolize alcohol due to her age and the changes that the magic wrought in her blood, she was drinking too much if she was going to safely land the plane in case of emergency.

Morgana was nearly finished with her second book when the plane started its descent into London Heathrow.

As soon as the captain turned off the seatbelt sign, Morgana was on her feet. She pulled her small carryon out from under the seat, then strode down the jetway into the airport.

When Morgana cleared customs and left the secured area of the airport, she retrieved her nondescript black suitcase from the baggage carousel, then walked towards the taxi stands but was drawn up short by a man dressed all in black holding a sign with "M. Bellflower" written on it.

She considered. It could be a trap, but Bridget hadn't yet shown any propensity to send anyone else to do her dirty work.

Except Donovan. But now that Morgana knew what a human— or humanesque—familiar looked like, she wouldn't miss it again. She drew in a breath and looked deeper. He was brimming with power, but all of it was his own.

Warlock.

Morgana walked over to him. "Scales?" she asked.

He nodded sharply. "Silver Eye?"

Her nod was just as brief.

"If you want, I can take you to the prison." His words were clipped and emotionless.

"I didn't think I would be welcome, much less met and escorted," Morgana said. She handed the man her roller bag, even though he hadn't indicated he was planning on taking it.

He took the bag when it became apparent she wasn't going to take it back and led her out of the airport and to his waiting town car.

"We knew you'd show up regardless of your welcome. It's better if the visit is controlled." He opened the trunk of the car, slid her suitcase inside, then closed the door.

Morgana waited by the back passenger side door.

The man huffed, then opened the door for her. She inclined her head. "Thank you. I appreciate your courtesy."

He grunted, slammed her door a little harder than necessary, then walked around the car and got in.

"What's your name?" Morgana asked once they'd left the airport.

"Why do you want to know?"

Morgana rolled her eyes. Warlocks were always so touchy. Probably an inferiority complex. "It would be easier if I could address you by your name. However, if you would prefer to keep that to yourself, I will not push."

"Mark."

He was obviously a stellar conversationalist. It was probably why he'd been sent. Someone younger and more nervous around her might reveal more than he was supposed to.

"Mark," she said in her most pleasant voice, the one she'd cultivated when she was undercover for the Silver Eye. "Where are you taking me?"

"The prison. We want you in and out as quickly as possible. There is no reason to draw this out with social niceties and the pretense of courtesy." He glanced at her in the rearview mirror, then looked back at the road.

"I'm glad to get this part of the visit out of the way with quickly, but I haven't eaten since before I boarded the plane in Portland, Oregon, and if I'm going to get through the next few hours without sleep, I need something to keep my strength up." As if to emphasize her words, Morgana's stomach growled.

"I'm not authorized to stop anywhere."

Her stomach growled louder. "One hour delay will not change anything, will it?"

Mark grunted, then changed lanes and exited the M4 and drove down a progression of smaller and smaller streets, eventually pulling up in front of The Magpie and Crown. "Will this do?"

Sarcasm lay heavy on his voice, and Morgana smiled slightly.

"This will do nicely. Presumably, they will have a traditional pub menu. I will not linger too long, and of course, I would love it if you'd join me, my treat." Morgana sat in the back until he opened the door for her. She probably shouldn't tweak his pride and sensibilities this much, but this was a small enjoyment in a world that had consisted of little joy lately.

Mark followed her in. Morgana took mercy on him and didn't make him open the pub door for her.

The host station was unoccupied. Morgana strode up to the bar and pushed her American accent back, letting the speech of her native country take control. "Is your kitchen open?"

The bartender smiled at her. "Just opened. Take a menu and find a seat wherever you want. You can order with an app on your phone, or if you'd rather, I'll send Jamie over."

"Send Jamie over," Morgana said. "I've just come from the states and haven't had a chance to update my phone. Please pour me a Warner's gin and tonic and send it over with Jamie. My driver will have a Coke."

"One G&T and one Coke coming up. Jamie will be out in a couple minutes." The bartender winked at Morgana, then walked down to mix her drink.

Morgana looked around the pub. It was long and narrow. The bar ran nearly the length of the back wall, and tables were set against the other wall. Morgana chose a table midway between the entrance and back exit, situated her chair so she could see the entirety of the bar, then gestured towards the empty chair across from her. "Please sit, Mark."

"Your driver?" he asked.

Morgana shrugged. "You aren't my friend. Not even an acquaintance. What would you call our relationship?"

"We don't have a relationship," he spat out. "I would never attach myself to a *witch*."

"That's what I thought," Morgana said smoothly. "Therefore, since you have been employed to drive me from the airport to our destination, you are my driver. And since you are my driver, you will drink a Coke rather than this delightful cocktail."

A young person who must be Jamie set the drinks on the table. They had delicate androgynous elfin features, pale skin, sapphire blue eyes, and bright pink hair that just brushed their shoulders.

"Your hair is a wonderful color," Morgana said. "Quite fetching."

Jamie blushed. They smoothed their hands down over their grey t-shirt and denim jeans. "Thank you. Your hair is great, too. Your whole look." They waved their hand to encompass Morgana's long, dark hair, black leather pants, matching jacket, and a corset top with nearly imperceptible scarlet swirls.

"Thank you." Morgana glanced down at the menu. "I'll have the steak and ale pie."

Jamie nodded, then turned towards Mark. "And you?"

"Fish and chips," he said without looking up at them.

"Coming right out." Jamie took their menus, spun on their heel—black Dr. Martens over skinny black jeans—and disappeared into the kitchen.

"What can I expect?" Morgana asked Mark, taking a long drink of her cocktail.

He shrugged. "When was the last time you were there?"

Morgana smiled tightly. "I have few reasons to visit a warlock prison."

Anger sparked in his eyes. "I did not mean officially. We know the Silver Eye takes too great an interest in our prisoners, and no doubt has aided the few escapes we've had."

"I cannot speak to what other members of the Eye do or do not." It wasn't completely true. In cases where a prisoner was clearly innocent or able to be rehabilitated, action was taken to ensure the witch in question lived, but she was not about to admit that to Mark. "I have never been in the Scales prison, either as a guest, a prisoner, or a rescue party. And before you even ask, the Eye had nothing to do with Bridget's escape. They should have taken custody of her instead of allowing the Scales to hold her." Morgana took another drink, then set it down with a sigh of satisfaction. "This really is excellent gin."

Mark's hands trembled. Perhaps he wasn't as unflappable as she'd originally thought. That was good. Men who were angry and off-balance often revealed more than they'd intended.

"We didn't let her go," he growled.

"You didn't stop her, either, though, did you?" Morgana asked pleasantly. "You chased her all over Ireland and Canada and did not even know who you were chasing. One of your own was even bound to her as a human familiar, and you did not know. I figured out who she was within a month of meeting her face-to-face, and it was because of me she was captured."

Morgana didn't bother adding that she'd nearly been killed in the process, or that the power Bridget had stolen from her might be the reason the blood witch had been able to break free.

"Which of us was bound to her?" Mark asked, incredulity overtaking his anger.

Damn. Donovan clearly had not revealed his true identity to his employers nor fully reported on the events in Oracle Bay—the events that he had a hand in. She needed to be careful to guard her tongue, even if Mark could not.

Morgana shrugged and lied. "I do not know. I heard it from one of the men who was in Oracle Bay recently."

Mark glared as if he didn't quite believe her, but Morgana kept her gaze placid and her face expressionless.

"We didn't let her escape," Mark muttered. "Not on purpose."

Morgana tilted her head to one side and looked at him until he squirmed. He ducked his head, avoiding her gaze, and took a sip of his Coke.

"What do you mean by that?" Morgana asked. "I may have a poor opinion of the Scales as an organization, their ability to successfully contain and punish witches who are truly dangerous, to tell the difference between a blood witch and a witch who uses their own blood in ritual, and their lack of curiosity to learn. But I would never have accused you of letting her escape."

Mark didn't look at her and remained silent.

Jamie returned with their food. "Anything else?"

"I would love another gin and tonic," Morgana said. "And a bottle of sparkling water would be appreciated as well."

"I'll be right back with those."

"Mark, what did you mean by your statement? It feels important, and if I am going to track her down, I require all possible information." Morgana picked up her fork, took a bite of steak and flaky pastry, and waited.

"You will not be tracking her down. That is our job. You are only allowed in now so that you will not force your way in later." Mark picked up a piece of deep-fried cod and tore a piece off with his teeth.

"There will be a carefully crafted message," Morgana said. "I am aware of this, as you must be. Then there is no harm in telling me now what I will hear again from your superiors. The benefit of you sharing the story now is that it will be from the perspective of a man who knows what happens in the prison rather than a superior officer who only sets foot inside the facility for trials, executions, and emergencies."

"Awright, then," Mark said. His voice roughed, and his accent slipped almost imperceptibly into Scottish. "You know she escaped, taking out almost twenty of her guards. Seven dead, the rest injured. Two more have died since. She drained their power, but before she killed them, she forced one to unlock the door and hand over the keys."

"You cannot mean physical keys, surely," Morgana said.

"Not entirely. There are physical keys, electronic safeguards, and magical barriers on top of those. No single guard has access to more than two of the three, and most of us have only one, if any at all. The electronic safeguards are keyed to me. I cannot unlock a cell, but I could take down the power that electrifies the door to each cell."

"Did anyone else escape when Bridget broke out?" Morgana asked.

"No. Hers was the only door that opened. There were six guards assigned to her. They worked in pairs in overlapping eight-hour shifts, so there was a new team on every four. Each of us were among the strongest, magically speaking."

"If there were only two on duty at any given time, how was it that so many were killed?" Morgana asked. She doubted she would get nearly this much information from whoever she met with at the Scales prison.

As if he'd realized the same thing, Mark stuffed another piece of fish in his mouth and washed it down with Coke, refusing to meet her eyes.

nine

"No." Morgana crossed her arms and glared at Mark. He hadn't spoken another word to her in the pub, not even to thank her for the meal—not that she needed thanks—until now.

"You have to put on the blindfold," he said in a reasonable tone that was as far away as the anger that'd punctuated his words in the pub.

"Why? I already know where we are," Morgana said. After Mark had ushered her back to the car, he'd driven away in silence. Morgana had given up trying to keep track of where they were by watching the streets roll by and grabbed her phone out of her pocket and pulled up her map app.

It was as she'd expected. Mark was deliberately driving in circles and spirals, probably to disorient her. Perhaps the Scales believed the common rumor that witches eschewed technology whenever possible, and she would be lost. But she was not only able to pinpoint where they were, she could save their location and send it to Paska.

Mark took a deep breath and looked up at the sky. Morgana had the distinct impression that he was counting to ten and asking his gods for patience.

"You might know the general location," he agreed, then gestured behind him. "It is hard to disguise the Thames as anything else. However, you do not know how the prison is accessed, and that is a secret we will not share with you. Either put the blindfold on and let me lead you until we're inside, or stay here, in which case, I thank you for the meal and wish you luck finding a flight back to the United States."

Morgana narrowed her eyes. His attitude and conversation were distinctly different than they'd been up to this point, and she began to suspect he'd been playing her all along. Perhaps he was further up the chain of command than she'd originally thought, and he was feeling her out the same way she'd been doing to him.

She mentally kicked herself. She should have seen it. She hadn't given away anything—she had assumed she'd been dealing with a common security guard—but she did not like the feeling of having the wool pulled over her eyes.

Morgana weighed the pros and cons of giving in to his demand she be blindfolded. After a moment, she shrugged. The Silver Eye might have cut off all communication, making it even more likely they did not anticipate her coming out of this situation alive, but they knew she was here. The Scales would be unlikely to do anything stupid. She pursed her lips. Anything terribly stupid.

"I agree," she said.

Mark's eyebrows shot up for a moment, and Morgana enjoyed his look of surprise before he schooled his expression.

"Very well." He pulled a blindfold out of his pocket and walked over to her. "Turn around."

She did as commanded and held still as the cool silk cloth slid against her skin. "Silk blindfold? Kinky."

Mark grunted, but Morgana could swear she heard an undercurrent of laughter in it.

He pulled it tight. "Can you see anything?"

"Not a thing," Morgana said. "You must have paid a witch a pretty penny to have your blindfolds enchanted."

"You're not the only ones who can harness the darkness," Mark said, all amusement gone from his voice now.

Morgana smiled. "Of course not. My apologies. I had forgotten."

"I'm sure you did." He grabbed her arm. "Don't fight me and stay close. The path is narrow in places, and you don't want to wander away."

Morgana nodded her acquiescence. She might be known to the Scales, at least in part, but she doubted they knew the full extent of her powers, especially not after Paska's gift. Neither earth nor water would pose any danger to her unless they cuffed her as well as blindfolded her, and even then, there were no guarantees she wouldn't have enough power to save herself.

But she had no intention of stepping off the path to test her abilities or tweak Mark any further. It was always better to be underestimated, and she was not about to give them even a minor show of power.

They walked down a slight decline for approximately twenty minutes, the only sounds their footsteps on the cobblestone path and the steady drip-drip-drip of water. Morgana breathed deeply, feeling the moisture in the air cling to her skin. They were some distance under the Thames.

A couple minutes later, they started back uphill at a much greater incline than they'd gone down.

Mark was huffing beside her before they even hit the stairs. "Thirty stairs. They are stone and slippery and not uniform," he wheezed. "I'll be right behind you."

"Is there a railing?" Morgana asked.

"No railing. Get going."

Morgana walked forward until a toe hit the rise of the stair. The climb was awkward with no eyesight and no railing. She stumbled every couple steps when the rise of the stair didn't match her feet's expectations, but the grip of her boots kept her from slipping.

Finally, she hit the thirtieth step. She paused, felt out with her toe experimentally, then shuffled forward and out of the way of Mark, who, judging from his panting, was only about halfway up.

A hand grabbed hers. Morgana clasped the unseen hand hard, yanked the person down towards her, and when she heard their muffled exclamation of shock and pain, she swept one boot-clad foot under theirs. She was rewarded with the thump of a body hitting the floor. Immediately after, she felt a vibration in her chest that suffused her body with pain, amusement, pride, and love. Her breath left her in a sigh of relief. "Donovan?"

Donovan stood and untied her blindfold, letting the silk slide down her neck and brush against her breasts. She bit back a gasp; this shouldn't affect her this much. It was only a scarf over three layers of clothes. Nothing erotic about that.

He leaned close to her and whispered, "We are not, nor have we ever been, involved."

Hurt pierced her chest at his words, even though she'd been the one to close the door on their relationship. She knew the words were a warning, a signal that they could not acknowledge their past in front of anyone she was likely to encounter, but somehow, it still stung.

Then his tongue traced the shell of her ear, and the pain of rejection melted into the heat of arousal.

The cords between them vibrated a very different song now. If this was the way they resonated together with the hint of intimacy, she could only imagine what it would feel like when they were naked in each other's arms again.

No. That could not be, not unless she knew it would make no difference to hers or Paska's fates. But until their deaths became inevitable, she would do what she must to stave off the end. And that meant not giving in to the attraction between them that would strip away all walls she'd built between her heart and his.

She took a step forward and turned just in time to see Mark, red-faced and puffing, reach the top of the staircase.

"Davies," he said neutrally, although distaste curled his lip.

"Lloyd," Donovan replied cheerfully. "Thank you for retrieving Ms. Bellflower for us. Your zeal in leaving before I was ready to accompany you is noted."

Donovan turned and gave Morgana a slight bow, gesturing towards the center corridor. "If you wouldn't mind accompanying me. We'll stop first in a conference room so you can speak with the surviving guards on duty, and we can attempt to answer any questions you might have. Then, I will take you to Bridget's cell. After that, I'm afraid we will have to ask you to leave."

Mark took off in a different direction, leaving her and Donovan alone in the stony corridor.

Morgana walked forward, careful to keep plenty of distance between her and Donovan. "I appreciate you meeting with me at all. If you don't mind my asking, can you tell me your rank within the Scales? I had previously been under the impression that you were more of a contractor for them, not officially affiliated, nor indeed highly enough ranked that you could speak for the organization."

Donovan sped up until he was walking next to her, then slowed and matched his stride to hers. "I'm not speaking for the organization, and my work with them is less formal than Mark's, for example. And I'm not responsible for any assumptions you made about my job. I never lied to you or misled you."

There was the anger Morgana had expected, and she felt an answering flare. "Did you not? I seem to recall some very surprising information that came to light towards the end of our previous association just before I subdued Bridget for you so you could take her into Scales' custody."

Donovan snorted, and his amusement washed away whatever rancor existed between them. "You sound like you're an extra from Downton Abbey. Not only are you stressed and formal, you've pulled out a posh accent. Love the outfit, by the way. It's no sweater set and pearls, but the leather works for you."

Morgana lowered her voice. "If we have never had anything but a professional relationship, shouldn't you keep your conversation a little more focused on work and less on my clothes and accent?"

She glanced at him when he didn't immediately answer and took a moment to drink him in. He was almost six inches taller than her not-inconsiderate height of five and a half feet, and his grey-streaked dark hair was pulled back by a rubber band and trailed down his back. Light, honey-brown eyes glowed against his russet skin, only lightly lined, making him appear at least a decade younger than his actual early sixties. He was wearing dark denim jeans and a kelly green t-shirt that stretched tight across his chest and encased his strong, muscular shoulders. There were no signs of any lingering injuries, no scars that she could see, and no weakness.

He looked like the in-focus version of the man who'd sat next to her on the plane.

"My look hasn't changed much," Donovan said.

"Good," Morgana said. "It makes you easier to identify in case you ever become a target."

He laughed as they approached the end of the long corridor. Donovan opened the last door on the right and ushered her into a beige-on-beige room that would have fit into any corporate office. "The others will join us soon. Would you like tea? Water? Soda?"

"I would love a water. Sparkling if you have it." Morgana set down her bag and hoped her other suitcase survived whatever search the Scales were presumably conducting. There was nothing in there unusual, but they might be extra thorough when they found there was nothing to discover.

Donovan cracked open a bottle of sparkling mineral water and poured it into a glass for her. "You must be exhausted. How long have you been up?"

"Long enough that I cannot perform those calculations right now." The longer she sat alone in a room with Donovan, the less she remembered why she had to stay away from him, despite his amorphous connection to the Scales. Surely if she and Paska were doomed anyway, she might as well enjoy the last months of her life with the man she'd fallen in love with.

Her phone buzzed. She pulled it out of the inside pocket in her jacket. Paska had texted her. She didn't really want to open it but felt like she had no choice. She tapped the message app.

Don't do it. I'm working on a solution, so don't fuck this up any more than you already have.

Morgana shoved her phone back in her pocket and scowled at nothing in particular.

"Problem?" Donovan asked.

"Nope," Morgana replied as cheerfully as possible, which was not very cheerful right now. "Just Paska checking in to make sure I got to London." She pulled her phone back out of her pocket and fired off a quick response.

I appreciate you looking out for me for the last sixteen hundred years. The goddess has blessed me more than any mortal man could ever curse us. I will take care.

She put her phone away and inhaled deeply. The weight of the curse that had lain on her for centuries released. The curse itself was still there—she could feel it wrapped around her soul—but she would no longer give it the power to hold her down. She would do nothing rash—like rip off her clothes and ask Donovan to take her right then and there on the large conference room table—but she was finally able to breathe through the curse and maybe, just maybe, see something on the other side.

ten

Five men, all in black, filed into the room, interrupting Morgana's rather elaborate fantasy she'd been concocting while watching Donovan from underneath her lashes. Based on the flush on his ruddy, tanned skin, he was getting the echoes of what she was imagining through the bond they'd formed, for all that it was nascent and tenuous.

Donovan jumped to his feet, then just as quickly sat down. Morgana smirked at him when she saw the obvious source of his discomfort. Either his imagination had been putting in the same overtime as hers, or he was getting the gist of what she was thinking. It did neither of them any good in the long run as they could not, in good conscience, further consummate their relationship. Nor were they likely to have the chance to do more than think lustful thoughts at each other.

It wasn't the release she craved, but it was something. One small connection between them.

The five men sat in near perfect synchronization, and power rolled off them and across the table, crashing into her.

Morgana rolled her eyes. She might not want to ensure they were aware of how powerful she truly was, but she would not put up with this feeble attempt to cow her magic. They might have power, some of it might even be innate and not spelled, but she was a witch and lived by traditions that had been passed to her over centuries, was blessed by her goddess, and had lived for hundreds of years growing her power and refining her control over the elements.

She held up a hand—a gesture was unnecessary, and she generally considered them ostentatious, but there was a time and a place to show off—and the roll of smoke of their power visibly coalesced, broke against the barrier she'd set, and flowed back towards them like a wave retreating into the sea.

They barely had time to dissipate their own testing before it covered them.

"Gentlemen," Morgana said. "Let us not waste time playing games. I will acknowledge the Scales as an entity powerful in its own right. I'm sure you are some of the strongest members and are not easily defeated. I do not blame you for Bridget's escape, nor do I think that makes you weak. In return, I would ask of you to believe there is nothing you can do to me, singly or together, that would end well for you. Can we agree so we can move on? I am eager to hear the abridged story you have prepared for me and see the cell Bridget escaped from, likely cleansed of all magical residue. After that, I will leave you to your work, and you can breathe easily again."

The man in the center of the group of five leaned forward and stared at her with an intensity that signaled he was expecting her to squirm. He had ebony skin, deep brown eyes, and a shaved head. He was dressed in the same tactical long-sleeved black t-shirt and trousers as the others. Morgana grimaced slightly. She might mock the all-black uniformity of their clothing, but she was little better, clad as she was in black from head to toe.

Donovan was the only bright spot in the room.

After another moment of scrutiny, Morgana grew impatient. "Are you finished intimidating me? I would like to get on with business. I rose at five o'clock in the morning on the west coast of the United States, and I am exhausted."

The Black man, who looked like he was in charge—or would have, if Donovan wasn't sprawled in his chair ignoring the man—stood.

"I am John Smith."

Morgana snorted, an inelegant sound but an unavoidable one. "Seriously?"

He raised an eyebrow at her, and she stuffed her incredulous amusement back down and attempted to look suitably interested in whatever he was going to say.

"The other men in this room were all present for the blood witch's escape. You know Mr. Davies from your earlier association when we attempted to work with the Silver Eye to find the witch and bring her into custody." Smith's gaze didn't leave her face.

Morgana steadfastly kept her gaze on the man in front of her, resisting the urge to look at Donovan, assess him for any injuries he might be hiding, and assure herself that he was okay.

"And the others?" she asked steadily.

"Minor injuries only. They were not the guards assigned directly to the blood witch, but rather were on the floor making regular patrols between the secure cells we have for all our most dangerous criminals. They will answer your questions, but you do not need to know their names." He glared like he was expecting her to leap across the table and shake the names from the row of pale white men with sandy hair, light brown eyes, and sprinklings of freckles who looked as if they could be cousins.

"I will not ask for their names. I appreciate you giving me the opportunity to ask questions." She pulled out a notebook with her list of questions. She wasn't sure if she'd be given the chance to ask, but she wanted to be prepared.

"Did you notice anything unusual about Bridget the day she escaped, such as a change in food consumption, sleep habits, conversation topics?"

"No," operative number one said, the other four shaking their heads in agreement.

Morgana paused for a moment, but no one elaborated.

"What was the usual schedule for Bridget?" Morgana tapped her pencil against the notepad while the men exchanged glances.

"Next question," Smith said.

It was going to be that kind of questioning, then. She would have to ask carefully since she would get few if any answers, and most of the information she'd be able to gather would be through reactions and expressions rather than any verbalizations.

"Did she say anything when she escaped?" Morgana asked.

Operative number four shuddered, then blurted, "She didn't say nothin', but she laughed, and it made me feel like me nightmares had come to life."

Operative two nodded emphatically. "It chilled a body to their very soul."

"She did say something, though," operative three said quietly. "Just before she ripped Jenkins's heart out and disappeared."

"Next question," Smith said. "And make it count, because it'll be your last."

Morgana considered carefully. She was used to being exact in her questioning—looking into the future required conciseness and specificity—but she felt an extra level of pressure here.

"You spent weeks with her in your custody at the behest of those who hold higher rank than you. Knowing what you now know about Bridget and her capabilities, would you use magic or modern weaponry to execute her immediately?" It wasn't a great question, and it wouldn't give her answers, but she was interested in their thoughts.

"Both," Smith said. "I know that guns aren't something the Silver Eye employs, so it's a good thing they aren't pursuing her." He stood and the rest of his men, with the exception of Donovan, did the same.

Morgana waited a couple beats, long enough to make it obvious that she cared little for their protocol, then finished her water and stood up.

"Presumably, you'll blindfold me again and escort me to the exit. May I also assume that my suitcase will be waiting for me?" Morgana picked up her black bag and slung it across her body.

Smith didn't answer. Rather, he turned on his heel and marched out of the room.

Donovan stood, nodded at Morgana, and said, "Mark will be in shortly to show you out. He will have your suitcase with him as well. Take whatever you've learned back to the Eye, then go home, Morgana. There is nothing safe or easy about this search, and you can do nothing that the Scales can't."

Morgana smiled at him. "I will certainly report this information. I will also ensure the Eye knows not to pursue Bridget because the Scales believes they are not properly equipped to handle her capture."

Donovan winced, then grinned slightly. "I look forward to hearing the conversation between representatives from our two organizations when that message is delivered."

Morgana cocked her head and regarded him. "Is that something you're likely to hear? Because I wouldn't have thought you positioned to be privy to that kind of conversation."

"There are ways to listen without being seen, although I would never do anything like that." He winked broadly and left the room.

Morgana sat on a surprisingly comfortable deck chair on the balcony of the hotel she'd booked that morning. The river view was lovely, and she sipped the wine she'd ordered from room service as she scanned the Thames, trying to figure out where the island prison was located.

When she'd had her blindfold removed and her suitcase

returned, Mark had disappeared, leaving her to find a taxi to take her to her hotel.

In the end, she had not been able to secure a ride before a cold drizzle started, so she'd walked the three blocks to the nearest Tube station and rode in the crowded carriage to her destination.

She'd arrived at the hotel damp, travel-stained, and exhausted. The hotel receptionist had taken one look at her, expedited her check-in, upgraded her to the nicest suite they had available, and sent up a bottle of wine.

She stretched and adjusted the warm blanket around her body. She was tired but loathe to let herself fall asleep before the sun went down. She suspected that she would not be returning home immediately, and it would be better to adjust to the seven-hour time difference as quickly as possible. That meant staying up until a reasonable bedtime and remaining in bed until at least six o'clock in the morning, her usual waking time.

She sighed in defeat. There was nothing immediately visible, either through regular or her enhanced magical sight. They must have had a witch hide the prison the same way Morgana hid the Irish town of Kilnamanagh where the coven she'd started three hundred years ago was housed.

Morgana went back into the room, stripped off her clothes, and turned the water in the shower up as hot as she could stand it.

Once she was clean and the ache in her muscles that had shown up during the flight relaxed, she dressed in loose, dark trousers, a black blouse, and put her leather jacket back on.

She headed down to the main floor and stopped at the concierge desk.

"Do you have a recommendation for dinner?" Morgana asked.

The woman behind the desk tucked her light brown hair behind her ear. "It depends on what you're looking for. Do you have a particular cuisine in mind? If you want traditional British and French cuisine, the Grill is very good, and they have an excellent wine selection."

"That sounds perfect." Morgana smiled at the young woman. "Do I need a reservation?"

"I can take care of that for you. What's your room number?"

"I'm in the River View suite. Is there a bar I can wait at until my table is ready?" Morgana kept her smile in place and the exhaustion that plagued her away from her expression.

"Of course," the woman said. "I'll let the bartender know you're on your way. Your table will be ready in about fifteen minutes. Will anyone be joining you for dinner tonight?"

Morgana started to shake her head, but before she could answer, a deeper voice behind said, "We'll need a table for two, and my thanks."

eleven

Morgana sat at the bar, ignoring Donovan and concentrating on her gin and tonic. He hadn't said anything, either, since walking in behind her and claiming to be her dining companion.

She was determined not to be the first to speak, but when he finished his beer and signaled the bartender for another, Morgana broke the silence.

"Why are you here?" she asked quietly.

"You're not going to ask how I found you?" Donovan countered.

Morgana shifted her gaze to him but kept most of her attention on the cocktail in front of her. "You work for the Scales—more than just work for them if appearances are anything to judge by. That gives you access to all sorts of information. I'm not trying to hide. I've checked into this hotel with a credit card and using my real name. The how isn't important."

Donovan raised an eyebrow. "Your real name?" Skepticism laced his tone.

"This name is on all my legal documents and financial accounts," Morgana said. "So yes, my real name. You are avoiding the question.

After the warning that we should not appear to know each other any better than two people who have worked together in the past, it seems unwise to follow me to my hotel. If you can find me, so can any of your colleagues."

Donovan was again saved from answering when the host arrived to show them to their table.

Morgana pasted a smile on her face and pretended she wasn't bothered by the idea of sitting across from Donovan for an entire meal. It wouldn't be as easy to ignore her feelings when she couldn't avoid his eyes.

Their table was tucked into the back corner, adding an air of intimacy to an already intimate restaurant.

Morgana ordered another G&T, and Donovan ordered a bottle of grenache blanc and two glasses.

When they were alone again, Morgana delayed having to look at Donovan by studying the menu, even though she already knew what she was ordering.

Donovan set his menu down. "I'm coming with you."

Morgana's eyebrows flew up to her hairline. He couldn't have said anything that would've made him more unattractive in that moment. If there was anything she hated, it was being told what to do and how things were going to go with her. "I don't recall asking you to go anywhere with me."

"You didn't, and I know you wouldn't, even if it meant you'd be in danger. You are too damn proud, and not good at asking for help." Donovan drained his beer.

"I do not need an escort back to Oracle Bay," Morgana said, placing her menu on the table and smiling up at the server who was delivering their drinks.

After ordering and taking a long drink, Morgana turned her attention back to Donovan. He was smiling at her over the rim of his wineglass.

"What?" she demanded.

"You're not going back to Oracle Bay," he said.

Morgana let the affront she felt at his audacity show in her expression. "I most certainly am returning to Oracle Bay. It is my home."

Donovan quirked one eyebrow. Morgana dropped her gaze to avoid getting caught in his honey-brown eyes. That was a mistake. Now, she was caught by the play of muscles under his crisp red button-down shirt and the way his suit jacket fit like it had been made for him.

She jerked her eyes back up to his face when she heard his low chuckle.

"You might fight what's between us, but you can't ignore your attraction to me, can you?" His lips curled upwards, and her toes curled in response.

"Never mind that," she said, wishing she could dismiss her rising lust as easily as she could dismiss his words. "You know why things are the way they are. Why don't you tell me what it is you came here to say and then leave so I can finish my meal and my evening in peace." Morgana tipped back her gin and drained it in three swallows.

Donovan filled her wine glass from the bottle on the table and slid it across to her. "There's no reason to hurry. I've already ordered dinner, and I'm planning on dessert." His eyes dipped lower, lingered on her lips, then scanned down the length of her body.

Heat scorched her skin in the wake of his gaze, and she took a gulp of the wine to cool herself down.

Morgana flushed and felt the blush staining her pale skin. It'd been centuries since she had met anyone who could disconcert her like this man.

"Where will you go next to pick up the trail?" Donovan asked, then held up a hand. "Don't lie to me, Morgana. There've been too many of those between us already."

"I'd rather not tell you," she replied. He was right; they had so many lies between them. And too many truths to bridge the gap.

"It would be easier if you did. It'll save me the trouble of having to follow you. Being tailed is distracting. You're chasing a dangerous woman, and I wouldn't want you to be anything less than at the top of your game." He reached out and caught her wrist as she was about to set her wineglass down. He held her hand steady and refilled her glass, brushing his thumb against the pulse point in her wrist before letting her go.

"You could refrain from following me," Morgana said evenly, taking a small sip of her wine before setting it down. She ran her thumb up and down the stem of the glass and sent a prayer to her goddess that the food would arrive soon so she could find a way out of this conversation.

"You have to know that's not going to happen," Donovan said. "The Silver Eye said you're a free agent now, and they don't know what you're doing."

Morgana gritted her teeth. Nothing like being thrown to the wolves by the organization she'd spent the last century working for.

"You don't have a return ticket to the States. That means you have plans, and I want to know what they are." He leaned forward and placed his left arm on the table next to the wall, briefly touching her arm before she pulled away.

"Perhaps I am planning a week in London? The Savoy is a lovely place to stay—it's been too long since I was last here. It is always nice to take advantage of their spa services, not to mention the shopping in this area."

"Shopping? You could at least do me the courtesy of coming up with a plausible lie." Donovan's eyes jerked up and focused on something behind her, then swore under his breath.

"What is it?" Morgana asked. Her pulse accelerated, then steadied. "Bridget?"

"It's my boss." Donovan relaxed back into his chair, but a muscle clenching and releasing in his jaw belied his stance. "I thought I'd have a little more time."

"You had to have known you'd be found here," Morgana said reasonably. "As previously noted, if you were able to find me, so could anyone else. And it is likely that there are others as disinclined to believe that I would be returning home immediately after this visit, as untrue as that assumption may be."

Morgana leaned back to make room for her plate of risotto. The server refilled their glasses and took an order for another bottle of wine before walking away.

Donovan eyed his duck à la'Orange with a grin. "Maybe the boss'll wait until I'm done eating, at least. Even he wouldn't want to ruin this duck and that wine."

Morgana resisted the urge to turn around and look. She was not violating any rules by eating dinner in her hotel, although Paska would not be thrilled to know who she was dining with.

Donovan groaned, then stuffed a bite of duck into his mouth.

"Is he not waiting?" Morgana asked with a smile. The lemon and asparagus risotto was perfectly creamy, and the last glass of grenache blanc was an excellent accompaniment. If things between her and Donovan could be different, this dinner would be nearly perfect.

The server returned with a half-bottle of Côtes du Rhône and a bottle of Laurent-Perrier Grand Siecle No. 25. "The gentleman at the bar sends the Champagne with his compliments," the server said, presenting the label to Donovan.

Morgana twisted around in her chair. A white man with straw-blond hair leaned against the bar in a perfectly tailored suit. He towered over everyone around him, and when he saw her looking, he smiled and saluted her with two fingers. Something about him made her uneasy, but not so uneasy that she wouldn't drink Champagne.

Donovan looked at Morgana. "The lady knows a lot more about Champagne than me. It's her opinion that will matter."

The sommelier nodded and turned the bottle towards Morgana. It was one of her favorites.

"That looks delightful," she said. "I haven't had any for a few years. Is this as structured as the No. 24?"

"Better in some ways," the som said, untwisting the cage. He popped the cork, then poured some into a flute and handed it to Morgana.

She took a sip and let the soft bubbles of the sparkling wine melt on her tongue. She closed her eyes in pleasure as the rich, biscuity taste suffused her mouth, then swallowed. "Oh, this is magnificent."

The som smiled and filled both glasses, then set the bottle in an ice bucket the server placed on the table. "I'm glad you enjoyed it. Please let me know if you require anything else."

Morgana took another sip of the Champagne. "This is the most wonderful thing I've had in my mouth in a long, long time."

Donovan snorted.

Morgana opened her eyes and looked at him. "Is something funny?" As soon as she asked, she replayed the words she'd just uttered. A flush washed across her face.

"I wouldn't call a couple months a long, long time," he said with a wink.

"Neither would I, and I stand by my original statement. It has been a very long time." It would be too easy to give into her amusement and relax. He was as infuriating as he had been when they'd first met; the heat between them had not gone away. If anything, it had intensified. But if she enjoyed herself now, it would be easier to make an excuse to do it again. And soon, it would be easy to justify not just a meal, but after dinner drinks seated next to each other in the bar, a walk along the Thames holding hands, and a goodnight kiss at the door to her suite.

And if she let her lips touch his, her defenses would crumble. She had to keep her distance. If Paska was to be believed, she'd already set it in motion when she'd fallen in love with Donovan, but if she could keep from binding their hearts too closely together, maybe it would be slow to reach completion.

"If my boss wasn't watching us, this evening would be just about perfect," Donovan said, unconsciously echoing her thoughts. "It's a stupid power play." Donovan took another bite of his duck, then a sip of the Champagne. "This really is good. I don't know a lot about Champagne. Or wine at all, really. I'm glad you do."

"Would you prefer a beer?" Morgana asked. "I'm sure they have an excellent selection. You could get a glass of whiskey and a beer, and I will finish the Champagne on my own."

"I appreciate the offer of self-sacrifice, but I'll just keep plowing ahead with the bubbly. I understand it's the traditional drink at weddings." Donovan took another, longer drink of his Champagne.

Heat followed by ice flowed over Morgana's body, and she froze with her fork halfway between her mouth and the plate. She'd never considered the ties he had beyond the Scales and her. He probably had family, and at his age, his nieces and nephews would be old enough to get married.

"Do you have kids?" she blurted.

Donovan tilted his head to one side and set down his fork. "We never really talked about family, did we? We skipped a lot of the 'getting to know you' stuff people do when they're working together"—he winked—"in favor of 'how do we not get killed by this crazy witch?' Why are you asking now?"

Morgana worried at her lower lip with her teeth, then forced herself to let go. "At your mention of weddings, I realized you were of an age to have nieces and nephews, as well as the children of your friends getting married and wondered whose wedding you would be attending. It then occurred to me that you might also have children. Hence the question."

"It's a perfectly normal question, even for professional acquaintances," Donovan said, a smile playing around his lips. "Even for professional acquaintances who show their nerves by becoming excessively formal when speaking."

Morgana clamped her lips shut and waited for him to continue.

"I have three kids," Donovan said finally.

Morgana nodded, determined to let it go at that. She had the knowledge she had requested, and there was no reason to look further into it.

"Dakota is twenty-eight. She lives in Seattle with her wife Valerie. Benjamin—Ben—is twenty-five. He lives wherever he happens to be at the moment and is not getting married any time soon. My youngest, Sara, is twenty-three. She's in grad school at the University of Washington, studying to be a librarian. I talk to her almost every day, and she would've told me if she was getting hitched. As far as I know—and she might not tell me this unless things were getting serious—she's not even seeing anyone. Too focused on her school and learning to manage the gifts she's inherited from my side of the family." The smile that appeared on Donovan's face when he talked about his children warmed Morgana's chest.

"I wasn't thinking of any of their weddings," Donovan continued. "I was thinking about mine."

Morgana inhaled the sip of Champagne she'd been taking. "You're engaged?" she hissed. She may have ended things between them before they could really get started, but if he knew someone well enough to be affianced, he should never have kissed her in the first place.

"Not yet." His smile didn't waver, even in the face of her increasing anger. "But I have my eye on someone. She's worth any wait and all the patience."

Morgana's anger sputtered and died as quickly as it'd erupted. He was quite probably talking about her. There was no reason to ask for confirmation, even if he was being ridiculous and naïve about his chances with her. "Are you speaking of me?"

Donovan's grin widened, and his eyes softened. "Who else would be worth this much heartache?"

twelve

Morgana had made her escape as soon as she could without breaking the bounds of politeness, leaving Donovan with the rest of the Champagne and instructions to the server that anything he wanted would be covered on her tab.

She changed into wide-legged black pajama bottoms and a shell-pink chemise left over from her last undercover job and too comfortable to get rid of and opened a bottle of sparkling water. Five minutes later, there was a knock on her door. She should not answer it. No good came of a man—*that* man—being at her door.

Another soft knock, nearly deferential, broke the silence. That was not the way Donovan would knock.

She opened the door. A young, uniformed man stood in the doorway with a bottle of Champagne in an ice bucket.

"This is yours, madam," he said. "The gentleman you dined with had it sent up since neither of you finished it this evening."

"Thank you." She set down the bucket and pulled a few bills from her wallet. "Have a good evening." She closed the door behind him, found a glass on the sideboard, and poured herself some Champagne.

Morgana walked out onto her balcony, massaging her left temple and sipping her wine. A warm early summer breeze swept over the Thames and caressed her face briefly before dancing off to see what was happening on the next block over.

Raised voices caught her attention. She was too far away from the riverfront walk to clearly hear most conversations, but the volume on this one made it easier to eavesdrop.

"You're an idiot!"

Morgana stood and leaned over the balcony, scanning the area below. Donovan stood, arms crossed, almost out of view in the shadow of a large tree.

"You're the one who followed me and sent over the Champagne, and you call me an idiot?" Donovan's voice returned.

"Someone had to keep you out of trouble." The clipped British accent of the man Donovan had claimed was his boss froze Morgana in place.

Their voices lowered, and Morgana could no longer hear them. She leaned further over the balcony and concentrated. When she wanted to, she could hear much more than most, even including the magically inclined.

"You've seen her file; she's not going to be content with the song and dance Smith and his men gave her today. She'll take what she's learned and make her own plans, none of which will involve leaving this investigation to the Scales." Donovan sounded almost bored.

An uncomfortable sensation roiled Morgana's stomach. Donovan had already betrayed her once by not telling her Bridget had bound him as her familiar—something that wouldn't have been possible if he'd been purely human and didn't have the ability to borrow the shape of any passing felines.

She couldn't doubt his love or attraction—it was hard to lie through the bonds that formed between two people—but countless betrayals had happened despite love, sometimes even because of it.

But no. She would not let her insecurity overshadow what she knew. He was playing a game just as his boss was, and even with the tenuous bonds between them, he knew she was listening.

"Do you think you're the only one who believes he knows what Morgana Bellflower is up to? She's no longer working for the Silver Eye, which means she wasn't here in any kind of official capacity." The man snorted contemptuously. "But you knew that already, didn't you? Lloyd saw the way you interacted with her in the tunnels, and he reported your overly familiar behavior. The men who are still surveilling Oracle Bay asked a few questions. It seems that you and Ms. Bellflower were closer than you revealed in your official report. You were supposed to gain her trust, not seduce her."

"How do you know she wasn't the seductress?" Donovan asked. He uncrossed his arms and leaned against the tree. The only thing still visible were his boots. "She's a beautiful woman; she'd be difficult to resist. And you know she can be ruthless in her quest for information. I told her I worked for the Scales. Luring me into her bed, taking away my ability to walk, and draining me of my physical energy could have been a plot to get access to my stuff and hack into my electronics while I was in a post-coital stupor." Amusement tinged his voice, and Morgana relaxed.

"Did she hack into your electronics?" the boss asked curtly, then answered his own question. "She did not. You may have forgotten to report your intimate relationship with Ms. Bellflower, but you would have let us know if you'd been compromised in any other sense. It is possible she was the instigator of the dalliance, but having met her, I doubt very much that she would unthaw enough to perform a seduction."

"But you think I could heat the ice queen up solely with the power of my charisma and raw sexuality?" Donovan asked. "You have a lot more faith in me than I do."

Morgana rolled her eyes and took another drink of her Champagne.

Donovan's boss let out an explosive sigh loud enough for

Morgana to hear. "I don't care who seduced who. What matters is you didn't report it, and now you've met her for an intimate dinner at a very expensive hotel. Unless you have some intelligence about her plans, and if you do, you need to tell me right now, what you were doing violates the orders given to you."

"I asked her about her plans. She said she was returning to Oracle Bay now that she's satisfied we have things well in hand." Donovan pushed himself up from the tree, bringing his face into the light. He glanced up towards her so quickly, Morgana would've missed it if she hadn't been watching him like a hawk.

"And you believe her?" the boss said incredulously.

"Of course not. But you didn't ask me if I'd gotten anything believable out of her. You asked me what she said." Donovan ran his fingers through his hair, pulling out the tie that held his hair back and shaking it out around his shoulders. "Now, if you don't mind, I would like to go home. It was a long day and as much as I enjoy our working relationship, I'd rather be in my bathtub with a pint of bitter and an audiobook."

Morgana was seized with the desire to know what kind of books Donovan listened to, then was sidetracked by the image of him reclining in the bath, his pint on a shelf next to the tub. Condensation from the heat of the water steaming the mirror and the glass enclosure.

Donovan glanced up towards her again, and an answering surge of heat pulsed through their bond.

"My office, nine o'clock tomorrow morning." Donovan's boss stalked away without waiting for an answer, leaving Donovan watching him until he disappeared from sight.

Morgana leaned back into her chair before she gave into her desire to reenact Shakespeare's famous balcony scene.

She stood and refilled her glass. She thought about curling up in the chair near the fireplace. It was too warm, but there was something comforting about it, nonetheless. But the Thames, the lights of the Millennial Wheel and the Houses of Parliament, and the sounds of London traffic were too great a lure. She loved the quiet of Oracle Bay and the darkness of a small town on the western edge of the North American continent, but London would always be her second home, more-so even than Kilnamanagh.

Morgana closed her eyes and let the sounds of the city as it wound down for the evening pour through her, energizing and revitalizing her. She was too tired to come up with anything concrete now, but no longer tired enough to fall asleep.

Tomorrow, she would take what little she'd learned from the Scales and decide where to go next.

Her phone pinged, interrupting her reverie, and she cursed.

Morgana thought about leaving it unanswered. There were few people who had this number, and most of them could wait until morning.

She opened her eyes and grabbed her phone.

There was one message from an unknown number. She nearly deleted it unread—she got occasional spam or wrong numbers—but curiosity got the better of her.

I can tell you what the witch said for the right price. Meet me at The Bloomsbury Tavern at 2300.

Morgana pursed her lips. It could be a trap set by Donovan's boss. The timing fit. But the chance that it was the man who'd heard Bridget's last words before her escape was too great a chance to give up.

Morgana shivered. A third possibility of the message's origin presented itself.

Bridget must know that the promise of information about her whereabouts would prove irresistible to Morgana.

And she'd be right. If there was a clue in what Bridget had said, Morgana had to take a chance to find out. She set her Champagne down with a regretful sigh and opened the closet where the Savoy's butler had hung her clothes. She liked to imagine that they'd been shocked at the number of corset tops she'd packed but knew that probably wasn't the oddest thing they'd ever seen.

For tonight, though, Morgana required a different costume. She put on her black leather pants and a flowing black tunic top with a low neckline, completing the look with a pair of low-heeled black leather booties. She brushed out her hair and pulled it back into a low ponytail. She seldom wore her hair anything but loose, and it felt weird to expose the back of her neck like that.

A swipe of mascara and a touch-up of her red lipstick, and she was ready to go. It was only nine o'clock, but according to her phone, it would take at least a half hour to walk to the pub, and she wanted to be there long before her contact arrived.

She texted him back. *2300 confirmed.*

Then she grabbed her wallet and passport and shoved them in a small black purse along with her phone. She immediately pulled her phone out of the purse and shot off another text.

I'm going to meet an informant at the Bloomsbury Tavern at 11pm. If you don't hear from me by midnight, something has gone wrong and I'm in need of rescue. Donovan is in the city. Text him.

Paska's reply came seconds later. *Don't go alone. I know I told you to stay away from Donovan, but if you don't contact him now and ask him to meet you there, I'll do it.*

Morgana huffed. She'd known Paska wouldn't like the idea of her going alone, but she would not give into his demands. *Good idea. I'll text him now,* she lied.

No, you won't.

Morgana didn't reply, she just dropped her phone in her bag and headed out the door.

thirteen

Morgana sat at the furthest end of the bar with her back to the wall, drinking a glass of sparkling water. It was almost eleven, and she was on high alert, covertly studying the face and aura of every person who walked in the bar. She hadn't paid much attention to any of the Scales men in the meeting earlier that day, and at this point she'd been awake for thirty-six hours, so she wasn't sure she'd recognize him, anyway.

But she was positive she'd recognize Bridget, regardless of any disguise or glamour she wore.

A magical signature she recognized entered the bar, and Donovan made a beeline for her.

"Again? I understand you finding me at my hotel, but here? I walked here and paid cash." She knew the answer already. Her meddling brother.

He held up his phone and displayed the most recent text message from Paska.

Morgana is headed to the Bloomsbury Tavern to meet some Scales operative. The meeting is at 11, so she'll probably be early. I don't like you and want you to stay out of her life. Go keep an eye on her.

"Mixed messages," Donovan said, tucking his phone back into his pocket.

Morgana sighed and stirred her water. "I told him I'd text you."

"You lied?" Donovan sat next to her.

"Yes. And for a very good reason. You need to leave. If the person who is showing up sees you, he will not talk to me. You are ranked higher than him within the organization, and by speaking to me, he will be going counter to the wishes of the Scales." Morgana held his gaze without blinking.

Donovan's shoulders slumped slightly, and she knew she'd won.

"Fine. I'll go. But I won't be far away. If you need me..."

Morgana smiled at him, then reached out before she could stop herself and touched his face. "If I need you, you will know."

Donovan bowed slightly and got off the barstool. The front door opened again, and a warlock walked in. Morgana didn't recognize his face, but his aura was unmistakable—ashy grey with a ring of red. Some witches liked to say those colors were the mark of evil, but Morgana knew better. Red only marked the source of power, not the intent of the wielder. Red denoted spellwork; a deeper red would identify a warlock who traded with demons. Powerful witches had silvery-blue auras ringed with colors representing their magical affinities. Morgana's was silver with swirls of blue and green dancing around her. Paska's was light blue with darker blues and oranges dancing like flames. Donovan's was light grey with green and brown, a stark contrast to those of the organization he worked for.

She turned to urge Donovan to hide or look for a back door out of the pub, but he'd disappeared without her noticing. That was the most impressive thing she'd witnessed him do. A tendril of heat rose in her chest. *One* of the most impressive things.

She smiled into her water and waited for the Scales warlock to spot her and come to sit down.

He took his time, scanning the bar slowly while he waited for the bartender to pour him a Guinness.

Eventually, he must have been satisfied that he was anonymous, and she hadn't laid a trap. He sat next to her, placing his beer on the bar with too much force and sloshing some of the foamy head of the beer onto the polished wood surface.

Color rose in his neck as he grabbed a bar napkin and wiped up the mess.

"What do you know and what do you want?" Morgana asked. Something about this situation made her uncomfortable, and she didn't want to linger.

He looked at her, and the rage and madness in his eyes hit her with an almost-physical force. She leaned back to escape the torrent battering against her.

A second later, his expression turned to one of determination tinged with a bit of fear and avarice.

Morgana slid her barstool a little further away from him and opened the well of her power, readying a magical defense in case she needed one.

"I heard what the blood witch said after she killed George and Gordon and the others. No one else heard her, but I was right next to her. I'll tell you, but you have to pay me first." The man looked around, twitching with nerves, then took a gulp of his beer.

"If you were so close to her, why are you still alive?"

If she hadn't been watching for it, Morgana would've missed his eyes dart away from her face for a fraction of a second. Whatever he was about to say next would be a lie.

"She thought I was dead," the man said. "I thought I might be, too, for a moment. When she blasted us with power, I collapsed with the others. I wasn't unconscious for long, but when I woke up, I kept still and kept my eyes closed. I listened, though."

"What's your name?" Morgana asked as she processed his words, trying to untangle any truth that he'd woven into his lies.

"Why would I tell you that?" he asked. He picked up his beer and took a long drink.

She shrugged as if it meant nothing either way. "You know mine, after all. It seemed both polite and fair."

The struggle evident in his expression was too great for such a simple question, but eventually, he came to a decision.

"Patrick," he said roughly. "Nice to meet ya'."

Morgana inclined her head and waited for him to look her in the eyes again. It only took a few seconds of silence for him to grow uncomfortable enough to fill it.

"Are you going to pay me or what?"

"I haven't decided if what you hold is valuable enough to barter for. If you were feigning death, why wouldn't she drain your power along with the others? It is either because you are lying about the events you witnessed or because you have too little power to bother with." She tapped her index finger against her cheek as if trying to decide which it was.

"I'm not a liar," he spat, then seemed to realize what he'd implied about himself.

Morgana didn't give him a chance to recover. "Powerless, then," she mused. "It is possible she would have left you there, although it seems unlikely she believed you dead."

Patrick sputtered, flecks of spittle flying out of his mouth and spraying the bar in front of him.

Morgana leaned back and raised her eyebrows at him.

He flushed. "Do you want to know what I heard or what?"

He was getting impatient. She needed to move quickly before he imploded under the pressure of his own deceit.

"What is your price?" she asked.

"One million pounds," he replied promptly.

Morgana tilted her head and regarded him quizzically. A demand for money was the last thing she'd expected. Magical artifacts, protections, curses... She'd been prepared for any such requests, as ludicrous as they might be. But money?

"Why do you ask for money? The Scales is not only one of the wealthiest organizations in the world, it is well-known for its generous salaries and benefits. Scales warlocks want for nothing."

Morgana had the money—she hadn't always used her foresight for good, and investing could be exciting—but she seldom parted with it unless she wanted comfortable flights, luxurious lodging, or expensive wines.

"I want to leave the Scales," Patrick blurted, and for the first time since they'd started speaking, she heard the ring of truth in his voice.

"They have a generous allowance, regardless of your active status," Morgana said. "The only reason you would need money to leave is if you were leaving before the end of your ten-year contract." The Scales paid a generous retirement bonus that reflected the number of ten-year contracts a warlock completed, but breaking a contract rendered the one in breach anathema at best and hunted at worst.

Patrick's eyes darted back and forth, and Morgana could almost see the wheels in his mind spinning as he looked for an explanation that would make sense and not paint him in a dishonorable light. "I just want to be on my own. Not watched over the rest of my life."

It was a good answer, and one she could almost believe. Almost. "Is your information worth a million pounds? Or will I feel cheated when you tell me she uttered a mundane curse when she stumbled over the body of one of your compatriots?"

Patrick blanched. "No, no! It's not nothing like that!"

Morgana was sure he was too nervous to deliberately attempt to mislead her by employing a double negative, but she couldn't discount it completely. She already knew she would pay for the information, no matter how unhelpful it proved to be. She wasn't about to let him know, though. Better to make him sweat while she pretended to consider it.

When Morgana determined he was on the verge of either collapsing in on himself, exploding in a fireball of anger, or running away, she nodded. "Okay."

His mouth dropped open like he could scarcely believe it. "Okay you'll pay me?"

She nodded and pulled out her phone. "Provide your bank account information to me, and I will transfer the funds."

He shook his head. "It's too much. It'll raise suspicion."

He was correct. That much money changing hands would be flagged by the financial authorities of both the United States and the United Kingdom. "That is an excellent point. I do have financial interests in banks that are…outside the business interests of our respective countries."

He nodded eagerly. "Yes. Here." He pulled a piece of paper out of his pocket and shoved it across to her. It was damp, and the ink on it was smeared.

Morgana smiled tightly. Other people's bodily functions were something she never wanted to encounter. She snapped a picture of the five account numbers with her phone. "I will begin the transfer immediately. It will take some time for the transfers to be complete. Do you require confirmation that the full million has reached your accounts and is available to you before you reveal the information, or is evidence that I have initiated the transfers satisfactory?"

He chewed his lip for a moment. "How long will it take?"

For someone who had five offshore accounts, he knew very little about how the processes worked.

"A week, at least," she lied.

His face fell.

"But I can request the transfers now and provide you with screenshots immediately," she said.

"Oh. Okay. That will work."

Morgana opened her banking app and initiated five individual transfers for two-hundred-thousand pounds each to his accounts. When the list of pending transfers appeared in a row on her app, she took a screenshot and sent it to the number he'd texted from earlier. She took an extra minute to send it, along with the picture of the account numbers, to Paska. He was masterful at computer-based theft, and if this information turned out to be worthless and it was too late to cancel the transfers, Paska could get it back with interest.

Patrick picked up his phone and looked at the photo. He nodded once, then looked at her. The nerves that had permeated him dissipated, and the cunning and fear that she'd seen when he first walked in reappeared.

Without further preamble, he said, "As she was leaving, she looked around the room and said, 'Oracle Bay will burn for what they've done to me.'"

"How do you know she looked around the room?" Morgana asked. "I thought your eyes were closed because you were playing dead."

"Well, I opened them, didn't I?" he said. "You got what you want, and I got what I wanted." He stood up, drained his beer, and slammed it down on the table. "If that money doesn't go through, you'll be sorry."

"I'm already sorry," Morgana said sincerely.

He ducked his head, then walked out of the pub.

Morgana flagged down the bartender and ordered another gin and tonic. Then she picked up her phone and sent two texts, the first to Donovan and the second to her brother.

You need to tell me everything. Now.

Cancel all but one transfer and send the recalled £800.000 to the Oracle Bay fire department.

Morgana drained her gin and tonic, thought longingly of her bed, and ordered another while she waited for Donovan to come back in.

fourteen

"We need to go somewhere I can't be tracked or recognized, and you need to ditch your phone," Donovan said.

Morgana finished her gin and tonic and looked at Donovan.

He sighed, pulled several twenty-pound notes out of his pocket and dropped them on the bar after catching the bartender's attention.

"I'll wipe my phone and drop it in the nearest bin," Morgana promised. She might not be as technologically adept as Paska, but she knew enough to ensure her personal information was backed up before reporting her phone lost and wiping it. "We'll walk back to my hotel. No one will see you in my room, although if they're tapped into the CCTV, they will be able to follow our progress."

"Are you saying you don't have a way to avoid being seen on camera?" Donovan asked with a teasing note.

"My skills don't lend themselves well to disarming cameras without raising suspicion, and a trail of disabled cameras would identify our path as surely as maintaining visual contact."

"Fine," Donovan grumbled. "I'll take care of it."

Morgana smiled at him and let him hook his arm through hers and lead her out of the pub. She dropped her phone in the first bin they walked by.

Donovan pulled her into an alley. "Give me your purse."

"This has been a very long game just for a mugging," Morgana said, handing over her purse.

Donovan snorted. "You're worth the work, sweetheart." He closed his eyes. "No bugs or trackers that I can find. Ready to be invisible?"

Morgana raised her eyebrows at him. "Impress me."

His grin was cocky and knowing enough that she blushed. He pulled a piece of paper and a long pin out of his back pocket. He smoothed out the paper, pricked his finger with the pin and let one drop fall on the paper, then stared at it.

Morgana tried to get a look at it, but he angled it away from her. A moment later, her awareness of him disappeared, and she gasped at the sudden loss of him in her subconscious.

"Okay," he said. "No one will notice us now." He crumpled up the piece of paper and tucked it into his jacket pocket.

Morgana slipped her arm through his, snagged the paper out of his pocket, and leaned into him. "Let's go then, before your magic words wear off."

Donovan led her down side streets and dark alleys reeking of urine and garbage before suddenly pulling her onto a brightly lit street a half block away from the Savoy.

Morgana looked down at herself. She was presentable enough to access her rooms without a raised eyebrow. She took a deep breath, tightened her grip on Donovan's arm, and started forward. She stumbled over a raised cobblestone, and a wave of dizziness rushed over her.

Donovan's arm slipped out from hers and slid around her waist. "Are you okay?"

"Of course," she said. "I am merely exhausted." That had to be it. She was paranoid to think it was anything else. Except... Had there been a moment when she'd taken her eyes off her cocktail while sitting with Patrick? Yes, when she was transferring the funds. She shook her head, and another wave of disorientation washed over her. "Get me to the room immediately," she commanded while swaying on her feet.

Donovan didn't ask questions, and he didn't hesitate. He swept her up into his arms and strode down the wide path to the hotel. "Key?" he asked.

Morgana dipped her hand into her bra and pulled it out. She thought she heard him groan, but the world was swimming too much for her to be sure. She closed her eyes and calmed her breath.

Donovan slowed as he walked through the lobby, but after a buzz of conversation, continued to the lifts. She didn't open her eyes again until he put her on the bed.

"What's wrong?" he asked.

"Patrick put something in my drink," she slurred.

"Shit. What do you need me to do? I can track him down and find out what it was," Donovan said. "I might enjoy that."

"Bath," Morgana said. "Please."

Donovan didn't answer, but moments later, the sound of water echoed through the room. She'd never had anything slipped into a drink before—at least not something that wasn't a poison designed to kill her immediately—but she was familiar enough with popular culture to know she had been "roofied."

Donovan's arms slipped around her body again, and he carried her into the bathroom. "Clothes off?" he asked.

"Yes." That was all she could manage to say; later she'd have to explain that she needed to be stripped to save her clothes, and not so she could be nude in front of him.

His hands trembled as they tugged off her leather pants and pulled her blouse over her head, but she barely felt the touch of his skin on hers. He lowered her into the bath, and the warm water slipped over her skin.

As soon as she was immersed up to her neck, some of the fog dissipated. She was still limp and could not move of her own accord, but her mind was more awake.

Bathwater would not heal her as effectively as being immersed in water at its source, but she balked at the idea of asking Donovan to take her to the Thames and dip her in. This would have to do.

She closed her eyes and visualized the light of her being slowly pulsing outward. With each exhalation, she expelled a little of the drug, and with each inhale, she brought in the cleansing, healing power of water. After about ten minutes, she opened her eyes. "Change the water," she rasped.

She shivered as the water drained, and only Donovan's arm kept her upright. This drug was not as dangerous as some of the poisons that had been administered to her over the centuries, although it had been nearly a thousand years since someone had dared attempt to assassinate her. It would work its way out of her system, but she did not want to be vulnerable right now.

Morgana choked out half a laugh as the tub refilled with steaming hot water. She never wanted to be vulnerable, but she was naked in a bathtub with Donovan Davies holding her. This was more than mere physical vulnerability—she had no doubt he would remain honorable and not take advantage of her—this was bareness in another sense.

Donovan drained and refilled the tub three more times before Morgana was able to sit up on her own.

"I need to go under," she said. Her voice was hoarse, as if she hadn't used it for days instead of a couple hours. "Just for a minute," she added when she saw him hesitate.

Donovan nodded and removed his arm from around her shoulders. "I trust you to ask for help if you need it."

Morgana didn't bother answering. She slipped under the water and let it flow over her face while she pushed out the remainder of the drug.

When she emerged from the bath, Donovan was waiting for her with a towel and a robe. He offered his arm to help her stand and step out of the tub, and even though she did not want to appear weak in front of him, this was a silly place to stand her ground. She grasped his hand and let him steady her, then wrap her in a towel.

He dried her off. He didn't skip over areas of her body she expected him to miss, just treated them with the same gentleness and thoroughness as the rest of her. When she was dry, he helped her on with the robe. It was soft, white, and plush, and it brought to mind the last time she'd been in a robe in front of him. That robe had been silky and black, and just as decadent as this one. She waited for the heat that usually suffused her when she recalled the single night they'd spent together, but there was nothing left in her to call up even the vestiges of desire.

Once Donovan tied the robe around her, he snagged the towel again and reached up to dry her long, black hair.

"Comb?" he asked when her hair was no longer dripping.

"Toiletry bag is on the counter," she said.

He grabbed the bag, then led her to a chair in her room and pushed her into it. He rubbed leave-in conditioner into her hair, massaged her scalp until her eyes drifted shut with the pleasure of it, then used her comb to untangle her hair.

"Do you want me to braid it?" he asked.

"Can you?" She wasn't sure why this, of all things, surprised her.

"I not only have daughters, I have long hair, too," he answered, then used the comb to separate first the top half of her hair from the bottom half, then to create three equal hunks of hair. He plaited it quickly and carefully, then slipped the hair tie from his own ponytail to secure her hair at the end of the braid.

"I know you wanted a conversation when we returned to the hotel, but I think rest is a better option," Donovan said. "Do you have pajamas?"

Morgana flushed a little. She hadn't planned on sharing a room with anyone on her trip and hadn't packed the pajamas she reserved for especially chilly nights in Oracle Bay. She shook her head. "Help me to my suitcase, please."

Donovan helped her stand, and she walked to her case on increasingly steady legs. She pulled out the packing cube that contained her underthings, slipped out a pair of pants, and eyed the rest of her suitcase. She didn't have anything that would serve as a nightshirt.

"Do you want my t-shirt?" Donovan asked.

Wearing his shirt to bed would immerse herself in his scent. She might as well admit that she was accepting the course fate had laid out to her if she did that.

She shook her head and snagged a soft bra devoid of the dreaded underwires. It would have to do. "I'll be back in a moment. If you're staying, you should call to request a toothbrush. I will not share mine, and I did not bring an extra." She walked into the bathroom and closed the door. She washed her face to remove the makeup, finishing the job the bath had started, then brushed her teeth before taking off her robe and putting on the bra she'd grabbed on a whim.

She put the robe back on and walked to the bed.

Donovan was sitting in the chair she'd vacated when she came out, toothbrush in hand. He brushed by her with nothing more than a look more of concern than lust, although there was a little desire hidden behind his care.

Morgana appreciated his lack of flirtation, although a very small part of her chafed under the idea that the events of tonight had removed his attraction to her. It was ridiculous—he was not the type of man to be effected that way by her incapacity, no matter the cause, any more than he was the type to revel in her need for him and strive to put her into more situations where she would become dependent. He'd simply cared for her, supported her when she needed it, and not left to seek out the one who'd drugged her, no matter how much he likely wanted to.

Morgana shrugged out of her robe and slipped between the soft sheets with a groan of exhaustion. She barely registered the bed shifting when Donovan got in beside her.

"Good night, sweetheart," Donovan said.

Morgana closed her eyes and let herself drift into sleep.

fifteen

Morgana woke up slowly, aware of her consciousness before she opened her eyes or moved. Something was wrong.

She frowned slightly without opening her eyes, then remembered. This wasn't her bed.

The bed shifted, and a heavy arm draped over her.

Morgana's eyes shot open, and she rolled away, then sat up. The covers pooled around her waist, and she stared at Donovan.

He blinked sleepily at her. "Good morning," he said. Her reserves must have replenished themselves while she slept, because his gravelly voice, deeper with the vestiges of sleep, tugged at something deep inside.

Morgana didn't say anything. Instead, she racked her brains for her memories of the night before but came up mostly blank. "Did we...?" She hated not knowing. The uncertainty and blankness pushed away the first hints of desire and replaced them with a cold, panicky sickness.

"No. Not even a kiss," Donovan said. He swung his legs out of bed, and the comforter fell away from him. He was dressed only in a tight pair of pink boxer briefs that hugged the tops of his powerful thighs and contrasted nicely with his ruddy tan skin.

Her gaze traveled upwards past his narrow hips, soft stomach, and broad chest. She licked her lips as her gaze snagged on his shoulders. She'd always had a weak spot for shoulders, and Donovan's were perfect.

He cleared his throat, and her eyes made the rest of the journey to his face in a nanosecond. He raised his eyebrows at her, and she blushed.

"Sorry," she said.

He just grinned, grabbed his shirt and jeans off the floor, and disappeared into the bathroom.

Morgana slid out of bed, pulled on the robe that lay in a heap on the floor, and walked to her suitcase. She grabbed the first clean clothes she found—the leather pants she'd worn the night before and a blood-red blouse covered with black lace that let only a little of the red peek through—and waited for her turn in the bathroom.

She turned her head and glimpsed herself in the mirror. She reached up to touch her hair. It was loosely braided and still damp in places. She frowned at her reflection and tried to gather her memories.

She'd met the Scales man at the pub, and after paying him a million pounds, received Bridget's parting words. Donovan had met her at the pub, done something to make them unnoticeable, and they'd walked back to her hotel.

Somewhere between the pub and the Savoy, her memories faded.

Clearly, she'd made it here, showered, had her hair plaited, and climbed into bed with the man she loved and needed to stay away from. But there was nothing there but vague memories of water interspersed with fear and anger.

Donovan emerged from the bathroom, and she brushed past him. When she was dressed, made up, and her hair was brushed out, she walked back into the room and picked up the room service menu.

"We are going to eat, and then we're going to talk," she said, passing him the menu after making her selections.

"I'd like to go home and change," Donovan said. "You can check out of here and come with me. It is probably a good idea, anyway. You've already been targeted once."

Morgana opened her mouth to tell him where to put the insinuation that she needed to be taken care of and kept from harm, but he held up a hand before she could say anything.

"I know you're more than capable of taking care of yourself, but as we saw last night, the Scales—or at least someone or someones from the Scales—are willing to cross boundaries they shouldn't in order to take you down." He handed the menu back to her. "I'll have the full English, coffee, and orange juice."

Morgana picked up the phone and ordered before saying anything.

"I don't remember much of anything from last night past you using blood magic to hide our tracks," she confessed.

Donovan stood and walked over to her with his arms held out. Just before he stepped into the space she allowed no one but her brother into, he stopped, and his arms dropped to his side. "I'm sorry. I can fill in the blanks if you want."

Morgana dropped her eyes. "How many of the blanks involve nudity?"

Donovan hesitated, then reached out and tipped her chin up with one finger until she was looking into his eyes.

The touch, deliberate in the way his arm over her hadn't been, pulled at something deeper than her heart, deeper than her body. Her soul reacted to it, and she stepped forward. She reached up and placed her palm on his cheek.

"Tell me," she whispered.

Donovan's cheeks flushed, and heat flared in his eyes. Before Morgana could take the step that would have them pressed chest to chest, he took a step backwards, and his expression turned to one of regret.

"There was nudity." His voice was full of flirtatious mockery, and none of the seriousness she'd seen from him in the last day. "You needed to be in the water. You were there for hours, purging the drugs from your body. I'm surprised you don't remember what happened after you decided you'd healed yourself enough to leave the water."

"Why did it take so long?" Morgana asked, more to herself. "If it was a simple drug to ensure my compliance and make it easier to take me in for whatever purposes either Patrick or the Scales had, the effects should not have been more severe nor lasted so long."

Donovan pursed his lips. "You're right. You shouldn't have had to do anything other than sleep, but you were certain you needed more."

Morgana growled in frustration but was saved from trying to break through the wall around last night's blanked memory by a deferent knock at the door.

Donovan's gaze caressed her face once more, then he answered the door. Their breakfast was wheeled in by a suited man who placed the silver-domed trays on the table near the balcony.

Morgana pulled a few notes out of her purse and tipped the man. Once he'd walked out of the room, she took the domes off the food; her mouth watered when the aroma of her food wafted up to her.

"Do you have a way to check it for drugs or poisons?" she asked Donovan. She did, but it wasn't easy, and if he could do it easily, that would save some time and get the food in her stomach quicker, provided it wasn't tainted.

Donovan licked his lips and sighed. "I do. There are enough poison averse animals in the world that a combination of them can detect most poisons and drugs. I spent a few years seeking them out and asking them to share parts of their spirits with me."

Morgana's eyes widened. This was the most he'd ever told her about what he was. She wanted to know more, but his expression didn't invite questions.

He smiled at her; the intimacy of five minutes ago was

completely gone, and the absence of it left her feeling more bereft than she'd anticipated. "I might as well tell you. I was born a cat. Or rather, I was born human. Mostly. But cat is in my DNA. Basically, I'm a werecat, I guess, although that's as accurate as calling you a Wiccan."

Morgana waved towards the food, trying to process what he'd told her. Paska had called him a beast, but she hadn't truly believed him. "I'll save my follow-up questions. I would appreciate your skills now; I am quite hungry but do not want to trust any food or drink right now. I do not know how much the Scales know about my location."

Donovan walked forward and sat in the chair nearest Morgana's food. He looked up at her. "Would you mind checking out what's happening outside from the balcony?"

Morgana nodded through the pang of hurt that accompanied his request. It made sense he didn't trust her with everything he was. She wasn't sure she trusted him, either, not even with her heart. *It was too late for that*, she told herself. She walked outside and leaned her forearms on the balcony railing.

The late morning crowds were just as thick as any other time. The bustle of London didn't ebb and flow with the hour as it did in other, smaller cities. Between the residents of the city and the flocks of tourists who permeated the streets, it was nearly impossible to pick out any individuals who might be surveilling the hotel. She'd assumed she'd be trailed but hadn't thought they'd resort to drugging her.

Her increased metabolism that allowed her to rapidly metabolize alcohol worked on most drugs, too. If what Patrick had put in her drink was enough to knock her out and steal her memories, it might have been enough to kill her.

She turned around without thinking to ask Donovan the symptoms she'd exhibited. She might not be familiar with drugs that were instantly dissolved in liquid but not lethal enough to kill instantly, but Paska would be. He'd made a particular study of drugs and poisons, often dosing himself to understanding the effects and trying out antidotes he'd crafted to somewhat mixed results, at least at the beginning of his experiments.

Donovan was crouched in one of the chairs, sniffing the food and looking more feline than human. His face had flattened, and his ears had lengthened, narrowing into points, and were covered in fine hair. He didn't look like a cat, not exactly, but he didn't look like a man either.

She hadn't made a sound, but something had alerted him to her regard, and he looked up. His eyes narrowed, and the vertically slitted pupils contracted. He hopped off the chair, and when his feet hit the floor, he once more looked like a man.

Morgana walked through the balcony doors and tried not to let her discomfiture show. "I apologize. I had a sudden thought about the drug that was used on me last night and forgot your request to give you privacy. Your abilities are impressive, though."

Donovan didn't meet her eyes, but she glimpsed anger on his face before it smoothed out into what Morgana recognized as his neutral mask. Smooth with only small lines at the outside corners of his eyes and between his brows, slightly upturned lips, and light mockery in his gaze.

"I don't let anyone see that side of me. It's private. I'd appreciate it if you don't bring it up again." He sat down without looking at her and picked up a fork. "The food and drink are all safe, as far as I can tell."

Morgana sat across from him and took a bite of her breakfast.

They ate in silence for several minutes before Donovan cleared his throat. "You said you had an idea about the drug used on you last night?"

She nodded. Once she'd swallowed, she took a long drink of the breakfast tea that had finished steeping. "I need to know what symptoms I exhibited. If it affected me so much that I don't remember anything about last night, it must have been more potent than the type of drug that men slip unsuspecting women in bars. Paska will know, but I will need to describe everything we know."

Donovan closed his eyes and lightly snorted. "Of course Paska would know. He probably knows more about the seedy underworld than anyone else. If he didn't have more of a conscience, he would be directing the shadow side of the Scales."

"The shadow side?" Morgana cursed at herself. Of course, the Scales was more than their public face, well, public in the most secret sense of the word. The number of witches who'd disappeared after being apprehended—witches who'd never come close to the line, much less stepped across it and harmed anyone—was more than zeal and misunderstandings could explain away. She'd never paid much attention to the inner workings of the Eye—she preferred to work alone, do the jobs she was assigned to do, and avoid any of the political machinations that inevitably existed. But the Eye knew. There was no other reason to have an entire contingent of witches who specialized in breaking into Scales secure prisons on rescue missions. She'd spent too much time isolated from the world in front of her and had forgotten—or ignored—any clues that would detract from the good she was doing.

Donovan tilted his head. "You didn't know?"

"I should have. It was foolish of me in the extreme to believe the Scales was what they appeared to be." She laughed a little. "I do enjoy your assertion that my brother has too much of a conscience to stand in the shadows and direct men to cross lines they shouldn't. He likely isn't. Leadership is not something he typically enjoys; he's been a loner for fifteen hundred years, and it seems unlikely that he would allow himself to be burdened with the needs and wants of others."

"Just that, then? His lack of desire to be the boss?" Donovan sounded skeptical, and Morgana knew she needed to relieve him of his rose-tinted glasses, at least where Paska and she were concerned.

"He is old, Donovan. We are both old. The conscience you describe is not what either he or I would ascribe to. Working in the dark to take out those with power enough to disrupt the magical world before they can realize how much potential they have and be tempted to use it to harm innocents—or friends and family, regardless of guilt—would not be considered unethical. It is pragmatic." Morgana watched him carefully, looking for signs of acceptance or repugnance. She'd told him before that she would kill without hesitation if she deemed it necessary, but he persisted in believing she was still bound by some moral code he would recognize. She didn't kill unnecessarily, of course. Neither she nor Paska found pleasure in violence, but her view of necessary differed greatly from Donovan's.

Donovan shrugged helplessly. "I don't believe you'd lie about this, but if you're the kind of person who kills without remorse after serving as the only judge of their crime, you could be the kind of person who'd lie about it, too?"

"Have you never killed at the behest of the Scales?" Morgana asked.

"No." Donovan's answer was immediate and without hesitation. "I go after rogue witches, the ones who are violent and in danger of being discovered by regular humans. Because I can sense their power, it's easy for me to figure out who's the wicked witch and who's an innocent caught in the crossfire. I bring them back, go to their trials, and make sure the sentence matches the crime. Any who can be rehabilitated are, then released."

"Are you sure?" Morgana asked gently. She didn't want to shatter his belief that he'd been working for the greater good all these years, but it was far past time he let go of his presuppositions that others shared his morals. "And even if you are correct, and imprisonment is the sentence most witches are handed down, there are two other questions you need to consider. Does the jury consist of anyone but warlocks who already are predisposed to distrust those magic-wielders who have access to powers they can barely sense? And how do you expect a person to be rehabilitated successfully if they are kept in a magical prison without access to the very elements that feed their souls?"

To his credit, Donovan did not issue immediate denials. His brows creased, and he turned away from her, taking his coffee to the balcony.

Morgana let him go. He should not have made it to sixty without doubting the sincerity of men who hid in the shadows and refused to interact with others in the magical realm. Having his illusions shattered this late in his life would be painful. She sighed. *This late in his life.* Even if she could give in to her feelings for him and take a chance on the heat and love she felt growing between them, it made little sense to entwine her life even more with his. He would likely live longer than a mundane human, particularly if he lived in a place like Oracle Bay that was suffused with the kind of magic that increased the lifespans, not only of the supernatural among them. Even the regular mortals experienced the benefits of the town. There was little illness, and most lived to be quite old by human standards, with clear minds and whole bodies.

Morgana's phone buzzed. She turned it over to see a text notification from Paska.

Money taken care of. I'll monitor the one I didn't reverse. I'll know if it's accessed.

Morgana pursed her lips. She was often curious how Paska had learned so much about electronic crime but had never bothered to ask. His answer would likely be too technical for her to care about. She replied with a thumbs up, then followed it with a question. *What combination of materials would be able to incapacitate me and remove my memory?*

She didn't have to wait long for an answer.

Without a sample, I'm only guessing. Rohypnol is less available than it used to be, but my guess is that mixed with blood salt—salt with iron mixed in. Enough to dampen your will and inhibit your metabolism. Whoever planned it knew who they were dealing with. His text concluded with an emoji of a cat.

Morgana's thumbs flew over the keyboard. *It wasn't Donovan. He helped me to the hotel and let me immerse myself in water until I could sleep with no repercussions.*

And do you have any memory of last night? He could've gone through your phone and your possessions. I don't care how much he professes to care for you, he's a Scales operative. His entire career has been hunting people like us for the greater good. Morgana couldn't hear him snort, but she could sense it, nonetheless.

I cannot rule it out, of course, she typed reluctantly. *But I do not believe it. The Scales operative—or former operative now—I met with last night was likely an associate of Bridget. His message to burn Oracle Bay was a threat she wanted me to hear and was likely supposed to have me rushing home to protect my town.* She paused, then added a second text before her brother had a chance to reply. *Did you not send Donovan after me last night? You would not have done so if you suspected he was the type of man to poison me to break into my phone.*

There was no response from Paska, and Morgana put her phone away. He would not reply until he had something useful to say, and it was likely he only had supposition and sarcasm right now.

She returned her attention to Donovan. He was sitting in one of the chairs, sipping his coffee. She wanted to go to him, to find out what he was thinking. It didn't matter, of course. After this morning, he would go back to his life, and she would continue her search. Perhaps he would cast a more critical eye on the activities around him at the Scales, in which case she had done something to benefit him as repayment for how he'd helped her last night.

Her phone buzzed again, and Donovan's echoed the noise moments later.

She picked it up. There were half a dozen text messages. There were four new messages in the group text she shared with the other oracles in Oracle Bay and one from her brother. The sixth was from an unknown number. She closed her eyes and took a deep breath.

She scanned the text from the unknown number. *See you in Oracle Bay!* Morgana deleted it without responding. She didn't know if it was from Patrick or Bridget—and it likely didn't matter who'd sent it; she knew who was pulling the strings.

Donovan padded across the room in his bare feet and retrieved his phone; it had not stopped buzzing since the initial notification.

While Donovan scrolled through his phone, Morgana opened the next unread message.

Ceri: *You should check the news. There are unexplained murders that match Bridget's MO all across Europe. I don't get it, though. She has to know you're following her. Leaving such an obvious trail is stupid.*

Russell: *Unless she's baiting a trap.*

Ceri: *Paska said she was threatening Oracle Bay. Isn't that the trap she's baiting?*

Of course, Paska had shared Bridget's threat with Ceri. And he was right to do so. If it turned out not to be misdirection, they needed to be forewarned.

Paska: *She's playing a game with Morgana, but I don't believe the murders in Europe are the false trail. She did not intend them to be found.*

Two more messages had appeared in the thread before she'd gotten to Paska's.

Ceri: *You found them?*

Paska replied with a .gif of an animated mushroom pointing at itself with both hands and the words "Who has two thumbs and is awesome?" emblazoned over it.

Morgana turned her attention to the message Paska had sent her outside of the group chat. It was only one brief sentence. *The account was drained in Porto.*

They had their location, and she knew where she was going next. She stood and looked at Donovan to make an excuse and hurry him away so she could make her travel preparations.

He was watching her, and before she could say anything to hasten his departure, he smiled at her, although it didn't reach his eyes. "See you in Portugal."

sixteen

Morgana paced back and forth in the baggage terminal of the Porto airport, waiting for her suitcase to appear. She'd been waiting for over an hour and, based on the disgruntlement of other travelers who'd been present when she arrived, this delay had the potential to go on for some time.

She pulled her phone out of her pocket and checked the time. She still had another hour before the next flight from London on any airline arrived. She paused to appreciate the staff at the Savoy who'd found her the first flight from London and gave her a list of all other flights as a reference. She'd likely bumped someone from their seat, and she'd had to fly economy, but she'd been able to bypass most of the security checkpoints and leave London from Heathrow less than two hours after getting the message from Paska.

Donovan had purchased two tickets on an afternoon flight and made her promise to wait for him to return with his passport and a bag. She'd smiled, pushed sincerity into her eyes, and given her word. Ceri's warning echoed in the back of her mind, but she pushed it aside. Donovan would find her, either with his own instincts and investigative skills or with Paska's aid. Getting the jump on him, even if ill-advised, was not only entertaining, it was good for him.

Her phone announced two text messages in quick succession. Donovan and Paska.

Morgana grimaced, opened the text from Paska, and read it. *Ceri and Drew are working together to get a bead on Bridget's whereabouts. All we have so far is a starting location. Keep me updated.*

Morgana acknowledged the message, then turned to Donovan's.

Real nice, sweetheart. See you in a few hours. Don't think you'll escape me as easily a second time.

Morgana rolled her eyes and grinned. She was enjoying this more than she should. The chase was exhilarating, whether she was the hunter or the hunted.

A third message appeared before she had a chance to close the app, this from a number she recognized as one the Silver Eye used. *You are no longer a member of the Silver Eye. Whatever you do next, you will not have our protection. Stay out of Portugal.*

Morgana snorted. They'd sent her after Bridget on her own, then told the Scales she was no longer associated with them. When she'd accused the Scales of abusing their power and using underhanded methods as well as variable definitions of guilt or innocence, she did not reveal that the Eye trod near the same permeable line. She debated not replying, but it would be better for them to know she was here—although they likely did already.

I am in Porto on my time and to follow my own agenda. I have separated from the Eye. As a former contractor, I have no reason to adhere to the directives of a former employer. If you send someone to apprehend me, ensure you send your best. No one else will be able to come close.

Morgana tucked her phone away and resumed her baggage carousel vigilance.

It was another forty-five minutes before her suitcase made an appearance. She pushed her way through the small horde that had formed in front of her, elbowing aside an older man in a well-cut suit who glared at her and muttered something under his breath that sounded like an expletive attached to the word "American."

She grabbed her case and dashed through customs and out of the airport to wait impatiently for a taxi. She directed the driver to the hotel the concierge at the Savoy had reserved for her. It was not nearly as luxurious as the Savoy, and she hoped that would throw Donovan—and anyone associated with either the Scales or the Silver Eye—off her scent. She was well known for her preference for luxury hotels.

Morgana checked into her room and took a moment to look at a map and orient herself to the city. She hadn't been to Porto in over twenty years, and her memory of the layout was blurred with time and altered by structural changes.

She stowed her athame in a large shoulder bag. She would not go into this confrontation unarmed. Bridget had taken her by surprise in Oracle Bay, but Morgana would not give away any advantage she could muster.

She slung the bag over her shoulder, bound it to herself with a hint of magic that would deter any pickpockets, and looked at herself in the mirror.

She looked as she always did. Dark jeans instead of a skirt and ankle boots rather than knee-highs, but her long black hair and black blouse cemented her signature look, and her dramatic eye makeup and red lips did nothing to alter it.

She hated to admit that the suburban housewife disguise she'd maintained for a year at the behest of the Eye had served its purpose —at least for a while. She huffed out a sigh and peered out the window at the street below. Tourist shops were ubiquitous in this neighborhood; she was sure there was one nearby.

She was in luck. There was one across the street advertising souvenirs, including the roosters that were a symbol of good luck in Portugal and examples of the cork and tile the country was famous for. Morgana picked up her bag, tucked her passport into the interior zipper pocket, and grabbed a couple twenty-euro notes from her wallet.

She walked down the stairs and across the street, then bought five t-shirts and one hooded sweatshirt.

After paying for her purchases, she strode back across the street and sprinted up the stairs.

She eyed the t-shirts with disdain, then stripped off her shirt and replaced it with a bright red shirt with a blue rooster in the center.

She washed her face and reapplied minimal makeup—just foundation and a touch of mascara. Then, she took a deep breath and retrieved a comb from the same zippered purse pocketed where she'd stowed her passport. She ran her finger down the shaft of the comb and whispered an incantation. She pulled the wide teeth through her hair and watched as her long, black tresses were replaced by cotton candy pink hair that was shoulder length on one side and shorn close to her skull on the other. She shuddered. It was an attractive hairstyle on other people, and it didn't look unattractive on her, but this was almost as bad as her bland, brown bob.

Morgana turned from the mirror and slipped on the grey hoodie. There was nothing to be done about her jeans or boots, but hopefully the cheap clothing and modern hairstyle would be enough misdirection for any casual observers. She had no illusions that Donovan would recognize her, but he'd have to find her first.

seventeen

Morgana hefted her bag and adjusted the strap to a different place on her shoulder. She was in front of the Capela do Senhor de Além overlooking the Douro River and hidden from view from anyone on either the river or the road that ran behind the chapel. There were few tourists here, although the bridge and waterfronts on both sides of the river were bustling with tourists and locals enjoying the summer sun.

The chapel itself was in ruins, although some recent efforts at restoring the façade had been attempted. From her vantage point, she could see the crumbling walls around the former church yards and Muralha Fernandina's fortifications across the river.

What she did not see was any evidence that Bridget was nearby.

Ceri and Drew had given the area around the chapel as a starting place but had been unable to find anything more specific to direct her search. They pledged to keep trying, but it was the middle of the night in Oracle Bay, and Morgana didn't expect to receive any new information that day.

Morgana walked back up to the road, then slowly back towards the Luis I bridge to await the metro train that would take her back across the river towards her hotel. She was exhausted after two days of travel and the physical stressors of being drugged and having to question the representatives of the Scales. Her heightened tension by her potential proximity to Bridget did not help to calm her too-active nerves.

Although it was still early evening, she decided to find a place to eat, have a glass of the famous Douro Valley wine, and wind down so she could return to her hotel to sleep. A good night's rest would do wonders towards restoring her good spirits and heighten her powers of observation. Bridget could shield the dark magics she practiced well enough that she'd lived in Morgana's house for weeks without Morgana realizing who she was hosting, but now that Morgana had experienced the madness and rage that consumed Bridget, she should better be able to recognize her.

Morgana wandered down a street at random, heading away from her hotel, and stepped into the first wine bar she walked by that had an available table outside.

She settled in with her chair angled towards the street and perused the menu while strengthening the shields that would tell her if another magic-user approached. When the server came to take her order, Morgana smiled at the young woman. "¿Habla Español?" It was the only language besides English Morgana spoke fluently that was likely to be understood in a Portuguese bar, and she wanted to avoid the language she claimed as her native tongue as much as possible.

The young woman shook her head, and Morgana grimaced. It would have to be her fumbling Portuguese, then. "Desculpe," she apologized, then ordered a glass of alvarinho and a charcuterie plate.

She sipped the white wine, enjoying the notes of apricot enhanced with a hint of salinity, and ate her way through the variety of cheeses, sardines, bread, and lightly pickled carrots. When the food was gone and she'd finished her second glass of wine, the tension of the day had mostly unwound from her shoulders. She paid her bill in cash, then headed back towards her hotel. She took a circuitous route—nearly a requirement in the city with narrow alleys and only slightly wider streets that met at odd angles before plunging downhill or climbing steeply up. When she reached her hotel, she swiped her keycard to gain entrance to the building, then took the stairs to her room.

She dropped into the single chair and pulled off her boots. She seldom wished for sneakers, but the cobblestone streets of Porto did not marry well with the harder soles of her boots.

A tingle of awareness zinged through her being, and she straightened, her aching feet forgotten for the moment. Donovan was close.

"Damn that man," she muttered to herself. His ability to track her down was uncanny, and if she'd thought worse of him, she would assume he had secreted a tracker on her person somehow. She knew, though, that such dishonesty was anathema to the man.

He had to be close, and he'd likely used whatever cloaking spell he'd employed the night before to hide his presence from her until he was nearby. That meant he knew where she was, and he wanted her to know as well. She sighed and pulled out her phone.

532

If she couldn't avoid the man—and there was no evidence she'd be able to—she might as well welcome him for the length of her quest to find and neutralize the blood witch. She had, after all, been warned against working alone, and Donovan was the perfect person to work with. His service as her familiar, unwilling as it was, gave him insight into her mind Morgana didn't have. And his ability to use the strengths of multiple animals would complement her ability to call on the earth and its elements to enhance her natural magical abilities.

Between them, there were few places Bridget could conceal her presence once they'd located her.

Donovan knocked on the door. He stared at her for a second, eyes wide, then stepped across the threshold. "This is a very different vibe than the Savoy." He dropped his bag on the ground and raised a single eyebrow at her. "Nice look, by the way. It's a lot better disguise than the beige."

Morgana didn't bother acknowledging him. "I was about to go to bed. You are welcome to stay here if you must, but do not expect to interact with me until I wake."

Donovan nodded. "Of course. I can't imagine how tired you must be at this point. Before you hit the sack, can I ask one question?"

Morgana stared at him and pursed her lips.

He sighed noisily. "Fine. That was a question, but I'm sure you know what I meant. Did you find anything today?"

Morgana shook her head. "Nothing. My contacts in Oracle Bay gave me a starting point—the Capela do Senhor de Além—but I was unable to sense anything in that location. Unless I have new information when I wake in the morning, I will return and see if I am better able to find what I'm looking for when my mind isn't clouded from lack of sleep. Now, if you will excuse me." She didn't wait for a response, merely grabbed one of the t-shirts she'd purchased earlier and walked into the adequate bathroom.

After washing her face and brushing her teeth, she stripped out of her t-shirt and jeans and pulled on the oversized white t-shirt that proclaimed "I <3 Porto" in bright red letters. It fell to mid-thigh, which was almost enough to give the illusion of pajamas.

"I'll keep the first watch," Donovan said. He pulled a book and a manila folder out of his carryon.

"Wake me in five hours so you can get some sleep," Morgana replied with a yawn. She slipped into bed, pulled on the eye mask she'd left next to the bed, and wiggled until she was comfortable. She'd expected to lie in the darkness wide awake with the awareness of another person in her room, but sleep did not elude her for long.

<h1 style="text-align:center">eighteen</h1>

For the second morning in a row, Morgana woke with a heavy arm draped over her. This time, however, she was immediately aware of where she was and who was next to her.

She extricated herself from under Donovan's arm, selected clean underthings and another silly t-shirt, this one with three vertical sardines, two facing up and one looking down, emblazoned across the font, and went into the bathroom to shower.

Once she was clean, a feat that was not nearly as long without her waist-length hair to wash and condition, she dressed quickly, applied her minimal makeup, and left the bathroom.

Donovan was sitting on the bed, scrolling through his phone. "There's been another murder," he said.

"Where?" Morgana grabbed her phone, but she had no new notifications from anyone.

"Galicia."

"That's a three-hour drive north into Spain," Morgana said after plugging the town into her map app. "Ceri and Drew were certain she was here."

"My Scales contacts agree," Donovan said. "The murder in Spain matches the MO down to the symbols in the collarbones that have appeared on every other body, though." He slid out of bed. This morning, he was wearing long, loose pajama bottoms that were slung low enough that she could see his hip bones.

Morgana licked her lips. Tonight, they would have to get separate rooms. If she ended up in bed with him on a night she wasn't drugged or too exhausted to think, she might lead herself into temptation, and that was one thing she couldn't afford to do.

She tore her eyes away from him and focused back on her phone. "She's been able to kill from afar before. All it takes is one of her cursed beads on the person she has targeted. I don't know how she triggers the attack, but if she was able to take out Violet and Johanna simultaneously in Oracle Bay without being present and later kill Brandy through a letter while halfway around the world, she could be killing young women without being anywhere near them. There is no reason to believe she's left Porto."

Donovan disappeared into the bathroom and the shower turned on. "You're right, of course. I just can't help believing she's leading us by the noses. Why were we able to find her so easily here? Maybe this is just another red herring. She likes playing games."

Morgana steered her mind away from Donovan's naked body in the shower and the games she'd like to play. "You said it in Oracle Bay—she doesn't believe we can stop her, and she enjoys flaunting that. She murdered in Oracle Bay right in front of us. You watched Johanna die, and Violet died mere steps away from my shop."

"We caught her once, though," Donovan said.

"And she escaped mere weeks later. That might serve to increase her belief that she is unstoppable." Morgana exhaled the anger she'd held onto since Bridget escaped.

Donovan walked out of the bathroom with a white towel wrapped around his waist and a tight expression carving deeper grooves into his forehead than were usually there. "It doesn't make sense that the Scales wouldn't have executed her as soon as they got her. There was no question of her guilt. Even you could not fault them for that."

Morgana sighed. "Paska stopped them. He wanted me stronger before the stolen magic was released. He thought the Scales prison would be enough to hold her. Either he was wrong, which seems unlikely, or someone—Patrick seems an obvious choice—was already working for her and engineered her escape."

"You've made a lot of accusations against the Scales."

"Well-deserved, I assure you," Morgana replied. Her stomach growled. From her research, she knew there was an excellently reviewed cafe five blocks away—and several others between here and there—and she was eager to eat breakfast and resume her search. "Are you planning on accompanying me to breakfast, or do you want to meet somewhere later?"

Donovan dropped his towel.

Morgana uttered a strangled gasp, but she didn't close her eyes. Instead, she drank in the sight of him. The age that showed on his face was not apparent on the rest of his body. Strength radiated from him, and his muscles bunched and tensed as he unhurriedly reached into his bag and pulled out clothes. His body was covered with scars, but they didn't detract from his beauty. Instead, they told a story; she'd heard bits and pieces of it the night they'd spent together.

She nearly sighed in disappointment when he put on his boxer briefs—lime green today—and followed them with jeans.

He rummaged in his bag with a smirk on his face, and Morgana knew he was laughing at her.

Her stomach growled again. "I'm leaving in three minutes. Are you coming or not?" Despite her best efforts, her voice shook, and his smirk widened into a grin.

"I'll be ready whenever you are," he replied. He donned a dusky red t-shirt, then sat on the bed to put on his socks and shoes.

Morgana tucked her athame into the sheath she'd strapped around her ankle, tucked it under her jeans, and reluctantly grabbed her own footwear. As much as she was looking forward to breakfast and resuming her hunt, her feet protested the necessity of walking around in her boots any longer than necessary. She winced as she zipped her boots, and nearly stumbled when she stood. After breakfast, her priority had to be finding some alternative footwear, preferably something that would not have to be broken in.

She hobbled to the door. Donovan's hand at her elbow stopped her. "What's wrong with you?" he demanded.

"Blisters," she replied through gritted teeth. "Cobblestones are the devil's pavement."

"Why didn't you heal your feet the way you purged the drugs?" Donovan asked, drawing his eyebrows into a tee above his nose.

Morgana flushed slightly. It hadn't occurred to her to do so. "Physical healing is not something I do often, and almost never for minor injuries or illnesses. I use water to replenish myself magically and have aided others when the occasion called for it. But on myself? It seems a frivolous use of power." It sounded stupid, even to her own ears, and she mentally fumbled for something that made more sense.

"That makes sense, I guess," Donovan said. "It's the same way that many people won't take a painkiller for a headache because it simply never occurs to them to use medicine for such a mundane reason. Both are ridiculous, of course. But since I can't remember the last time I took an aspirin for anything less than a knife wound, I can't really say anything about what you're doing."

"You were stabbed?" Morgana asked. Fear flooded her system. Even though she could see him standing in front of her, hale and whole, the mental image was almost enough to bring her to her knees.

Donovan pulled her closer and nuzzled her behind her ear. "It was a long time ago, sweetheart. Before we met. No one's gotten the drop on me like that again, and with you by my side, it's pretty safe to say no one ever will again."

Morgana pulled away from him. When she felt him stiffen, she reached up and touched his face. "Thank you."

He raised his eyebrows. "For what?"

"Being here." She gestured behind her at the room. "This won't end well, but it's better than facing the witch alone."

Donovan snorted. "If we're going to lose anyway, we might as well die together?"

Morgana smiled sadly. They hadn't had a chance to become friends, not really, and they would not have the opportunity to again become lovers. There was little left for them. She opened her mouth, then closed it again. She couldn't offer empty promises nor false reassurance. But she could be honest, at least for a little while. "There are few people I'd rather die with."

nineteen

Morgana spotted a rare empty bench overlooking the river with a view of the ruined chapel and picked up her pace until she got to it, then sat down with a groan. Her frustration at not being able to sense Bridget was compounded by her increasingly agonizing foot pain.

"Feet?" Donovan asked.

"These hideous sneakers are not any better than my beautiful boots," she grumbled. "It is enough that I am wearing this ridiculous t-shirt and have pink hair. They serve a purpose, although probably not now that you're here. If these shoes are not going to alleviate the pain in my feet, there is no point in wearing them."

"I thought about saying something to you this morning about your disguise, but I figured if you hated it that much, you'd remember on your own. I think a part of you likes putting on another costume. Although how you've survived doing undercover work when you never change your personality to suit your disguise is beyond me."

Morgana glared at him. Her decision earlier to embrace what was between them, regardless of the consequences, waned in the face of his mockery. "I am very good at undercover work," she gritted out. "It is only you who sees me out of character."

"I fluster you?" he raised his eyebrows as he sat beside her and reached for her leg.

She swatted ineffectually at him. "You know you do. It is difficult for me to be vulnerable, but your presence is enough for me to forget who I am supposed to be."

"I like that you forget who you're supposed to be when I'm around. I'm much more interested in who you are." Donovan slipped off her shoe and dug his strong fingers into her foot. She groaned in pleasure.

"I don't know who I am." She meant the statement to come out jokingly, but the truth of it hit her harder than it should.

Donovan's massage stopped for a second. She looked up at him, knowing she'd see pity on his face. His expression held no pity, though. Instead, his eyes brimmed with compassion. After a beat, he resumed the massage.

She pushed a smile onto her face, more for his benefit than hers, and continued. "I have changed so much, yet not at all in the centuries I've been alive. When I was young, my world was so small. My village. My parents and brother. The priestesses who called me to the grove and the cloaked men who claimed Paska. There were other towns, some close enough to visit, but we were poor. It required a horse and cart to go far, and without coin for a room and meal, there was little call to go further than you could in a single day."

She closed her eyes and gave over to the pleasure of the foot massage. Clear blue skies appeared in her memories, and with it, the smells of her childhood. Fresh grass, fragrant trees, clear water. There were less pleasant smells, too, of course, but she did her best to filter out the smells of unwashed bodies and dung.

"Tell me about it. About where you grew up. What was it like?" Donovan shifted slightly and turned her body to get better access to her feet. They looked like any couple taking a break from their romantic stroll, and although Bridget knew about their involvement, it would take more than a first glance to recognize them. She pulled a tendril of energy from the river to aid in the healing of her feet.

"I'll tell you mine if you tell me yours," Morgana offered. "I don't know very much about you, either."

"It's a deal."

Morgana spread her awareness out around them. Just because she was traveling more than sixteen hundred years into the past didn't mean she should let her guard down. They hadn't found Bridget yet, but she was around. Ceri had seen it, and Ceri was never wrong.

Once she was satisfied that she'd know the moment anyone with magic, no matter how much they tried to hide it, was within a quarter mile of her, she allowed herself to be pulled back into her childhood.

"I don't remember ever being unhappy. My first memories are chasing Paska through the long grass near our village. I wasn't very old when play gave over to work. There was always something to do. Cleaning, cooking, mending. It was hard work, but everyone did it, and I didn't know there were any alternatives." Morgana's voice took on a dreamy quality. "I don't remember my parents' faces, but I know my mother had black hair like mine. And I remember how much she cried when my father didn't come home one day." She wrinkled her nose. "I don't know how he died—or even if he did— and I'm not sure if I ever did. Paska might know. Maybe I'll ask him next time we talk. He doesn't like to revisit the past, and I almost never push him to remember."

"How old were you when your father died?" Donovan asked. He set down her right foot, stood, and spun her one-hundred-eighty degrees, then sat on her other side to continue his ministrations on her left foot.

"Nine, maybe, or ten. I wouldn't have known my birthday at all if I hadn't been born at Midsummer, but my mother always told me that made me lucky." A soft smile ghosted across Morgana's face. "I don't know if she was right, but my life has been mostly good. It wasn't too long after father disappeared that the priestesses came for me. I cried when I left my mother. I never saw her again after that. She died before I finished my initiation."

"Was Paska with her when she died?" Donovan asked.

Morgana shook her head. "No. He was off getting his own training. There were more and more Christians all the time, and it was getting difficult to find new initiates into the mysteries."

"Was he a druid?"

Morgana pursed her lips and considered. "Yes and no, at least not the way you think of Druidry. We worshipped the gods and goddesses of the earth and air and spirit. The divine was in all things —trees and lakes were where I found them. Paska's gods were hotter and bolder. He found himself looking to air and fire. I don't know if the ability to take the form of a merlin was innate, or something he learned at the feet of the druids, for lack of a better word. But when we reunited, he was so powerful that he almost scared me."

"How old were you then?" Donovan reached down and pulled her other leg onto his lap, then scooted closer to her and wrapped an arm around her.

"Eighteen, newly handfasted, and hugely pregnant. He didn't recognize me, but I knew who he was immediately. His magic called to me. My husband and I followed Paska when he went to advise one of the local clan chiefs, and we were there when that clan chief rose to prominence through conquest. Eventually, he became tyrannical, and then he started losing. He was not a gracious loser." Tension crept into her body. The last three years she, Paska, and Gareth spent in the rough court of a self-styled king were some of the worst memories of her life.

"You don't have to talk about this if you don't want to," Donovan said, pulling her closer into his body.

"I've never told anyone. Not in all these years." Morgana laughed. "Of course, who would I tell? And who would believe me?"

"If you want to continue, I want to hear it."

Morgana turned her face into his shoulder and let his body serve as a buffer against the pain her memories brought. "We spent sixteen years with the king. I considered him and his wife to be dear friends, and Paska and Vortigern were even closer. But when Vortigern's luck turned, he didn't look for fault within himself. He blamed Paska, and to some degree, me."

"You said he was tyrannical. Would Paska sabotage his victories?"

Morgana smiled. "He absolutely would. And he probably was nudging things in the direction he wanted things to go." The smile dropped from her face as she prepared to relate the next happenings. "The king grew increasingly angry and more paranoid. He accused Paska of seducing his wife, then had her executed in front of us. I might believe Paska had a hand in the losses in battle, but he would never have betrayed the man he considered his best friend—possibly even more—by sleeping with his queen.

"We tried to reason with him after that. Vortigern was instantly remorseful and devastated by the loss of Sevira. We stayed another year. I was in my early thirties then and looked much the same as I do now." Morgana looked down at her body. "Well, minus the pink hair and novelty t-shirt."

"So almost too beautiful to be human?" Donovan asked.

Morgana grimaced. "I am not one of the fair folk who hide in the woods, no matter how I was called at the time. But still beautiful enough to catch the king's eye. He tried to lure me to his bed by playing on my sympathy and sadness over the loss of his wife, my friend. When I refused him, he was graceful in the rejection. A few weeks later, my husband died, the victim of a sudden fever. The next approach from Vortigern was an offer to comfort me as we were both in the same place now."

"Did Vortigern kill your husband?" Donovan asked.

Tears Morgana hadn't noticed forming trickled down her face. "I don't know. I think it likely, but I've always suspected he had help."

Donovan gasped, jarring Morgana's head from his shoulder. "You think your brother helped the man who'd executed his own wife kill your husband?"

"I don't know how else to explain a fever so hot and sudden that I could do nothing. I am not a healer, but I have some healing abilities, and I was never out of touch with the other women in my grove. There were many healers among them. I called for Wulfwynn, but she arrived too late to save him." Morgana took a deep breath. "It no longer matters if Paska helped kill my husband. What happened next overshadows any possible betrayal. When Wulfwynn arrived at my side, she brought my daughter with her. Elaine had been with the grove for six years. I traveled to see her eight times a year, but she hadn't come home once during that time."

A lump formed in Morgana's throat, and she couldn't continue for a long moment. Donovan said nothing, but the arm wrapped around her tightened again, and he stroked her shoulder.

When she could speak again, the words came out in a whisper. "When Vortigern saw Elaine, he was consumed with passion and the desire to possess her. At first, he attempted to seduce her with kind words and the offer of marriage and power. She refused him—she wanted nothing to do with men and even less to do with that man. She could sense his cruelty, and even if I hadn't warned her, she would have avoided him." Morgana swallowed.

"When seduction didn't work, he decided to take what he wanted. He had her kidnapped on the road not more than a quarter of a mile from my house as she and Wulfwynn began her journey to return to the safety of the grove. She fought him, and her screams had me on a horse and racing her way in seconds. Wulfwynn died first, a dozen arrows sprouting from her back where she lay on the road. I arrived too late to save her, but in time to see what happened next. Vortigern pulled Elaine from her horse and threw her across the saddle in front of him. He looked at me, and his expression was not the madness I expected to see. It was satisfaction. Guards appeared on either side of me and bound me with rope woven with magic, leaving me unable to use my power. While he was distracted, looking at me to let me know he had won, Elaine pulled a knife she had strapped to her leg and stabbed him, ripping the blade through his gut. She leapt off the horse. But Vortigern wasn't done with her yet. He chased her—him still astride his horse and her on foot. Elaine ran towards the edge of the world, as we liked to call the cliff that overlooked the sea below. She looked back at me when she jumped, and it was like she hung in the air long enough to say goodbye."

Tears streamed faster down Morgana's face. Donovan's lips brushed the top of her head. "Have you been carrying this memory alone for sixteen hundred years?"

Morgana nodded. There was only a little more to the story, but she had to tell him, to finish this purge. "When I collapsed in grief, unable to muster even a spark of power to take my revenge, I was taken to Vortigern's prison. It was there that Paska came to see me. I told him what happened, and a fury overtook him. He killed the men who guarded me, tore open the door to my cell, and burned the ropes from my wrists." Morgana rubbed a thumb over the slight burn scar that still remained on her left wrist.

"Why not have you killed the same way he'd killed his wife and your husband?" Donovan asked.

"He was afraid of Paska." Scorn dripped from her voice when she thought of Vortigern's cowardice in all things. "The king didn't believe Paska would protest my imprisonment—they were as close as brothers, and Vortigern believed he was nearer Paska's heart than I was. But if the king had executed me, Paska would've avenged me, and it had been foretold that any man who tried to take Paska's life would die horribly. And besides that, he wasn't sure if he could. Paska was not a warrior, but he was powerful. After walking out of the dungeon, I went back to my house to gather what few possessions I wanted to take back to the grove—I needed to return Wulfwynn's body and tell them what had happened to Elaine if they didn't already know. But Paska returned to speak to the king one more time. He greeted him like a brother, and when Vortigern leaned into the embrace, Paska shoved a knife into his gut, finishing what my daughter had started." There was no denying the fierce satisfaction she still felt all these centuries later when she thought about Paska gutting the monster who'd killed nearly everyone she loved.

"And that's when he cursed you?" Donovan asked.

Morgana nodded but didn't reply. She wanted to relish the gratification, not dwell on the consequences. It was enough that Donovan knew it existed. He didn't need the details. Not yet, at least. "I think I've talked about myself enough for the day." She sat up and swung her feet back to the ground. After glaring at the hideous sneakers for a moment, she gave up and pulled them back on, wincing as she laced them up.

"I can't imagine how long it will take to hear your life story," Donovan said. He stood and held out his hands to help her to her feet.

"Longer than we have, probably," Morgana said. "I don't know how long it will be until the curse takes effect. Less than a year, certainly."

"I'm sorry. I don't think I've said it yet, but I am. I should've stayed away, let you do this without me. Maybe then..." His voice trailed off, and he looked down to where their hands were still clasped.

"I think it was too late the moment I climbed into your bed. I've been deluding myself into thinking I could avoid it by avoiding you." Morgana dropped his hand but didn't step back. She looked up and licked her lips. She'd dreamed about kissing him again since she'd walked out of his apartment after their night together, and there was no reason not to anymore. Before she could close the space between their lips, a bell rang in her head. Someone had tripped her alarm.

Morgana jogged down the riverfront walk. The minor foot pain that lingered after Donovan's ministrations and her healing spell was pushed to the background; all her focus was reserved for finding the magic-user who'd come into her sphere of awareness. Donovan kept pace beside her. He hadn't said a word when she took off towards the Luís I Bridge. She liked a man who didn't ask questions when it clearly wasn't the time for explanations.

She skidded to a stop a few yards away from the bridge. She scanned the area; the magic user was close, and she didn't want to be out of breath when she confronted whoever it was. It probably wasn't Bridget—she was certain she'd recognize the blood witch's magical aura, entwined as it was with the magic she'd stolen from Morgana—but she'd made too many assumptions about what Bridget could and couldn't do, and she would not make that mistake again. For all Morgana knew, Bridget could have found a way to mask her magical levels, even from someone with as much power as Morgana.

A tall, white man with a fiery shock of red hair walked out of a wine bar and took one of the empty chairs on the sidewalk.

Morgana's jaw dropped.

"Is that who I think it is?" Donovan asked.

"Violet's husband," Morgana confirmed. She grabbed Donovan's arm and tugged him back towards another sidewalk cafe where they could keep an eye on Tom Masters without him looking up and spotting them. "Bridget was working with him this entire time, and neither of us figured it out."

"When Violet died, I questioned him. But he was barely a suspect to begin with, and his grief at her death seemed genuine." Donovan sounded as shocked as Morgana felt.

"Is he a warlock?" Morgana asked, then answered her own question. "He has to be—I felt his presence, something I wouldn't have done if he'd been an ordinary mortal. But I didn't pick up anything from him in Oracle Bay."

"Neither did I. We have to assume that Bridget can cloak others besides herself," Donovan said.

Morgana smiled tightly at the server who arrived to take their order. She requested a sparkling mineral water and a charcuterie tray. They might be there for surveillance, but she was hungry, and there was every reason to eat while she had a chance.

"How do you want to play this?" Donovan asked after the server walked away.

"We must assume he would recognize either of us, even with my ridiculous costume. I suggest we follow him when he leaves and hope he is too arrogant to pay attention to his surroundings."

"I can't think of a better plan right now. He has to be working with Bridget—it's too big of a coincidence that he'd be here otherwise, especially a month after his wife's funeral." Donovan angled his chair so he had a view of the street behind them.

"It could be a trap," Morgana said after the server dropped off their drinks. "Bridget must know we're here."

Donovan grimaced. "It probably is a trap, but I don't want to walk away from the chance to find her."

Morgana shook her head. "We have to spring it, but I don't want to jump in without knowing more. If Tom is bait and we don't bite, she'll fling him back out again tomorrow."

Donovan nodded slowly. "I don't want to wait, but we should make a plan rather than relying on your magical power and my strength and charisma."

Morgana smiled and rolled her eyes a little. "Perhaps you could destroy her and any other onions she might have collected by waving your giant ego around."

Donovan smirked. "Oh, I can wave something around…"

"Men," Morgana muttered. "Always bringing the subject round to the same place. So predictable."

Donovan's smirk turned into a chuckle. "It's a gift." His laughter stopped abruptly, and he stiffened in his seat. "I see Bridget," he muttered under his breath. "She's walking right towards us."

"Has she spotted you yet?" Morgana asked, not voicing the curses that were in her mind. They weren't ready for a confrontation, and the busy riverfront was not the right place for that, anyway.

"I don't think so," Donovan replied. His voice was laced with tension, and Morgana was reminded that although Bridget had tried —and nearly succeeded—to kill her, she'd subjugated Donovan, taken away his will, and turned him into a pet and a repository for her power.

"Will she be able to reassert her control over you?" Morgana didn't want to ask, but if he hadn't considered it, he needed to know.

He shook his head emphatically. "Not without capturing me and performing the binding rituals the way she did before. Paska's work was too thorough to leave her a foothold in my mind."

Morgana wanted to turn around and see Bridget for herself, but that was the quickest way to get noticed. She also wasn't sure she could keep the fear that was churning her stomach and weakening her legs off her face.

"She's heading straight towards us," Donovan said.

Fuck. Morgana pasted a smile on her face, took a deep breath, and settled her mind. This wasn't the time or place she'd hoped to confront the blood witch, but it appeared she had little choice.

"Morgana, Donovan!" Bridget called. All hints of the softer voice she'd affected before were gone. Now, it was all hard edges and barely veiled anger.

A few people sitting near Morgana and Donovan turned towards Bridget when Morgana twisted around in her chair.

"What a surprise, seeing you here," Bridget continued. Her aura swirled around her, blue laced with green—her affinity for earth—and a murky brown. The brown muddied the waters of her power and her mind, and it pulsed on and off with each surge of emotion emanating from her.

Morgana didn't reply. There was no reason to pretend she was happy to see the woman, and every reason to stay quiet. Silence would irritate the other woman, and Morgana wanted her off balance—although not enough to tip her over into the madness that would precipitate an attack in public.

Tom trotted up to stand a step behind Bridget on her lefthand side. He grinned at Morgana and Donovan, showing every one of his too-large teeth. "Betcha didn't expect to see me here, did you?"

Morgana looked over at Donovan and mouthed, "showboats."

He nodded, then they returned their gazes to the couple in front of them.

Bridget shifted from foot to foot when Morgana continued watching her in stony silence.

"Aren't you going to say hi?" Bridget asked after a couple minutes of awkward silence stretched between them.

"Hi. Would you like to join us for a glass of wine?" Morgana forced a smile. She wanted nothing more than to take the offensive, but the streets were packed with people. She was counting a lot on the fact that Bridget wouldn't be so far gone as to attack her magically in front of a large crowd, something she couldn't be certain of based on the lack of balance the blood witch had demonstrated so far.

"Don't you patronize me!" Bridget shrieked.

More people stared at Bridget, and she was drawing a small crowd.

Tension gripped Morgana, and she forced herself to loosen her muscles and push her shoulder blades down and away from her ears. She met Bridget's eyes for the first time. "You would confront me here?" Morgana asked.

"Why wouldn't I? I'm not afraid of you. Not afraid of anyone!" Bridget crossed her arms over her chest.

Behind her, Tom imitated her stance.

Morgana permitted herself a small grin, then looked around. Bridget was the center of attention for the nearly three dozen people who'd been dining or walking on the riverfront. As enjoyable as it would be to watch Bridget unravel, it served no purpose. If the blood witch lost complete control, the bystanders might take the brunt of her rage. Morgana wouldn't be able to shield them all, not without raising even more questions than Bridget's attack would.

"Kill them," Bridget said to Tom.

The red-headed man hesitated, his eyes darting wildly between Bridget and Morgana.

Bridget turned and placed a hand on his arm. "Don't make me tell you again. Kill them."

People were realizing this was more than a crazy woman screaming at a couple having a quiet afternoon meal. The crowd around Bridget dissipated—the ones who'd been walking, picking up their pace. The diners overturned chairs and disappeared into the cafes that lined the street.

Tom pulled a gun out of his jacket and pointed it at Morgana.

"No!" Donovan yelled. He launched himself at Tom.

Time slowed down.

The report of a gun rang in Morgana's ears, and a sickening *whump* made her blood run cold. She was on her feet and at Donovan's side before Tom dropped the gun to his side, a look of confused triumph on his face.

Screams erupted and tables overturned as panic gripped the waterfront crowds, but it all faded to the background of her awareness when she looked at Donovan.

Bridget laughed. "Oh, poor kitty got hurt."

Morgana reached out to Donovan through the bond they shared. There was pain but not fear. She took the risk of dropping her gaze for a moment. Blood stained his t-shirt's left sleeve, but not as much as she would have expected to see had it been a devastating hit.

"'Tis a flesh wound," Donovan said. His voice was shaky, but the bravado he injected into it balanced it out.

Cries behind Morgana raised the hairs on the back of her neck. "Donovan, see what's happening," she said. Ice spread through her veins. She knew already—Tom's bullet had grazed Donovan and found another target.

Sirens in the distance announced that the Portuguese police would be there soon. There was no way to take Bridget now without more people dying, and the human police wouldn't help matters. She had to get Bridget to move; there had to be somewhere better to have this confrontation.

Bridget smirked. "What will you do now, Morgana? Take me out in front of all these people? I have the power to beat you and make my escape before anyone realizes what's happening."

"Walk away, Bridget," Morgana said. All the tension that had wracked her body earlier drained out of her, leaving behind cold steel and certitude. "Don't make the mistake of thinking I won't protect myself and defend the people standing here."

Donovan's footsteps echoed behind her. "A young woman is dead," he said flatly. "The bullet that missed me is lodged in her chest."

Bridget smiled, and a shiver ran down Morgana's spine. The blood witch reached into her pocket. Morgana flinched before she could stop herself, then flung her shields out as far as she could without weakening them. It was difficult to protect large numbers of people. Their emotions and movements disrupted her concentration at a time when she could not afford to be distracted.

Bridget laughed, grabbed Tom's arm, and pulled him up beside her. "See you later, Morgana," Bridget said. "And good luck." Bridget spun around and threw what she'd withdrawn from her pocket like she was in a heated ultimate frisbee match. A disk sailed out, and as it spun, beads dislodged themselves from the periphery and flew through the air.

Morgana flung her power out as widely as she could, trying to place a physical shield over the magical one she'd already created. She glanced behind her when more screams tore the air, and when she pulled her gaze back around, Bridget and Tom were gone. Her jaw dropped. They couldn't have disappeared. Only the divine had the ability to travel unseen, and only gods could travel instantly.

Screams erupted in the air, and Morgana turned her attention to the scene behind her.

Most of the beads had been stopped by her shields, but there were dozens of people on the ground writhing in pain.

She assessed the situation. There were too many, and if the beads had the same effect as the ones Bridget used to drain the power of a witch, then Morgana didn't have time to save more than one.

She scanned the downed people again, and her gaze caught on a child. At first glance, she'd thought the person on the ground was a young woman, but now she could see that the woman was kneeling at her child's side, keening loudly.

This was no kind of choice, but Morgana could not make any other. She sprinted to the child's side and placed her hands on either side of their head. They couldn't be more than five or six, and the power surrounding them had more than one signature.

Morgana rolled back on her heels and regarded the child with a more critical eye.

"What is their name?" she asked sharply, hoping the mother understood English.

"Luisa," the woman answered.

Morgana looked down at the little girl and smiled. "You are going to be okay, Luisa." She closed her eyes. The black magic was traveling through the girl's body much slower than Morgana would've expected. The child had more natural defenses than anyone Morgana had seen in a long, long time.

Sweat rose on Morgana's brow as she reached into the girl and bound the black magic, then drew it slowly out.

"Witch magic?" the young mother asked.

Morgana spared her a sharp glance, then nodded.

The woman reached out and placed her hands on Morgana's. With the addition of the young witch's power—power that recognized itself in her child—the work eased. Moments later, the spell was pulled out of the child, and Luisa opened her eyes.

Tears streamed down Luisa's mother's face. "Obrigada," she whispered as she drew Luisa into her arms. Then she added in accented English. "I can help with the others."

Morgana forced a smile. "Yes. Please." She pushed to her feet and held out a hand.

The woman gained her feet, Luisa still in her arms. "I'm Ana," she said. She turned and handed Luisa to a beautiful dusky-faced man behind her who was white-faced and swaying. "Her father," Ana whispered. "He is pretty but no good in trouble, you know?"

"I know the type." Morgana held out her hand and led Ana to the next person who was still screaming.

twenty-one

Morgana was exhausted by the time Donovan convinced her to take a break. The rest of the witches in Ana's coven had arrived by then, and although they weren't as powerful or skilled as Morgana, they were healers. Once Morgana had bound the black magic, the Portuguese witches were able to keep it from doing further damage and slowly pull it out of those affected, leaving her and Donovan to deal with the human police, a necessity she despised. It was fortunate that Donovan's credentials and manner inspired trust from fellow law enforcement officials, and his ability to spin lies with the truth enabled Morgana to melt back into the background.

"We didn't save them all," she said dully. Of the thirty people struck by Bridget's magic, only ten had survived until the paramedics had arrived.

"But you saved some." Donovan pulled her into his arms. "You need food and rest."

The crowd that had scattered in the aftermath of the attack was beginning to return now that the injured and dead were taken away.

"I need to find Bridget and take her out." The loss of everyone who hadn't made it weighed on her in a way death hadn't for a long time. She'd watched so many people die, some by her hand, in the last millennia and a half, but hadn't felt this crushing grief and guilt for as long as she could remember. Anger simmered in the background, and she needed to assuage it all today.

"You are in no shape for a showdown," Donovan said. "Let's find food and a place to sleep. We can firm up our plan and approach, and you'll be ready to fight her tomorrow."

He was right. She was already wobbling on her feet, missing the healing energy she'd expended. "I should not be this exhausted," she said.

Donovan raised his eyebrows. "You've used a lot of energy in the last few days between recovering from being poisoned, searching for Bridget, keeping yourself constantly shielded, and healing so many people now."

Donovan was right. She hadn't properly refilled her stores since before healing herself in London. If she wanted to ensure her victory over Bridget, she would need to replenish her powers and ensure she was tapped into a local source, especially since Bridget was still carrying her stolen power. "Okay."

"Okay? That's it?" Donovan's expression was incredulous.

Morgana shrugged. A lump formed in her throat, and she swallowed it back. If she was too exhausted to control her emotions in public, she was too tired to have a magical fight. "You are correct. I need rest, and I need to make a better plan than 'follow her magical signature and attack.' I do not want to return to our hotel, though."

Ana approached Morgana with another woman in tow. Their faces were pale, damp with sweat, and pinched with exhaustion. "You can stay at our safe house," the second woman offered in English accented with a slight southern drawl. She was tall and slim —all sharp angles and minimal curves—and had deep mahogany skin and dark brown eyes. She was wearing jeans and a colorful, patterned blouse. Her hair was hidden by a fuchsia scarf.

"You have a safe house?" Morgana asked.

The woman smiled tightly. "This is not the first blood witch to use this city as a hunting ground, and the Silver Eye looks the other way. We have had to take steps to protect our own."

Morgana closed her eyes. She'd accused Donovan of being blind to the inner workings and machinations of the Scales, but she was just as guilty as he was. "I am sorry," she said. "My name is Morgana."

"Sydney," the Black woman replied.

"Do you have water and earth?" Morgana asked. It would be an odd question to ask anyone but another witch.

"Of course," Sydney replied. "There is a large unpaved courtyard with a stream running through it. If you need salt water, that is available nearby."

"Fresh water is my preference," Morgana said. "Thank you."

Sydney smiled tightly. "Don't thank me yet. You don't know the price of our aid."

Morgana bowed her head slightly. "Unless the price is causing harm, no matter how slight, to an innocent, I am happy to pay."

"Depends on if you think that blood witch is innocent." Sydney's eyes were hard as onyx, and anger radiated from her.

"She has been stealing power from those with unrealized magic, then killing them. She's left a trail of bodies in her wake. This"—Morgana waved her hand, indicating the riverfront promenade—"is only the latest in a series of depredations. She is far from innocent. And she will pay for her crimes."

"Why haven't you stopped her yet?" Sydney asked bluntly.

Morgana growled in frustration. "I had. After she nearly took my power and my life, she was remanded into the custody of the Scales. Two weeks ago, she broke free, stealing the power and lives of several warlocks. That is why I am here."

"And the man?" Sydney asked, narrowing her eyes at Donovan.

"He is my companion and was once held in thrall by the blood witch. He has his own score to settle and his own power to wield in the name of justice." A rush of love and surprise hit her from the bond she shared with Donovan.

"He's not a warlock."

There was no question, so Morgana didn't reply. It wasn't her place to share the details of Donovan's magic. Either he'd be welcome in the safe house, or she would find alternative lodging.

Sydney and Ana eyed Donovan with expressions that were nearly identical, a sight that would have been amusing under any other circumstance.

"Okay," Sydney finally said. "Y'all are both welcome." She turned to Morgana. "You are responsible for him. Any wrong he commits, you will pay for."

"Understood," Morgana said, nodding gravely. It was no different from any condition she would have set in the same situation.

"Ana. Take them to the safe house, then go get Luisa. Tonight, I want us all hidden as well as we can. That witch might not know who we are, and I don't want to give her a chance to find out." Sydney turned and walked back towards the witches still working in tandem with paramedics on the few remaining injured who were likely to pull through.

Morgana eyed the cooperation between medical and magical persons and filed away questions for later.

"Come with me," Ana said. "Do you want someone to go to your hotel for your things?"

Morgana thought about it while Ana led them up what looked like a crooked alley, but based on the number of cars parked along the narrow sidewalks, might have actually been a street. She had her comb and her athame with her, and there was nothing else that was irreplaceable. "I don't, although it would be nice to have my clothing back, or at least anything else." She looked down at her t-shirt, jeans, and sneakers with a huff of disdain.

"I can send someone," Ana said hesitantly.

"No. It's not worth the risk. These clothes will serve for a battle."

With any luck, there might be a witch of a similar size who could lend her a clean shirt. There was no point in warning Bridget that Morgana was near by the smell of sweat.

Donovan spoke for the first time since Sydney approached them with her offer of safe haven. "I have a manila folder in the hotel room safe. It won't do anyone any good if they're not magical, but if it falls into the wrong hands, they could do some damage."

"Why did you not bring it with you?" Morgana demanded. Leaving implements of power in a hotel safe seemed to her the height of stupidity. "Especially since there was a chance we would encounter Bridget today."

Donovan grimaced. "It was a combination of not having a way to safely carry them and sheer forgetfulness."

"Will it help to have them with you tomorrow?" Morgana asked. She kept her eyes on Ana. The young woman was leading them up another twisted path of sharp turns in a city that already had few straightforward roads.

There was a long pause while he considered before he answered. "I don't think any of them would have any effect against Bridget, although some might be useful against Tom. They are written warlock spells that were given to me by the head of the Scales, like the one I used when we needed to escape notice in London."

He held out his arm to her, and she took it gratefully, leaning into him to take some of the weight off her feet.

"Ana, If you have a healer who can spare a little time and energy, I would like her to spend some time with my feet. The combination of unfamiliar shoes and the cobblestones and hills has made them very sore." Morgana was already limping again, and she wasn't sure how far she had to go.

"There will be someone there who can help you," Ana replied. "And it's not far now. Only a few more blocks."

Considering how long the blocks were, that might not mean much.

Fifteen minutes later, the narrow path they were on abruptly dead-ended at a red door set into a high stone wall. Citrus trees waved at them over the top of the wall, and the scent of orange blossoms wafted down.

Ana glanced back at Morgana and Donovan.

Morgana took the unspoken hint and turned her back to the door, pulling Donovan around with her.

"Thank you," Ana said. "You may come in now."

Morgana and Donovan followed Ana through the unassuming door and into a lushly wild garden paradise. Palm trees rose up between orange trees and brilliantly pink bougainvillea trailed over the walls. Birds of paradise grew near the walls and encircled the trees, and the air was redolent with honeysuckle.

"It's beautiful," Morgana said. She toed her shoes off and removed her socks as soon as the door closed behind them. She heard the snick of the lock and felt the wards close again to hide their passage. "No one will see the door if they're not with one of your coven, will they?" Morgana asked.

"They must be with one of us, and we must be a willing guide. There are ways any of us can warn the others if we are being controlled. If you follow me, I will show you first to your rooms, and then to the courtyard. Our healer will join you there." Ana led the way along a small gravel path towards the first of several adobe buildings decorated liberally with blue and white tiles that created the image of a woman standing in a pool of water, holding a torch in one hand. A bird was taking off from her other hand, and a massive tree grew behind her.

The peace of the goddess fell over her, and the tension and fear that had ridden her since Bridget had approached fell away.

"You look different," Donovan said, brushing away a wayward strand of hot pink hair from her forehead.

"The only way this would be better is if it was my backyard sanctuary. It is imbued with peace, and the earth mother and her elements protect it and replenish those who are connected to her." Morgana spread her arms wide, closed her eyes, and tipped her head up to the sky. She let the evening sun warm her face and breathed deeply. A smile grew on her face, and for a moment she was one with the earth, guilt and fear forgotten.

She dropped her arms and opened her eyes, then smiled at Ana. "If you would show me to the room where I'll be sleeping, I would appreciate it. If there is anyone who has a shirt I can wear instead of this one, that would be wonderful. I need a moment to feel myself again, then will make my way to your coven's sanctuary."

"Of course," Ana said. "Follow me, please." She led Morgana and Donovan through a maze of corridors past living areas and a large dining space with adjacent kitchen that buzzed with activity and emanated mouth-watering aromas.

Ana stopped in front of a nondescript room and pushed open the door. "Our rooms aren't much. Some sisters live here all the time. They have large, comfortable rooms. The rest are nothing more than a place to sleep." She gestured Morgana into the room and added apologetically, "There are no private bathrooms; yours is across the hall. And, since we are calling all our sisters and their families in tonight, there are not enough rooms for both of you, and he cannot wander the halls alone. You will have to share and stay together."

Excitement thrummed through Morgana's veins, and fear gripped her heart. She kept her voice steady and replied, "We will be fine, thank you. If you provide us with an extra blanket, he will be quite comfortable on the floor."

Donovan choked back a laugh, and she glared at him out of the corner of her eye.

Ana's eyes widened, but she didn't reply. "As you wish, Morgana. Now, would you like me to show you to the courtyard?"

"Could you give me directions instead? I need to freshen up first, and I don't want to keep you from retrieving Luisa." Morgana's hand twitched towards her purse and the comb within. She might not have her preferred clothing, but at least she could fix her hair. She had to admit, though, denim jeans and a t-shirt were comfortable garb for long walks in a hilly city. Leather trousers might give her more range of motion, but she would be soaked in sweat in fewer than fifteen minutes of walking.

Ana provided towels for the bathroom and written directions to the courtyard, then took her leave.

Morgana walked across the hall, took a brief shower, then pulled out her comb and ran it through her hair with the words that would change her hair. Instead of pulling the comb the full length, returning her long, inky tresses to a stopping point midway down her back, she left it just below her shoulders. It would be easier to pull back and more practical for battle. Even more practical would be a style that stopped at her ears and left nothing to grab or singe, but vanity was an indulgence she was loath to give up.

She dressed in the same clothes she'd been wearing and wrinkled her nose against the faint smells of sweat and blood rising from them. In the future, she would be sure to carry fresh undergarments with her, even if nothing else. She returned to her room. Donovan was stretched out on the full-sized bed. His eyes were closed, and he was lightly snoring.

A smile touched Morgana's lips. She closed the door gently and followed Ana's directions to the courtyard.

twenty-two

A touch at her elbow brought Morgana back into herself. She let go of the vision she held—lying in the embrace of the moss-covered roots of an ancient tree with her feet dangling in a stream while dappled sunlight played over her body, birds singing their sweet melodies accompanied by the sounds of the wind rustling the leaves, and the golden light of the divine self encompassing her.

Morgana opened her eyes. The sight that greeted her was not the familiar place she visited during her meditative states, the place where she was first introduced to the love of the earth goddess, but the Portuguese garden was not disappointing. The trees and flowers that had greeted her when she'd entered the compound were redoubled in the courtyard, the earth was sun-warmed, and the promised stream clear and cold.

Morgana stretched and stood. The healer had rubbed a pungent salve over her feet that had warmed to an almost uncomfortable degree before sinking into her flesh, unknotting the cramped muscles and tendons and healing the blisters that had formed where her ill-fitting sneakers had rubbed against her skin. She'd left

Morgana with an admonishment to soak her feet, then stay off them for a couple days and be kinder to them in the future, a command Morgana wished she could follow.

"Are you back yet?" Donovan asked. She looked up at him. The setting sun flared behind him, creating a halo-like effect and catching the tapetum lucidum in his eyes. His feline nature was seldom in the forefront, and her breath caught at the reminder of who and *what* he was.

"Yes, I think so," she said. Her voice had the dreamy quality it often took on when she had been meditating for a great length of time. "Did you have a good nap?"

Donovan sank to the ground beside her and stretched out his legs, placing his bare feet into the water. "I feel so much better now. I didn't realize how exhausted I was until I woke up an hour after sitting down on the bed to wait for you to come back from the bathroom." He reached over and ran a hand through her hair. "It's not as long as it was."

"Do you like it?" Morgana was surprised to find that she cared about his response. She'd never given even a fleeting thought to the opinions of anyone else on her appearance.

"I do. I like everything on you, of course, but this suits you. You are less severe with the shorter hair." Donovan wrapped a fist around a large chunk of hair and tugged lightly.

"Less severe? That really might ruin my image," Morgana replied.

"Sweetheart, if you think anyone believes you're the hard-ass you pretend to be, you're fooling yourself. Your friends know you're all soft and gooey under that hard candy shell." He let go of her hair and ran his thumb along her jawline.

"I am not candy," she replied stiffly. "And they do not consider me a friend. Drew told me, during the midst of everything, that he and I were not friends. I do not believe there are any in Oracle Bay who would consider me a friend."

Donovan leaned back from her and held out his hand, then starting ticking names off on his fingers. "Antonia?"

Morgana nodded. "But she…"

"If you say she doesn't count, I will tell her you said that," Donovan threatened.

"Fine. She counts. That's only one." Morgana crossed her arms. It was impossible to be angry in this miniature paradise, but she was going to give it her best.

"Andy."

Morgana opened her mouth to protest, but Donovan's finger pressed against her lips before she could say anything.

"You wouldn't have such a great give and take if you weren't friends. He threatened me, you know. Before I left town when he found out who I'd been, what she'd made me do." He grinned, but the pinched look around his eyes belied his casual attitude.

Warmth spread through Morgana's body, even though she knew she should be angry that the demon had been so presumptuous. "Do you want me to talk to him?"

Donovan laughed. "No. He loves you, and I would issue the same promises of bodily harm and eternal damnation were our situations reversed."

Morgana's eyebrows raised. "Eternal damnation?" Had Andy revealed his true nature to Donovan?

Donovan shrugged. "He was sporting enormous silver wings when he made the threats. I assumed he wasn't just blowing sulfurous smoke up my ass. You've got witches and seers and prophets. Why not demons?"

"He's not a demon," Morgana said, hoping Andy never heard her say that. "He's…neutral now. He fell, but then Hell kicked him out."

Donovan nodded. "Of course. Nothing so straightforward, then. But I was listing your friends. Ceri is your friend, or she would be if you opened up even a little more. Her partner and your brother love you both, and she would have you over for wine and gossip in a minute if you gave her any hint at all you were interested." He ticked off the last couple names quickly. "Sandy and Russell."

"Four friends are not very many," Morgana pointed out. "I am also not convinced you are correct. You barely know any of these people."

"It is five more than you thought you had a couple minutes ago," Donovan replied. "And I'm right. I spent enough time with your group as a whole, and even more time with everyone one on one when I was doing my rounds to interview them, and I heard how they spoke to you. You'd have more friends if you were open to it. Misty would sign you up for even more committees if you let on how much you liked it, and Jezebel would love to talk to you about some of the weird shit she's seen in the last couple years."

Morgana tilted her head and regarded Donovan. "What kind of 'weird shit' are you talking about? Has she confided in you?"

"Nothing more than 'I've seen some weird shit in the last year, and I bet Morgana would get it.'"

Morgana worried at her lower lip. If Donovan was correct, and she had to admit to at least the possibility of it, she might actually have the kinds of relationships she'd avoided and believed she would never experience.

She was saved the worry of forming a response when soft footsteps behind her interrupted her thoughts.

"If you're hungry, we're serving an evening meal in the dining room."

Morgana stood. The water rose to mid-calf, soaking the denim encasing her legs. For the first time, she missed the horrible capris she'd worn so often in her year of undercover work.

The woman who'd announced dinner had medium-toned brown skin, dark hair streaked with blond, and a generous curvy figure enhanced by her low-cut blouse and figure-hugging skirt. Her English was flawless and enhanced by an accent Morgana couldn't place.

"That sounds wonderful," Morgana said with a smile. "And if it tastes anywhere near as good as it smelled earlier, we are in for a treat." She walked out of the stream and let the soft, natural grass that grew in the rich loam dry her feet. Before she stepped out of the courtyard and into the building, she sank to the ground in a deep squat, buried her hands in the earth, and thanked the earth goddess for the gift of power Morgana had received. When she stood, her jeans were dry.

· · ★ ★ ★ ★ ★ ★ · ·

MORGANA EYED THE CLOTHING THAT HAD BEEN LEFT IN THEIR ROOM WITH pursed lips. A long, cotton shift that would serve as a nightgown, a pair of white cotton panties that would probably be better than nothing under her jeans, but were uninspiring in every other way, and a small, black t-shirt that would enhance the size of her breasts rather than conceal them.

"At least you got a nightgown," Donovan said. "I have an over-sized shirt."

Morgana glanced back at him and bit back a laugh. The t-shirt that'd been left for him hung down almost to his knees.

"You have a nightgown as well," she said. "Now turn around."

Donovan did as instructed. "I've seen you undressed before—more than once. I think you can trust me to be a gentleman."

"There are times when a woman doesn't mind being seen and times when she does. It has nothing to do with the other person's familiarity with their body. I do not often like changing in front of others, even if at other times I don't mind undressing to inflame desire and initiate sex." Morgana pushed off her jeans and pulled the grimy t-shirt over her head. She unhooked her bra and put the night-gown on. "Okay. You may look now. I am appropriately clad."

Donovan turned around and groaned.

"What?" Morgana asked, looking down at herself. "Is there something wrong?"

"That nightgown is nearly transparent," Donovan replied in a choked voice. "I...I should ask for a different room."

Morgana looked down and smoothed the nightgown down her body. The same wild abandon that'd caused her to straddle him in his pickup weeks ago had her reaching out to him. "You really shouldn't." She took his hand and pulled him towards her, backing up until the bed hit the back of her legs. Then she slipped her arms around his neck and fell backwards, pulling him down on top of her.

"Are you sure?" he asked, hands already tangled in her hair.

She hooked her leg around his hip and tugged him closer until there was nothing between them but the diaphanous material of her nightgown, then she reached up and took his mouth with hers, letting her body answer his question.

Dawn came too early. Morgana groaned at the knock signaling it was the time she'd requested to be awoken.

"Thank you," she called, then sat up and took stock of herself and her surroundings. She was alone in bed, but the warmth that still lingered beside her indicated she hadn't been for long.

Morgana climbed out of bed and raised her arms over her head. Her body was delightfully sore, and although she had gotten little sleep the night before, she felt refreshed. Sometimes marathon sex could exhaust a person and drain their resources, and then there were times when a witch could harness the sexual energy, feeding it back into the participants, heightening endurance and pleasure, and claiming the power created through sex magic to further boost her energy levels.

Morgana snagged the nightgown from where it'd been tossed the night before and pledged to write a note of gratitude to whomever had lent it to her. When she was clad, she picked up the clothes she intended to wear for the day and walked across the hall to the shower.

Thirty minutes later, dressed in the same denim jeans she'd worn the day before and wearing the tight black t-shirt someone had given her, she picked up her socks and shoes and followed the aroma of coffee and sizzling meat to the dining room.

Donovan was sitting at a table surrounded by half a dozen young women, likely initiates, chattering away at him. He wore a bemused but tolerant expression as he listened, nodding often and occasionally offering a comment of his own.

She watched for a moment, delighting in the knowledge that this man was hers, at least for a little while. He might be the vehicle that would drive her off the cliff to rejoin her daughter, but she could no longer imagine living without him.

He glanced up, and the smile he'd had for the women at the table broadened. His face lit up with joy, and the knowledge that his glow was for her—because of her—brought an answering smile to her face.

She walked towards him, and the women at the table shuffled to make room for her at his side.

"Good morning," he said, his voice low and growly.

Shivers of remembered pleasure ran up her spine. "Good morning to you," she replied. Then, she leaned forward, cupped his face with her hand, and kissed him hard, much to the amusement of the watching women.

Sydney appeared at the table and looked down at Morgana. "When you're done with breakfast, come over to my table, and we'll talk about our plans."

Morgana fixed the other witch with a stern look. "We can talk about plans as long as you understand that you and yours will not be involved in more than an advisory capacity."

Sydney flashed a smile, her white teeth a stark contrast against her black skin. "I'm in no hurry to run into battle, but you aren't the boss of me, so don't try to talk to me like you are." She turned and walked out the large glass doors leading towards a smaller courtyard than the one Morgana had used the day before.

Morgana pursed her lips and hoped that Sydney was just answering Morgana's domineering tone with a challenge of her own. If she could, Morgana would keep everyone but her out of the fray. She glanced sideways at Donovan and wondered how to convince him to stay behind.

"Don't even think about it," he replied to her unspoken contemplation.

Someone set a large cappuccino and a plate of fruit, cheese, and pastries in front of her. "Thank you," Morgana said to the young woman—one of at least two dozen she'd seen. This coven was one of the largest she'd ever seen. So many held to the modern tradition of thirteen full members, although there were often younger initiates into the mysteries at the periphery.

But a group this large brought to mind the grove where Morgana had first come to worship her goddess and learn to weave the elements around her. She hoped to have a chance to return to this coven and spend time after everything was finished and Bridget was returned to the earth, never to be reborn.

She ate quickly, then went to find Sydney. The other witch was sitting in one of eight chairs on the lawn. There was a second chair facing Sydney and three each on either side of her.

"You will not accompany me," Morgana said sharply, sitting in the chair directly across from Sydney.

"I have no intention of doing so," Sydney replied. "But you need to remember that whoever you think you are back home, you're not the one in charge here. Your blood witch is in our city. She murdered people under our protection—both regular humans and potential witches we were keeping an eye on. We are involved whether you want us to be or not, and we are going to be a part of this."

"We?" Donovan asked, settling onto the ground at Morgana's feet and leaning against her legs.

Six other women stepped forward and took the remaining empty chairs. With seven witches in a rough half-circle facing her, it could have been intimidating.

Instead, a grin rose on Morgana's face. "I like you, and I hope to return to live among you for a while when this is finished. I think we can learn much from each other."

Sydney nodded, a faint grin flirting at the corners of her mouth. "That sounds like a great idea."

Morgana leaned forward and put her hands on her knees. "Now, tell me what part you would like to take in the justice I bring to this blood witch and murderer."

"We know where she is," the witch to Sydney's right said. She was dark-skinned and so slight a figure she looked like a strong wind could blow her away, but the wave of power that emanated from her when she spoke proved her more powerful than Morgana would have guessed, had she been in the business of assuming people's power levels based on appearance.

"How, when I could not find her myself?" Morgana asked, her voice sharper than she'd meant it to be.

"You are clearly powerful," the woman continued in heavily accented English. "But we are many where you are only one." She tilted her head and regarded Donovan, who was still seated at Morgana's feet. "Or two," she added rather uncertainly.

"Two," Morgana confirmed. "And of course you're right. What do you want in exchange for this information?"

Sydney snorted. "Nothing. Not everything is transactional."

"That is not exactly true," said a witch with the lilting accent and brightly colored sari that marked her from the Indian subcontinent. "We want proof you've killed her."

Morgana thought for a moment. "What kind of proof would you accept? It will be impractical to bring you her head on a platter."

Donovan snorted, but none of the witches reacted.

"You are correct," the saffron-sari clad witch agreed rather reluctantly.

"Your word is good enough," Sydney said, shooting the other witch a look that Morgana couldn't interpret. "What we want is for you to swear that you won't disappear without coming back and telling us what happened."

Morgana nodded. "I so swear. Do you require me to bind myself to the earth?"

Sydney shook her head. "If you don't come back, I'll just assume you're dead and send someone out to find your body. And if you don't come back and I find out, I'll send someone to find your body." She shrugged, good humor sparkling in her eyes. "Meg"—she indicated the small Black woman with a jut of her chin—"can take you almost all the way to the blood witch's hideout. She knows all the secret paths through the city."

"I've always been a sneak," Meg said with a wide grin.

"And she'll stand by with a dozen or so of our sisters, so if you need help or a quick escape, they can be there in moments." Sydney crossed her arms under her large breasts, pushing them up and straining the material of her blouse. "They are not coming to your rescue, and they won't put themselves in danger. But we'll give you a way to contact them. If you call for help when it's not safe for them to show up, you'll be on your own."

"Understood," Morgana said. "I do not anticipate that we will need to be retrieved from harm, but it is good to have plans in case that eventuality, no matter how unlikely, comes to pass."

"Then there's only one more thing to decide," Sydney said.

"And what is that?" Morgana asked. So far, this had gone even better than she could have expected, but she tensed, waiting for the one thing that might make her refuse their help.

"When will you be ready to leave?"

<h1 style="text-align:center">twenty-four</h1>

Meg led Morgana and Donovan through an extensive tunnel system that was part of Porto's hidden "under city." They were damp and smelled of must and mold but were largely abandoned other than a few rats and one or two humanoid creatures, likely undead, who scurried away with the rest of the vermin when the large group of witches approached. There were hidden entrances all over, if one knew where to look, including a doorway under the Luís I bridge near the scene of Bridget's attack.

Meg stopped at the edge of the tunnel, handed Morgana a brilliant piece of diamond-shaped blue porcelain—the same color as the ubiquitous tiles found all over Porto. "If you need us to retrieve you, break this tile. It is almost impossible to break accidentally. You'll need to either use magic or smash it against the ground as hard as possible; there will be no accidental summonings. And, Sydney said, if you are still in danger, we will not come to your aid, and you won't have a second chance."

"Thank you, Meg," Morgana said, accepting the ceramic and slipping it into her pocket.

"The exit from the tunnel is about ten meters ahead, around the next bend. Once you leave the tunnel, you will be in an alleyway. Walk downhill. There is a large, abandoned building surrounded by a wall. Your blood witch is in the caves under the building."

Ten minutes later, Morgana was peering up at the eight-foot-high wall surrounding the old building across the Douro River from Porto. The building was crumbling stone and tile with huge gaping holes in the roof and a For Sale sign advertising a four-bedroom home in need of minor renovations.

"Is she here?" Donovan whispered.

Morgana shook her head. "I do not feel her, but I trust Meg and Sydney. They would not steer us wrong."

"Unless they are in league with Bridget," Donovan said. "She has surprised you before with the allies she's tied to her side."

Morgana heard the pain and guilt in his voice, and she took the time to reach over and caress his face gently. "You were caught unawares by someone you trusted as a friend. Tom is power hungry and would have sought out someone like her eventually. But the women in Sydney's grove are free from her influence. I know what to look for now. Bridget may be powerful, but she is not subtle."

"You believe she's here?" There was no skepticism in Donovan's voice, but Morgana felt the need to defend her trust anyway.

She clamped it down. "I do. She will know we are here as soon as we breach her shields, if she doesn't already. However, she may not be able to pinpoint our location, so it is best if we proceed in silence."

Donovan nodded, then reached out and took her hand, squeezing once before dropping it. He squatted down and laced his fingers.

Morgana stepped into his hands and allowed him to boost her to the top of the wall. She balanced astride it for a moment and reached down to him. Donovan took her hand, but from the way he leapt up, he didn't need it.

"Cat," he mouthed at her, amusement twinkling in his eyes. "Good jumper."

Morgana rolled her eyes at him, then jumped off the wall,

landing lightly on the balls of her feet, knees bent slightly to absorb the impact. Donovan landed beside her, even more silently.

Morgana took the lead. Donovan might be imbued with his own magic, but he was not a witch and had no skill in breaking wards and absorbing the power released. If Bridget had layered shield upon shield, Morgana would drain a good deal of her power, making it her own, before they even encountered each other. Normally, she would not take what wasn't hers, letting it instead drain back into the world, but she was not here to play nice or fair with the witch who'd stolen power from dozens of others.

The air shimmered slightly in front of her, and Morgana held up her hand.

Donovan stopped immediately.

Morgana sent out a whisper-thin tendril of power, testing the ward. It was as delicate as a soap bubble and would be easy to rip open, the kind of shield a child might construct when first learning. This was a trap.

Morgana took a step back and sent another probe out ahead of her, looking for what was hidden by the gossamer curtain that was the first layer of shielding. After a moment, she spotted the second ward. This one was offensive rather than defensive and would catch an unsuspecting intruder in sticky silk like a spider's thread. Whether they'd be held, cocooned until they died of dehydration, or Bridget would retrieve the unfortunate soul for her own amusement did not matter. Either way, it was a formidable ward, but one easy to break now that Morgana knew it was there.

Both wards were set independently and not directly connected to Bridget. If Morgana was careful and quiet, they could avoid detection a little longer. She took a step back and called on the earth around her. Rocks rose at her command and came together to form a shape roughly reminiscent of a human. She floated them forward. As they approached the first shield, Morgana "ripped" it apart, triggering the second ward.

The ward flared into visibility, a white-hot blaze that swiftly greyed and coalesced around the rocks. They froze in place, then slowly fell to the ground, pulling the sticky silk down with them. Morgana stepped around them, then paused again.

"This is like an Indiana Jones movie," Donovan breathed.

Morgana smiled back at him. "When we get home, I'll show you my whip collection," she whispered.

Heat flared in Donovan's eyes, and for a moment, they glowed amber.

Morgana turned around and continued slowly forward. She didn't encounter another ward until the doorway of the building. She'd been eyeing it askance. It did not look safe, no matter what the renderings on the sale sign aspired to. But if Bridget and Tom went in and out regularly, it was likely safe enough.

Unless they had an alternative entry point.

She sighed and once again sent a narrow probe to test the energy covering the doorway. There was power in this one, likely designed to warn of intruders and deal as much damage as possible. But it was crude; the magic going into the strength rather than the design.

Morgana sighed. If she broke this one, no matter how careful she was, Bridget would know. The time for subtlety might be past.

She reached forward with her power, prepared to take it out with one directed blow when something else teased at the edge of her senses.

"Duck!" Donovan yelled.

Morgana dropped to the ground. A shape flew over her and crashed into the ward. It sizzled, and the smell of burning flesh curled around them in the acrid smoke that rose from the body.

"Vampire." Morgana wrinkled her nose in disgust. "It's unusual to see them in the daylight. It was either highly motivated or is very old, and I've invaded its territory."

The smoking husk of what had once been a man slid to the ground. "Please," it said through blackened lips.

"How is it not dead?" Donovan asked in revulsion.

"It takes a lot to kill an old vampire," Morgana replied. She crouched down next to the vampire, close enough to converse without being easily overheard but not close enough to put herself within arm's reach. "How many people, including the undead, work for the witch?"

The vampire bared his charred teeth and hissed.

Morgana sighed. "I will take your head if you answer without lying. If you do not answer or you lie to me, I will tie you to that tree over there and let the afternoon sun take care of you. One death is swift. The other will let you experience the exquisite suffering of the full-body burns that ignite every nerve ending with excruciating pain with the certainty that the creeping sun will finish the job. It is your choice."

The vampire glared. Then, he made a noise that sounded like a dying bellows.

The undead was attempting to sigh through his charred lungs, rendered unused by his vampiric status and unusable by the magical fire that still licked at the edges of his body.

"Donovan, do we have anything that can serve as a rope?" Morgana asked.

Donovan opened the knapsack he'd been carrying and uncoiled a rope. Morgana blinked in surprise at him. She'd assumed they would have to bluff.

"Will this work?" he asked.

"Perfect." Morgana crouched down next to the vampire. "I apologize if me lifting you up to tie you to that tree causes any of your skin to flake off. You are rather badly burned." She slipped her arm around the vamp's shoulders and began to lift him.

The vampire groaned in pain. "Fine. I'll tell you."

Morgana laid him back down, more gently than she'd lifted him. "Please continue."

"You'll kill me quickly?" the vampire asked.

Morgana looked down at him. "If you are clear and honest with your answers, I will grant you a swift death. If I sense any lies, omissions that could eventually cause me harm, or dissembling of any kind, I will leave you here to die."

"I can't know everything that might eventually cause you harm," the vampire protested. "And you can't either. You can't just leave me here forever in case something I don't tell you comes back to bite you in the ass."

"That is a fair point. I will make my decision before I walk away from you. I will, however, know if you tell me a lie, and it will go better for you if you are completely honest." Morgana stood and looked down at the charred husk in front of her and spared a second to be relieved that she would not have to let the sun kill him. He would not have been able to call her bluff, for she was not bluffing, but the thought of subjecting anyone, even a bloodthirsty undead, to that kind of torture did not sit well with her. "How many undead work for the blood witch know as Bridget?"

"There are fifteen of us vamps," the vamp said. "Most are young, though. My children, if you want to call them that."

"Most?" Morgana asked.

"How old are you?" Donovan followed up.

The vampire looked between them as if deciding who to answer first, or if he even had to reply to Donovan.

"Tell us your age first, then the ages of the other fourteen," Morgana said.

"I'm a hundred- and ten-years dead. There are two other my age, and the rest are between five- and fifteen-years dead. There are also a couple warlocks, but they're not very powerful, I don't think. She gives them guns, and they don't really do any magic." He slumped in on himself, and a large piece of skin sloughed off his forehead.

She had to finish her questions quickly, or the vampire would be too far gone to talk. Even now, she could see his chest sinking into his body as the magical fire continued its path of destruction under the vamp's skin.

"Are there any more traps or snares between here and the witch?" Morgana reached out with her magic, sparing a small amount to keep the vampire conscious and blocking some of his pain so he could answer her question.

"Yes," the vampire gasped. "Not all magic. False floors. Trip wires. And magic stuff I don't know."

She would get nothing more from him, and he had given her enough to be better prepared. "Thank you. I will kill you now."

He nodded and closed his eyes.

Morgana grasped his face between her hands. More skin flaked off, and she felt the soft flesh underneath. She shuddered and twisted. His neck broke with a resounding snap. It wouldn't be enough. If she didn't remove his head, there was a chance, however slight, that his body would eventually heal.

She looked around, but there was nothing nearby that would aid in a quick decapitation. He was likely beyond the point of consciousness and pain, but she'd promised a swift death, and did not relish prolonging it.

"What do you need?" Donovan asked. His voice was lower and steadier than Morgana would have expected.

"Something to remove his head," she answered. "I do not want to use my athame—it is sharp enough to cut flesh, but is not designed to cut through bone, and it's not long enough to make an easy job of it." She stood and brushed off her knees, then scrubbed her ash-covered hands against the thighs of her denim jeans.

Donovan opened his knapsack again, placed the rope back inside, and pulled out a hatchet. "I don't have anything else that would work. I didn't plan on decapitating anyone today."

Morgana reached out to take the hatchet, but he didn't immediately let go.

"Do you want me to do it?" he asked. Now his voice was shaky.

"I have experience with this sort of thing," Morgana said.

He let go of the hatchet. "It's sharp," he said.

Morgana turned back to the vampire, hefted the hatchet a couple times in her hands to get a feel for its weight and balance, then braced herself. It was no executioner's axe, designed to be larger than a human neck to remove a head with a single blow. The best she could do was to chop swiftly.

She brought the hatchet down. Thick blood oozed from his neck but did not splatter as she'd expected. A second blow nearly severed his head, and the third completed the job. She pushed the head a few yards away with her feet as if she was playing a macabre game of football, then went back to his body. He did not have any clothing whole and uncharred enough to serve as a cloth to wipe the blade of the hatchet, but she did not want to return it covered with vampire blood.

"I have a rag," Donovan said.

"Of course you do," Morgana replied with a smile, passing the hatched back to him.

Donovan cleaned the blade, then put it back in his knapsack.

Morgana eyed the sack. "I did not see your bag until you retrieved the rope. You returned to the hotel for it, didn't you?"

Donovan didn't even have the grace to look abashed. "The spells were too valuable and dangerous to leave behind. I bought the backpack and most of the things inside at an outdoor store one of the witches took me to this morning."

"How'd you know what to buy?" Morgana asked absently. She was peering at the ward that'd taken out the vampire. She spotted the weak spot almost right away. There was broken masonry at the bottom of the doorframe, and the ward did not completely cover the crumbling mortar.

"I got a text from Paska," Donovan said. "He gave me a very specific shopping list."

Morgana reached between the ward and the stone, pushed in a sliver of power, then yanked up hard, ripping the ward.

The backlash nearly knocked her over. As it was, she staggered back several steps.

Donovan caught her and kept her upright. "You okay?"

Morgana nodded, then shook her head to clear it. "If it hit me that hard, hopefully it did at least the same amount of damage to the one who set the ward."

She took a deep breath and pulled her athame out of its sheath. "Are you ready to go inside?"

"Not even a little bit," Donovan replied.

Morgana smiled tightly, grabbed his hand, and walked through the door.

twenty-five

By the time Morgana found the trapdoor and dispelled the shields on it, she was dirty, sticky, covered with spatters of blood—both her own and that of the undead—and more tired than she would prefer while preparing to confront a blood witch brimming with stolen power and mad enough to use it without regard for the consequences.

Morgana ran her hand the length of her athame and felt the strength of the earth that had created the stone fill her body. Then, she opened the trap door and looked down into the darkness. There was a rope ladder, but climbing down that meant leaving herself vulnerable during the time it took to descend. And without seeing how far down it was, jumping was unwise.

"I didn't know when you were going to get here." Bridget's voice floated up out of the darkness. "Aren't you going to join me?"

Donovan silently pushed Morgana aside. "I'll carry you," he mouthed.

Morgana looked at him askance. It sounded like a monumentally bad idea, not to mention impractical.

He grinned, scooped her up in his arms, and jumped.

Morgana barely restrained a scream of shock and wasn't surprised that her knees wobbled a little when he set her down.

She turned towards where Bridget's energy was emanating from and ensured her shields were at top strength and covered her and Donovan.

Wards snapped shut above them, sealing them in the basement and making the way out more difficult to access. Light flooded the room, and for a moment, Morgana couldn't see anything. When she blinked away the afterimage, the space took on a familiar shape.

The basement was, down to the last detail, an exact replica of her workroom in the basement of her house in Oracle Bay.

There was an altar along the north wall, and the space was surrounded by layers of shields designed to keep magic in.

"Nice room," Morgana said dryly. "Do you create this design yourself?"

Bridget smirked at her and didn't take the bait. "That's a stupid question." She didn't waste her breath on any additional repartee and launched into a magical attack.

A bolt of lightning ricocheted off Morgana's shields, and as it did so, two men walked out of the shadows, chanting in Latin.

Morgana snorted. The warlocks' obsession with that particular dead language was both predictable and ridiculous.

"You worry about Bridget. I'll take care of the warlocks," Donovan said.

"Hey kitty!" Bridget called. "I've got a saucer of milk with your name on it."

So, the blood witch was not going to completely forego the traditional taunting.

The floor had been left bare, whether by virtue of Bridget's replication of Morgana's space or the nature of this basement, and she could feel the earth beneath her. Morgana reached into it and through, gathering strength and asking the elements to come to her aid.

The response was immediate, and the ground trembled beneath

their feet. Morgana kicked off her sneakers and let her sock-clad feet curl into the dirt. Spikes of rock shot out of the ground, surrounding Bridget in a stone cage.

The earth shook again, and the stone splintered, turning to pebbles.

"Did you really think you'd be able to defeat me so quickly?" Bridget jeered.

Morgana hadn't thought so but kept that to herself. The more Bridget's confidence grew, the more careless she would become.

More lightning shot from Bridget's hands and was stopped by Morgana's shields. Before Morgana could mount the offensive she'd planned, the lightning strikes became a barrage, and it was all she could do to keep her shields strong and whole. She spun them, ensuring that the lightning was not hitting in the same place every time.

The earth continued to buoy her, keeping her reserves filled, but even with that, she was tiring. She daren't check on Donovan to see how he was faring with Bridget's warlock bodyguards, but from the sounds reaching her ears, it was now a physical fight.

Morgana asked the earth to again aid her, and the response was instantaneous. It split open beneath Bridget, and she sank to her armpits before the ground closed up again. Only her head, shoulders, and arms were visible.

Bridget laughed, and the sound raised the hairs on the back of Morgana's neck. The madness that ran through her hysterical laughter was beyond anything Morgana had ever heard.

The earth shook again, and Morgana braced herself. This quake was not at her behest.

The ground split open again, and Bridget rose slowly from the ground as if on a slow elevator.

Morgana pulled her athame from her sheath and darted forward. A physical attack in a magical battle was often enough to throw an opponent off-balance.

Bridget held up a hand, and Morgana froze in place.

Bridget cackled again and pushed.

Morgana stumbled backwards and nearly lost hold of her athame.

"Haven't you figured out by now that you can't beat me?" Bridget said. "I'm so much stronger than I was last time we met, and I almost killed you then. I would've if it hadn't been for that stupid friend of yours. But he's not here now—he's safe and sound in Oracle Bay. There'll be plenty of time to deal with him and the rest of your stupid friends. Convincing Hazel to rejoin me probably isn't possible, so I'll have to kill her. Shame, really. She was useful." The entire time Bridget was talking, she paced back and forth, never taking her eyes off Morgana.

Morgana used Bridget's interlude of premature self-congratulations to break through the magical ropes binding her. Once she was free, she took a moment to reach down into the earth again. Bridget might force the earth to bow to her will, but the earth had known Morgana for centuries, *loved* her, and would gladly aid her when asked, and only reluctantly help Bridget when commanded.

A wave of regret greeted Morgana's request. If she took anymore from the earth, she would cause an earthquake that would go beyond this room and destabilize the fault that ran perpendicular to Portugal between the Azores and Gibraltar. The resulting tremor had the potential to be even worse than the one that had nearly destroyed Lisbon in 1755, the result of two warring factions of witches.

Morgana reluctantly withdrew her request and reached even further to the river that accompanied the tunnels Meg had led them through, but the answer was the same. She reached even farther to the Douro. There was no way to call on the elements she knew best without putting everyone in Porto and Gaia in danger.

She would have to do this on her own. She took a deep breath and massed all the power she held within herself. She had access to more innate power than anyone she'd ever met, but Bridget had gone beyond what was possible and could command more than

Morgana could even comprehend, although she did so at the cost of her physical and mental health.

Already, the blood witch was panting with exertion and a sheen of sweat dampened her brow. The shields she maintained to protect her from physical attack were cracking.

Morgana gripped her athame tightly until her knuckles whitened. She forced herself to relax, then poured almost all the power she had at her command into the blade. She ran forward, stabbed first at the shield surrounding Bridget, then aimed the knife at the blood witch's heart. Morgana's blade slowed when it shattered Bridget's shield, and that minuscule delay was enough to save her.

The blood witch stepped backwards, too slowly to stop the blade, but quickly enough to cause it to miss her heart.

The knife sank into Bridget's shoulder, and the blood witch screamed in pain.

Before Morgana could pull the blade out and stab again—into Bridget's heart this time—the earth shook again, and pieces of rock and wood rained around her. Something hit her in the head, and she stumbled backwards and fell.

She blinked, trying to revive her vision. Heat followed by searing pain started in her chest and spread out throughout her body. The earth was breaking, and she could not let that happen; too many would die if Bridget triggered an earthquake. She reached down into the earth and used the last of her strength to heal it and hold it together as well as she could.

Bridget's face swam into focus. "How's it feel to be killed by your own weapon?" An expression of faux concern fell over her face. "I wish I could stay and watch you die, but this building is about to fall around our ears, and I don't fancy being here when it collapses. You don't have enough power left in your body to be worth taking." She stood and snapped her fingers. Tom appeared at her side, one arm hanging uselessly from his body. Deep scratches ran the length of his arm and across his chest, and bone jutted through the skin of his forearm.

Warmth spread through Morgana's body as the earth, unable to act offensively on her behalf, but no longer in danger of destroying the city, cradled her. Pain was replaced by comfort, but she was careful not to show any relief.

Bridget waved. "I hope your soul rots in hell, never to be reborn. I'll say hi to your friends in that stupid little town for you and tell them you died weak and blubbering like a baby."

The lights blinked off, and the ceiling fell.

· · ★ ★ ★ ★ ★ ★ · ·

Light filtered into the basement through the holes in the floor above and the roof above it. By the quality of the light and the shadows cast by broken beams, Morgana judged it to be late afternoon or early evening.

Morgana took a breath, and a sharp pain accompanied it. Perhaps she had broken ribs. That would be difficult for the earth to heal, depleted as it was.

"Donovan?"

"Here," he replied.

She lifted her head and saw him sitting at her feet. "You're okay?"

He nodded. "When the building started falling, I changed shape and hid myself under her altar. I couldn't answer you; I can't speak in that form. I was trapped under there for a while. It was too small a space to shift back and move the beams and stone surrounding me, so I had to burrow my way out. And let me tell you, cat paws are not made for burrowing."

"Can you help me sit up?" Morgana asked. There was something blocking her ability to sit on her own, but she was tired of lying in the dirt.

"Do you want me to pull your athame out first?" Donovan asked.

"I didn't want to do it until you woke up in case it caused more damage."

Morgana felt around on her chest with her right hand until she found the handle of the athame. The blade had sliced into her chest, barely missing her heart. It'd penetrated her left lung, but the blade was keeping the hole sealed.

"We should call for help first," she said. "Can you reach into my left pocket and remove the tile Meg gave me? I don't have the magic to shatter it, but if you throw it at one of the concrete pillars hard enough, that should work. Help should arrive soon. Hopefully, there will be a healer among them. The earth repaired most of the damage, but I'll need water to complete the job."

Fifteen minutes later, footsteps echoed across the floor, causing what remained of it to shift and groan.

Meg's face appeared in one of the many holes. "Is she dead?" she demanded.

Morgana shook her head. "No, but she thinks I am. She will leave Porto now and return to Oracle Bay. She is single-minded in her revenge. After she lured me away from my base of power and destroyed me, as she believes she did, she will go to the town where she saw her first defeat and take her revenge on my friends now that I am not there to protect them." Morgana didn't add that the rest of the residents of Oracle Bay were not unprotected. That was information she wasn't ready to share with this grove, no matter how friendly and powerful.

Meg dropped into the hole, followed by three more witches. With Morgana instructing them, they removed the athame a millimeter at a time, letting the blade heal her in its wake.

Donovan refused to let her stand on her own. He cradled her in his arms and walked under one of the larger holes that had formed when the building collapsed. Then he crouched low and leapt. He landed less gracefully than when he'd jumped down into the basement. His legs wobbled, and the floor shifted beneath them.

As soon as he steadied, he strode out of the building.

A crowd had formed near the building. Murmurs of conversation Morgana didn't quite understand reached her ears.

"They're glad there were survivors," Meg translated for her. "The building's collapse shook the ground nearby. There were a few broken windows, but no serious damage or injuries. They're blaming the builders trying to sell this property without making sure it was safe first."

"I'm glad she didn't kill anyone else," Morgana said as Donovan placed her carefully on her feet. "Now, please tell me we don't have to walk back through the tunnels."

Meg laughed. "No. We have a car, and now that we're no longer worried about stealth, we can drive."

MORGANA OPENED HER EYES WHEN SHE HEARD HER NAME. SHE WAS immersed in the stream that ran through the courtyard garden. Donovan sat beside her, keeping her company and handing her bottles of water whenever she asked. He'd completely escaped injury, and before the house fell, had dispatched two of Bridget's bodyguards. He'd been battling Tom and had just broken the warlock's arm when everything went to hell.

Sydney stood in front of Morgana. "You didn't kill her."

The statement wasn't an accusation, but a thread of guilt laced through her, anyway.

"I did not."

Morgana relayed the story of what had happened with Donovan filling in the blanks of his actions during Morgana's confrontation with Bridget. "I could not win against her, and I don't understand why. She shouldn't be able to best me." It made little sense. Even with Bridget's stolen power augmented with Morgana's, she shouldn't be able to defeat Morgana. She had centuries more experience and training. She was used to the flow of immense amounts of power through her and could wield it without going mad.

Sydney shrugged. "Should or shouldn't don't matter. Walking into any situation with 'should' in mind is a recipe for defeat. What matters are facts—what *is,* not what *should.* She beat you. She's powerful and from what you've said, she's completely crazy. Crazy people who don't care what the difference between right and wrong are always have more power than someone with morals. She didn't care if she destroyed the city. You did. That's why you're the good witch, and she's the bad witch."

"Should I have stopped her, regardless of the cost to human life?" Morgana asked sharply.

Sydney shook her head. "Of course not. But when you confront her again, you might need to push your morals aside, at least for a little bit. Or find someone who doesn't have any to help out."

Paska's face flashed in Morgana's mind, and she grimaced. Her brother might be ruthless, but he did have a moral code, although whether he'd adhere to it now that he knew Bridget was on her way back to Oracle Bay was anyone's guess. She huffed out a breath. "I'll see what I can do," she promised.

"You need to leave," Sydney said with what felt like an abrupt subject change. "It'll only be a matter of time before she figures out you're still alive, and I don't want her back in my city." She handed Donovan a small rectangular card. "That's my phone number. Face-Time me when she's dead. I'll give you twenty-four more hours to heal, then a ride to the airport."

She turned and walked back into the house without another word. Donovan pocketed the card and looked down at Morgana. "Guess we're going home."

<h1 style="text-align:center">*twenty-six*</h1>

Morgana unlocked her front door and pushed Donovan into her house. She toed off her shoes, dropped her keys in the bowl next to the door, left her suitcase in the hall, and walked straight through the house to the back door. She stopped on the porch to peel off her socks, then strode across the soft grass to her pond, shedding her clothes as she walked.

She stepped in, shivered when the chilly water hit her waist, and gasped out loud when she sat, and it rose to chest level.

She sank underneath the water and stayed there until she needed to breathe, then slid up the smooth seat until her head was leaning against the back of the stone seat. The water had replenished itself in the two weeks that Morgana had been gone and was almost as powerful as it had been when she'd left. The Portuguese witches' healing water had been strong, but it wasn't keyed to her the way this was. She felt wholeness creep back into her soul.

She heard Donovan come out onto the back porch, but he didn't walk over to her, and for that she was grateful. She needed to reclaim her bond with her earth and water...her elements.

Rustling in the branches of the tree above her brought her out of her meditative state.

"Hello, brother," Morgana said without opening her eyes.

Feet hitting the soft earth were accompanied by a breeze that caressed her face in what felt like welcome and the whisper of sound that announced his shift from bird to man.

Donovan made a noise that sounded like choked back laughter.

"You failed," Paska said bluntly.

"And you're naked," Morgana retorted. "Put some clothes on before Donovan can't hold his laughter back anymore."

"Fine," Paska grumbled. "I hate clothes in the summer."

Morgana opened her eyes. Paska was dressed in cut-off denim shorts so short the insides of his pockets peeked out below the shredded hem and a mesh tank top. She couldn't hold back her laughter.

"What?" he groused. "If you're going to make me wear clothes, they might as well be fun."

"You've been raiding Barachiel's closet, haven't you?" Morgana asked.

"Can you do that?" Donovan interrupted. "Magic clothes on, I mean?"

Morgana smiled and stood. She walked out of the pond, and by the time she was standing on the ground once again, she was perfectly dry and clad in an outfit nearly identical to Paska's, although her tank top was neon green.

"Now I see the family resemblance," Donovan said.

Paska and Morgana exchanged a look. A smile played at the edges of his mouth. She took three steps to bridge the distance between them, then wrapped her arms tightly around him. "I missed you," she whispered.

He hugged her back. "This separation seemed longer than the others," he said. "We've spent years apart, but I've gotten used to having you around."

Morgana took a couple steps back and gestured towards the porch. "I have things to tell you. Want a beer?"

Paska wrinkled his nose. "Do you have any whiskey to go with it?"

Morgana sighed. "You know where it is. I'm going to change. Open a bottle of whatever red is on the rack in the kitchen."

Morgana opened her walk-in closet and looked inside. Rows of black skirts, black shirts, blouses, and corsets sparingly interspersed with red greeted her. She flipped through her clothes, bypassing item after item. She didn't have anything that felt suitable.

She rarely wasted magical energy on clothing when it was easier to choose something from her extensive wardrobe, but today she wanted something different. Morgana looked down at the denim cutoff shorts, then pushed a wave of power into her hands. She ran her hands down the length of her legs. The denim lengthened and darkened until she was clad in dark-wash blue jeans. She found a bright red tank top in the back of her closet and exchanged it for her neon green shirt. A glance in the mirror made her smile. The tank top was tight enough to enhance her breasts in a pleasing manner without appearing improper to those people who cared about such things. She added a simple necklace and pulled her hair back into a loose bun.

Then she dug around in the back of the closet and found a pair of tall, low-heeled black boots. They wouldn't have more than one drink here before Paska herded them to the Pour House to meet with the rest of the group.

Morgana smiled at the idea of reuniting with her friends. It was an alien concept, but one she quite enjoyed.

A glass of wine was waiting for her on the back porch, and Paska and Donovan each had one small glass of whiskey and a pint of beer in front of them.

Paska raised his tumbler of whiskey. "We all might be dead in a week's time, but at least we can drink together now." He tapped his glass against Donovan's, then Morgana's wine glass.

Morgana took a drink. "As a toast goes, that wasn't one of the most cheerful ones I've heard."

"Can you do better, then?" Paska challenged.

She thought for a moment. "I have one, but I'll save it for the gathering I'm sure you're going to insist we attend soon."

Paska grinned and downed his whiskey in one drink.

"I have one," Donovan said. He raised his pint glass. "I am one lucky son of a—" he broke off at Morgana's narrowed eyes "—of a cat to know you both and will be even luckier to die in battle at your sides."

Morgana clinked her glass, then drank. She sighed dramatically, but smiled at the two men she loved best. "All this death. We aren't dead yet, and we may never be. Why not toast to victory, friends, and family?"

"You're a lot more relaxed than I've seen you in a long time," Paska said. "Near-death experiences suit you."

"It could be the head injury," Donovan suggested. "When my aunt had a stroke, she lost the ability to get stressed out anymore. Even after she recovered, she was always mellow. Of course, that might've been the pot she smoked to help mitigate her symptoms."

Paska snickered, then drained his beer. "Drink up. We have places to be."

Paska drove them, not to the Pour House as Morgana had expected, but to Ceri's house.

"There is something here you need to see," he said when she raised an eyebrow at him.

The front door opened before they were all the way up the sidewalk, and Ceri appeared in the doorway, a smile of welcome on her face, which glowed with health and happiness. "Thank you for coming!" She hugged Paska, who returned it with no show of hesitance.

Then Ceri hugged Morgana. Morgana stiffened for a moment, then put her arms around Ceri to return the embrace. "I'm glad you're back," Ceri said.

"Me, too." She turned and gestured Donovan forward. "You remember Donovan Davies?"

"Of course," Ceri said. She took a step back, and her smile morphed from genuine to stiff. "The witch hunter."

Donovan leveled his most devastating smile at her. It would've taken a harder woman than Ceri not to thaw a bit in the face of it. "Retired witch hunter," he said.

Ceri's face thawed slightly. "In that case, you are provisionally welcome." She turned and walked back into the house.

"Should I go?" Donovan asked. "I don't mind. After all, I think I still have a job here. I could go see if any good candidates have applied to replace those two walking testosterone bombs that I'm firing next week."

"Stay," Paska said. "She'll come around soon. She hugged Morgana. It won't be long before that baby softens her towards you, too."

"She's pregnant?" Donovan asked. "Cool. Baby witches in town."

"Don't let her hear you call her unborn spawn a baby witch," Paska advised. "After all, it's just as likely to be a baby demon. I'll put my money on Ceri's genes overpowering Andy's, though. He might be a ten-thousand-year-old fallen angel, but Ceri is a force of nature." He swept into the house. Morgana took Donovan's hand and led him in.

Sandy was in the foyer, obviously waiting for them. She took a step towards Morgana with her arms out, then dropped them and smiled warmly instead. "I'm glad you're back!"

Morgana braced herself; she was about to do something she had seldom done with anyone but Paska and an occasional lover. She walked towards Sandy and folded her into a hug.

After a moment, Sandy recovered from her shock and hugged Morgana back.

Morgana stepped back and smiled. "It's good to be back. Where is everyone?"

Sandy pointed through the arched doorway. "Dining room. I'm the welcome committee, here to direct traffic, but other than Russell, you're the last ones here."

"Has he come back yet?" Morgana asked.

Sandy's face fell. "No. No one's heard from him at all. He's not hiding out in Eden Valley with his cousin Bev, although she said Barachiel left for a sudden business trip, which probably means he went to find Russell. I hope he's okay."

Donovan opened his mouth, and Morgana said, "Later. There are a lot of things to share with you that I haven't had a chance to yet."

"C'mon," Sandy said. "Grab a drink on your way through the kitchen. I think you're going to need one."

twenty-seven

Morgana poured herself a glass of wine while Donovan snagged a bottle of Pour House pils out of the fridge and Paska grabbed a glass out of a cupboard and snagged a bottle of Scotch from where it'd been hidden behind three boxes of saltines, a large stack of butterscotch pudding cups, four bottles of vitamins, a box of pregnancy tests, and a huge bag of ginger candy.

Morgana side-eyed the stash. It was an unusual assortment of items to collect in such quantity.

"Morning sickness," Donovan supplied. "My ex-wife lived on crackers, gingersnaps, and lime gelatin for at least a month when she was pregnant with our oldest. She had a bag of oyster crackers by the bed and would eat a handful every morning before getting up. It was the only thing that kept her from throwing up for hours. I had to wash the sheets every day, though. That is a lot of crumbs."

Morgana smiled. "I don't remember if I had morning sickness when I was pregnant, but I can see the benefits of these items. Shall we continue on?"

Paska preceded them into the dining room.

"Are you wearing...jeans?" Drew asked, incredulity staining his voice. "Is this like the time you dressed in sweater sets for a year?"

"Not just jeans," Misty said. "She has on an actual color. And arms. She has arms."

Morgana felt a flush rise up her face. Even when she'd gone undercover, she hadn't gotten this much attention and ridicule from the other psychics.

"Don't be assholes," Andy interrupted. "Morgana can wear whatever she wants, and she doesn't need you guys to tease her."

Ceri smiled up at her partner and kissed him on the cheek before whispering something in his ear. Andy rolled his eyes, then nodded at Morgana over Ceri's head.

"Thank you, demon," she said solemnly.

Andy grinned at her. "Any time, witch."

Drew grimaced. "Sorry I was an ass. You look good. And I should know—and see good-looking every time I look in a mirror."

Morgana laughed, as she was sure he meant her to. She took a step forward into the group, rather than just outside it, and her friends parted in front of her.

She gasped as the reason for meeting here revealed itself to her.

In front of her was the layout they'd devised when trying to find the solution to Ceri's ever-worsening visions and the fracturing of her mind. The map of Oracle Bay, Jezebel's star charts overlaying one another, and the major arcana cards of Sandy's deck on top.

Sandy smiled at Morgana. "We have more people identified now. I wonder if we'll end up with the full complement of people by the time we're done? Wouldn't that be awesome?"

Morgana walked up to the table and looked at the cards. The ones not yet associated with someone in this group were off to the side, as were the ones belonging to the angels who'd helped save Ceri and the town, but there were two new ones placed among those that represented the people in this room.

"Me?" Donovan asked, pointing at the Chariot.

Sandy nodded, approval brightening her face. "That's you—

determined and with a great handle on his aggression—and the Sun, all that warmth and potential and positivity, is Hazel."

Morgana looked around. She hadn't yet seen the newest member of their group, and to her chagrin, hadn't noticed, so overwhelmed had she been with the greetings of the others.

"She's in the bathroom," Sandy said. "I think she's nervous about seeing you again."

Morgana's attention was drawn back to the table. It reminded her of maps generals used to plan war strategies on. She smiled wryly. This was not so different, was it? They'd used it to battle the forces attempting to tear Ceri's mind apart, and now they were presumably going to find a way to defeat Bridget.

"Are you sure she's coming here?" Morgana asked. She'd been certain three days ago after Bridget left her for dead in Porto, but she'd been wrong so many times before about Bridget that she was doubting her instincts.

Ceri nodded. "Obviously, I couldn't help last time we played 'Psychics Assemble!' but Drew and I can see almost anything if we put our minds to it."

"Even when certain people shouldn't be using their powers because they're in a delicate state," Andy said under his breath.

Ceri laughed. "I'm scrying for two, now. I am twice as focused and have so much more seer power—rather than the other stuff that hides in my brain—than ever before. We have things that belonged to her. She left everything in your house, and Paska broke in after you left and retrieved her stuff. Between my powers being turned up to eleven, the fact that Drew and I have worked together for decades, and the personal items Bridget left behind, we can track her every move."

Drew and Ceri exchanged smug smiles, then turned towards the table where a crystal ball sat inside a large, shallow bowl of water. They linked hands and stared down.

"Right now, she's in Los Angeles," Drew said.

"Why LA, do you think?" Ceri asked, confusion furrowing her brow.

"There's a lot of magic in LA. It's not as strong as the magic here, but LA draws people to it just the same. It's a prime hunting ground. Bridget's building up her strength," Paska said. "Morgana damaged her."

Morgana closed her eyes. She knew how Bridget built up strength. "How many dead?"

"Two so far that I know about." Paska looked at Ceri. "We need to draw her here quickly before she kills anymore."

"Can you taunt her? Find a way to send her a picture of Morgana alive and well with today's newspaper or something?" Sandy suggested.

"I can make that happen," Drew said, "with Ceri's help. We can push a vision out, especially if Misty can back us up and give us a boost."

"It won't be a photograph with today's date, though," Ceri said. "It's more of an image, like a dream. She'll *know* you're alive and that you're here, but she won't get a lot of details. Just certainty."

"That might be even better motivation than a billboard," Misty said from where she was sitting at one end of the table.

"You're not wearing gloves," Morgana exclaimed. Then she started laughing. "I'm as bad as the rest of you."

Misty grinned. "I have a lot more control now. Paska's a great teacher."

"That I am," Paska agreed, holding up his Pour House-branded pint glass full of Scotch.

Andy growled under his breath. "How do you always find the good stuff?"

Paska pulled the bag he always wore at his belt and shook it gently. "I'm psychic, and what better way to use my talent than to find your Scotch?"

A wave of laughter rolled through the room, and for once, Morgana didn't feel excluded from it. Her brother had friends for the first time in as long as she could remember, and rather than feeling apart from it, she felt included.

"I don't know why you wear that you have to wear that fanny pack everywhere," Sandy said.

"Ugh," Ceri said. "Can we please call it a bum bag?"

A debate on the pros and cons of "fanny" versus "bum" and the etymology of both continued behind Morgana while she studied the board, applying her knowledge of Bridget and the location Drew and Ceri had seen to determine how it would all play out.

"Do you know when you were born?" Jezebel asked, coming up to stand beside Morgana.

She shook her head. "Not exactly. Midsummer, but I don't know the year with any certainty."

Jezebel pursed her lips. "Do you have a rough idea? Having the exact time is helpful in filling out a star chart, but there are a lot of things that you can see in the stars without relying on the western ideas of astrology. The Greeks weren't the only ones to ascribe personality traits and events to the way the sun, moon, and planets move through the sky. They weren't even the first."

Morgana turned to look at the young Black woman. "What did they do to you when you were away?"

Jezebel's eyes flashed. "Nobody does anything to me. If something happens, it's because I want it. I've sometimes doubted my power, but I've never doubted my agency. I am a fucking goddess. Although not literally. Probably." She smiled at Morgana.

Morgana smiled back. "You are certainly that. My apologies for implying otherwise." She raised her glass towards Jezebel. "A goddess such as I should always recognize another divine woman."

Jezebel burst out laughing. "We should be self-esteem motivational speakers. We'd make millions."

Morgana laughed, too. She'd been so caught up in her image of icy severity, she'd forgotten how much a relaxed attitude and fun could free the mind to find the answers to the questions she was seeking.

Her gaze snapped back to the table. "I know when Bridget was born," she told Jezebel. "Or at least, I have access to the birth records of Kilnamanagh. Would that help?"

Jezebel clapped. "Yes! That would be fantastic."

Morgana looked at her watch. It was three o'clock in the afternoon, which meant ten in Ireland. Someone would still be awake. "Walk with me to the other room. I'll get the information about Bridget, and then I'll tell you what I know about my birth."

twenty-eight

Morgana sat in her kitchen glaring at the tea kettle as if that would make the water heat faster.

Donovan walked up behind her and rubbed her shoulders. "You're not as tense as I expected," he said.

Morgana shrugged, and he pushed her shoulders back down. "Despite everything, I had fun today. It was...nice. I don't enjoy feeling vulnerable and worrying about what other people are thinking about me."

"Sometimes that's the price you pay for opening up your heart to friendship," Donovan noted. The kettle beeped, signaling it was ready. "I've got it. You just sit."

Morgana watched as the man she loved made her tea. It was nice.

He set the cup with the tea strainer of loose-leaf peppermint in the hot water in front of her. "I'll let you know when it's time to take it out."

"I've decided not to worry," Morgana said.

"About the tea?"

She laughed. "No, about what other people think of me. If they liked me when I didn't care and wasn't friendly, I can't imagine they'd like me less when I am approachable. I am a wonderful person and have nothing to be worried about."

A wide grin split Donovan's face. "That's the confident woman I met in the airport. Even in your Stepford costume, you carried yourself like a goddess. It's good to see her back."

Morgana took the tea strainer out of her cup and placed it on a small saucer in the middle of the table. "Are you having tea?" she asked, standing up and walking into the living room.

Donovan held up his beer. "Nah. Andy sent me home with a six-pack of the pils."

"Home?" Morgana raised her eyebrows. She forewent her usual overstuffed recliner—the one she pretended to dislike when the psychics came to her home for their weekly wine nights—and curled up in the corner of the loveseat instead.

Donovan had the grace to look discomfited. For a moment. "I canceled my lease with that crappy apartment right after I left town, so I don't have anywhere else to stay. You wouldn't turn me out into the cold, would you?"

"It's July."

"On the Washington Coast. It gets chilly at night." Donovan widened his eyes and looked down at her.

"You grow fur." Morgana took a sip of her tea and smiled at him over the rim of her cup.

"If you're cold, I'm cold."

Morgana pursed her lips and looked at him. The last time she'd taken a lover that had lasted more than a few days was more than three hundred years ago, but she didn't remember ever having this easy teasing conversation. "I guess you can stay tonight," she said, feigning reluctance. "I would feel terrible if you froze to death on the harsh beach."

Donovan sat next to her and pulled her feet onto his lap. "My gratitude knows no bounds," he said. "Just tell me how I can repay you."

Morgana set her teacup down and scooted closer to him. He leaned over and kissed her softly. She took the beer bottle from his hand and leaned over him to put it on the end table. Her breasts pressed against his face, and she lingered a moment, enjoying his reaction and the tight control he kept himself under.

She leaned back, and he groaned in disappointment.

Morgana smiled at him, then brushed his lips with hers. Then, in one continuous movement, she pulled off her tank top, swung her feet around, and straddled him.

"Woman, you are going to kill me," he said. His hands were on the hook of her bra, and in seconds, her breasts were free. He tossed the bra, and then his hands were on her. He touched and teased, his lips following his hands' every movement.

She rocked forward, enjoying the physical evidence of his appreciation of her body.

"Bedroom?" he asked in a strangled voice as she continued undulating her hips against him.

She stopped to consider, and his hands fell to her hips, urging her into motion again.

"Too far away," she said. "The loveseat will have to suffice."

Donovan growled and stood, tumbling her backwards in a fall controlled by his arms cradling her. He lifted her and sat her on the couch, then pulled off her jeans and panties, gazing up at her in adoration. "You are so beautiful," he said.

"Strip," she replied. "I want to see if you're as lovely as I remember."

Donovan shucked off his jeans and boxer briefs, then dropped to his knees in front of her. "Let me worship you," he said. He didn't wait for a reply.

Morgana tipped her head back and smiled. Any response she would have made was lost in wave after wave of pleasure.

twenty-nine

Morgana woke to a crash from downstairs. She frowned and grabbed her phone to see what time it was. She was greeted with a half dozen text messages from Paska.

7:19 am: *New information from Jezebel and Ceri. Pour House now.*

7:25 am: *Why aren't you responding? You're always up at dawn.*

7:26 am: *Get out of bed and get over here. You're like a teenager with your out-of-control hormones. Anyone would think you hadn't been bedded in over a century.*

7:35 am: *If you don't answer me in fifteen minutes, I will come and get you. Don't think I won't.*

7:50 am: *I am letting myself into your house right now. I suggest getting dressed.*

7:51 am: *There is a naked man in your kitchen making tea.*

Morgana rolled her eyes and started dressing. She pulled on the same jeans from yesterday but paired them with a black t-shirt today. Her phone dinged again.

7:53 am: *Bring clothes for your man. And superglue if you have it.*

Morgana cursed. She grabbed her phone and a pair of jeans from Donovan's suitcase and walked out of the bedroom. At the top of the stairs, she yelled, "If you've broken one of my teapots, I will have your hide, old man. We'll see how good you look as a *fanny pack*."

There was a burst of laughter from downstairs.

Men.

Morgana marched into the kitchen. Donovan was leaning against the counter in a pair of eye-blindingly bright yellow boxer briefs that were suspiciously close to the color of the tank top Paska had put on the day before. She tossed him his jeans, then fixed her brother with a glare.

He gave her his best wide-eyed "I'm the picture of innocence" look. She wasn't buying it.

"I heard a crash. What broke?" She fixed Paska with a glare, then shifted slightly to include Donovan in her potential wrath.

"I dare you to look at anything in this kitchen and find one thing out of place, broken, or otherwise disturbed," Paska said. He sat down in the chair she favored and grinned at her.

Donovan pulled the tea strainer out of a cup and handed it over. "Chai spice."

Morgana took the cup and saucer and looked at them with a critical eye. They looked perfect. So did the five matching cups and the teapot that completed the set. But this wasn't the tea set she had out for everyday service. She narrowed her eyes and looked around the kitchen. She set her cup on the table and walked over to the garbage can. No glass.

She spun around, ignoring her brother's poor attempts at keeping his laughter to himself and steadfastly keeping her eyes off Donovan's chest. She spotted her everyday service in the cabinet she dedicated to her tea sets.

She opened the doors and examined the pot, then every cup and saucer. Nothing. She turned her attention to the other sets.

She started to close the cupboard when a thought occurred to her. She opened herself to look at the world with her *other* senses. She didn't use them much. The world could be overwhelming enough without seeing the magic that overlays everything—particularly in Oracle Bay. But desperate times.

That's when she saw it. One cup and saucer from her everyday set had been pushed to the back. It was bright with magic weaving around it and holding it together.

She turned accusing eyes on Paska.

He shrugged. "I told you to bring the superglue. You knew something was broken."

"Then why hide it?" she asked, returning to the table and picking up her tea.

"Fun. Obviously," Paska said. "I told you she'd find it within five minutes," he said to Donovan.

"I didn't argue with you. I would never underestimate Morgana's powers of observation—or anything else." He picked up the paper cup with the Caffiend Dreams logo on the side and took a long drink. "I love cappuccinos more than should be legal," he said. "Thank you."

"You brought him coffee?" Morgana asked. "You never bring me anything."

"You forgive me for everything; I don't have to work for that. If Donovan is going to be a part of our family for however long we have left, then I would like to have a cordial relationship with him." Paska picked up a second paper cup, removed the top, then poured a generous glug of something from a silver flask he pulled from his pocket.

"Do you always drink so much alcohol?" Donovan asked.

"Yes," Paska answered, then held the flask out. "Want some?"

"Um. No thanks." Donovan held his cappuccino a little closer as if afraid Paska would dose his coffee anyway.

"Probably best," Paska said laconically. "You won't have the metabolism for it the way we do."

Donovan looked at her, and she shrugged. "The older you get, the harder it is to get and stay drunk. Paska's body metabolizes alcohol almost as fast as he can consume it. *Almost.*"

Paska. "Are you ready to go yet? Jezebel has something new, and Misty has a plan."

Morgana finished her tea and looked at Donovan. "As soon as he's dressed, we can walk out the door."

Paska gave Donovan a long look. "You don't have to put a shirt on if you don't want to. Morgana shouldn't get all the fun."

Morgana shot him a look.

"What?" Paska threw his hands up. "You've always gotten the best-looking ones. It should be my turn, don't you think?"

"You've had plenty of good-looking men," Morgana muttered. "More than me, and you know it."

Paska grinned. "You're absolutely right. But that doesn't mean Donovan should wear a shirt."

Donovan laughed. "I'll be right back. I wouldn't want to distract you from plan-making, *brother*."

"Ouch," Paska said. "I regret everything I said about welcoming you to the family. You took what I said and made it weird."

Ten minutes later, Paska was pulling into the parking lot of the Pour House.

"Why here and not Ceri's? The board is there," Morgana asked.

"It's here now," Paska said. "Ceri refused to let anyone come there—something about not wanting to vomit all over us. Andy and Drew got the board and took it to the Pour House. It doesn't open until eleven today. It should be plenty of time."

"Have I been kicked off the group chat?" Morgana asked.

"Maybe if you shared your new phone number," Paska said.

"You have it. You could've added me back any time," Morgana pointed out. "And since I'm on my second new phone since leaving Oracle Bay, I didn't have anyone else's contact information. I've memorized your number, but I draw the line at remembering anyone else's."

"I don't know how you keep the fact that you're siblings a secret. You squabble like siblings," Donovan said as he opened the door.

"Not to mention it's an entire town of people who can see everything."

"Not everything," Paska said. "And you will do well to keep that information to yourself until such time as we *both* give you consent to share."

Donovan bobbed his head at Paska. "I'm not going to tell your secrets. I don't have a death wish." He winced and looked apologetically at Morgana. "Sorry."

"It's fine," she said, pushing down the fear she had of meeting her end. "I don't have a death wish, but it's not something any of us can escape forever."

"No point in talking about something we can't change," Paska said. "Let's go figure out what we can."

· · ★ ★ ★ ★ ★ ★ ★ · · ·

Morgana stared down at the charts Andy, Drew, Sandy, and Jezebel has spread out across the large communal table that was the centerpiece of the Pour House. Hazel and Misty hovered at the periphery, the former wide-eyed, and the latter practically vibrating with eagerness to share her plan.

With the additional information Jezebel had with Bridget's star chart and the rough positions of the planets when Morgana was born, the Fibonacci spiral that had been apparent when they'd first put everything together last year was broken.

"Bridget's chart, instead of complementing the rest of ours, breaks everything up," Jezebel said.

"She would break every one of us, then destroy the town and likely the whole peninsula out of spite," Morgana whispered. She didn't delve into the meaning with her sight but rather with centuries of experience of looking at divinations.

"But if we move you ninety degrees clockwise, see what happens?" Jezebel asked, shifting Morgana's chart. Sandy followed behind, ensuring the cards stayed in position except for Morgana's, Paska's, and Donovan's. "Your chart moves, which it would if the year you were born was off by a year or five, then you move. Donovan moves with you; his card is in orbit around you. And Paska moves, although I'm not entirely sure why." Jezebel looked at Paska but didn't say anything.

Maybe their relationship wasn't as secret as Paska thought it was.

"And when it all moves, that's when things start to look up!" Sandy took over the narrative, and Morgana was reminded of the last time they'd all worked together. What had she been thinking to ever try to do this alone? Hubris. Hubris and stupidity. "Bridget still barrels through everything, but now she… I'm not sure how to say this right, but she runs into you and Paska. But right behind you is —" Sandy pointed to the Empress card that signified Misty.

Misty walked forward. "And this is where it gets good," she says. "Because when Sandy redid the draw to make sure we were still all associated with the same cards, two were stuck together."

Sandy lifted the Empress card, and beneath it was The World.

Morgana's mouth fell open into an "O." "How is that possible?"

"I don't know yet," Sandy said with a helpless shrug. "I'll figure it out, but maybe we're not meant to have that answer right now. All I know is Misty is more now than success and energy. Before, I could see her ties to Oracle Bay, but now…"

"She's the world—or at least our world," Morgana said, finishing Sandy's sentence.

"It was weird at first," Misty said. "But since I accepted it, I can feel Oracle Bay running through me. It's more than a town. It was created by gods—I don't know which ones, so don't ask. Not just from one culture, either. Gods from all over came together to make this place here. Not Etruscan ones, though. Uni promises she knows nothing about it. Anyway, this town is old. Older than almost every-thing else in this area, and it is full of magic."

"It's much older than any of us," Paska said. "And its magic is almost beyond comprehension."

"Almost?" Morgana asked with raised eyebrows.

"Some of us are very wise. And by us, I mean Misty and me. She is the World, and she can channel the ancient magic." Paska smiled at Misty.

"Not perfectly," Misty admitted. "I need help, but I can do it."

"That's great," Donovan said. "But what do we do with it?"

Misty waved at Jezebel and Sandy again. This time, Jezebel took the lead. "Drew and Ceri know where she is and approximately when she'll arrive."

"We'll all know when she's here," Drew said wryly, speaking for the first time. "She's going to light the town on fire."

"Ordinarily, it'd be you and me fighting fire with fire and water," Paska said to Morgana. "But this time, we'll have to rely on the fire department. They're grateful for the million-dollar anonymous donation, by the way. Fortunately, there was a company manufacturing fire equipment that was enduring a hostile takeover, and they had to sell their overstock quickly."

"Hostile takeover? Hostile might be an exaggeration. I was very polite." Morgana smiled at Paska's snort of laughter and the surprised expressions that graced the rest of her friends' faces. "Okay. Fire. She said more than once she wanted to do that, so I'm not surprised you're seeing it."

"We're going to let the fire department put out magical fire with mundane equipment?" Drew asked.

"Who said it was mundane?" Paska asked.

Of course it wasn't. Her brother was terrifyingly thorough when he wanted to be.

"What's the rest of your plan?" she asked Misty.

"Drew and Ceri—if she's up to it—will stay here and scry, keeping us updated about Bridget's movements. You, me, Paska, and Donovan will be at the lighthouse. That's the best place for this. It's the easiest place for me to access the power of Oracle Bay, and it's far enough out of the main part of town that no one else should get hurt."

Morgana pursed her lips. Everything sounded reasonable, except... "Once she finds us and you've tapped into the deep, ancient well of magic that is this town, how do you use it? She does not care about anything. She would trigger the Cascadia fault if she thought it would help her win. It will be hard enough to keep her from destroying the world. How do we do that and defeat her?"

Misty bit her lip and looked over at the other psychics.

Paska grinned and rattled the bones in his pouch. "That's where I can help." He opened the pouch and tossed five long finger bones onto the table.

Four of them landed in what looked like equidistant positions from each other, and the fifth landed on Morgana's card.

"I'll bet if you get a compass, you'll find that the four landed on the cardinal directions," Paska said. "It's been like that every time I've thrown them. If I use more than five, it's the same, except the extra ones all gravitate towards the center—towards you. You and the elements are the keys."

"And I—or Oracle Bay, rather—am the lock," Misty said.

Ceri slid into one of the free chairs at the table and looked between Misty and Morgana. "This is either the beginning of a weird but strangely arousing porn movie, or you're ready to find out what happens when you open the door."

"You know my vote," Paska said. "But we can debate the cinematic merits of locks and keys later. Now's the time for a different kind of action." He gathered the bones up and returned them to their pouch, then held his hands out to Morgana and Misty. "It's time to go."

thirty

Morgana paced the length of the pier near the lighthouse as she had been for the last three hours. A stiff, cold breeze was coming in off the ocean, causing waves to break over the jetty and scuttling the few clouds that dotted the blue sky. She shivered with a chill that was half from the wind and half from fear.

Ceri and Drew had seen Bridget was in Astoria before they left the Pour House, and Jezebel's calculations put her arrival in Oracle Bay at noon. It'd been too long to wait at the lighthouse, but Morgana had been too tense to go anywhere else, no matter how suggestively Donovan had offered to help relieve her anxiety.

"I wish you'd sit down," Misty called from where she was perched on the metal railing at the end of the pier. "You're making me antsy."

"Well, I wish you'd pace with me," Morgana snapped. Her shoulders dropped, and she turned towards Misty. "Sorry. That was rude."

"It was, but I wasn't any more polite than you. I don't want to go into battle—again—but I'd rather be mid-fight than waiting." Misty hopped off the rail and walked towards Morgana.

The women leaned against the rail and looked down.

"At least neither of us are preparing for this by taking a nap," Misty said.

Paska cracked open one eye and glared up at the women. "Like I could sleep with all the pacing and jumping around." He closed his eyes again. "Sleeping before a battle is the best way to prepare. Being well-rested gives an advantage over any enemy, particularly one who's had to travel to you."

Morgana pursed her lips and looked down at him. "He's right, of course. But I've never been able to sleep before a fight."

"Not since the Battle of Heavenfield, when you decided to take my advice and ended up sleeping through the whole thing." Paska opened both eyes, then went from lying down to standing in one smooth movement that always made Morgana jealous.

Misty laughed. "You missed a whole battle?"

"I wouldn't have if someone had woken me up," Morgana groused.

"I'm not your alarm clock. And from the looks of things, you're not going to need one today." Paska pointed away from the lighthouse towards town. His entire body stiffened and vibrated for a moment.

A fireball was shooting through the air.

Morgana stood with her hand over her mouth and watched as it disappeared behind the buildings on the outskirts of town. Moments later, a loud boom reached them and flames shot up.

Misty moaned. "My town! I'd finally found a tenant for the wine shop, and now it's burning down."

Morgana glanced at her with interest before turning her attention back to the distant flames. "You can tell what's on fire?"

Misty nodded, tears streaming down her face. "It's already spreading. The empty building next door is catching."

Sirens rent the air as the fire department responded to the fire.

"At least it's empty buildings," Morgana said, slipping an arm around Misty.

"You're welcome, by the way," Paska said with a grumpy voice. "Do you know how hard it is to redirect a fireball into one of the three empty buildings in town when I can't even see them from here?"

Misty smiled at him through her tears. "Thank you, Paska. I'll make sure you get a special commendation from the town council."

"You are the town council," Paska said.

Morgana shrugged her shoulders. "I wish Donovan was here."

"He will be soon enough," Misty said.

Three phones beeped, indicating text messages. Misty pulled her phone out of her pocket and read the message aloud.

"It's from Jezebel. *'fire department on the job. Bridget just walked down main st all dramatically with like a cape of fire trailing behind her. D about to try to arrest her.'*"

"Wouldn't it be great if she just surrendered and let Donovan cuff her?" Misty asked. "If that's what happens, I'll give him a raise."

Morgana smiled tightly as her stomach twisted in knots. This was her least favorite part of the plan—using her boyfriend as bait. There were so many ways this could go wrong, and her mind was on a nonstop scroll through every single one, pausing on the ones where Bridget killed Donovan before he could say a word.

Their phones pinged again. Morgana pulled hers out of her pocket. It was Jez again.

Arrest did not work, but that bad witch is mad now. She's screaming something at him and just punched the weird redheaded guy that's with her.

Three dots blinked on and off at the bottom of the group text, and Morgana held her breath, waiting for the next update.

Your bf just turned into some kind of cat. Did you know that was going to happen?

Morgana bit her lower lip and responded. *It wasn't part of the plan.*

"I thought having a goat/goddess treat me like a daughter-in-law was weird, but a boyfriend who turns into a cat? That's next level,"

Misty said, reading over Morgana's shoulder. Her voice cracked with tension.

Morgana didn't answer, just waited for the next update—the one that would signal the plan was falling into place or tell them everything was falling apart. Relying on Bridget to take the bait and follow Donovan to the lighthouse felt like a long shot now that things were in motion, no matter how certain Ceri, Drew, and Jezebel had been that it would work.

He's running & she's chasing him. Get ready.

Morgana tucked her phone away and walked to the end of the pier with Misty at her side. Misty positioned herself between Morgana and the lighthouse and closed her eyes. Her face smoothed out, and she began to glow.

"Bridget is going to kick herself when she realizes what was right under her nose this entire time," Paska said at Morgana's shoulder. "Look at that woman. I've never seen one person channel so much power without blinking an eye, and this is with only a couple weeks of training. Imagine what she'll be able to do in a year."

"I hope we find out," Morgana murmured. She crouched down and unlaced her boots, then pulled them off. She balled up her socks and shoved them in the boots, then stepped off the wooden pier and into the rocky sand on the beach. The rough ground cut her feet and the ocean's waves lapped her ankles. The saltwater seeped into the cuts and her blood mingled with earth and water.

"I'll be on the lighthouse, ready to play my part." Paska waded towards her, took Morgana's face between his hands, and looked her in the eye. "Don't be a hero if you don't have to. There's no glory in dying in battle." He kissed her on the forehead, then rested his head against hers for a moment. He took a step back. "I love you, sister." He took rapid steps, then leapt into the air, turning from a man to a raptor in the blink of the eye.

Paska's merlin circled three times, then flew to the top of the lighthouse and perched to wait for Morgana's signal.

Morgana let the earth and water ground her body and center her mind. She opened herself completely to her elements and let the power cycle through her.

A large bobcat appeared on the edge of the road, running pell-mell towards them. He ran between Morgana and Misty, then skidded to a stop on the wet wood of the pier.

"Are you okay?" Morgana asked.

Before Donovan could shift back to his human form and answer, Bridget appeared. She looked like a middle-aged woman trying to cosplay Drew Barrymore in a low-rent version of Firestarter.

Morgana waited. For their plan to work, Bridget needed to commit completely to her attack, and if Bridget was going to commit, she needed to know she was going to win.

"Why won't you die?" Bridget screamed. The madness over-taking her was evident in more than her eyes and actions now. The fire storm that swirled around her burned her hair, and her aura was cracked and pulsing. Even without intervention, Bridget would prob-ably burn herself out within a few weeks. But if she wasn't going to take anyone else down with her, Morgana needed to stop her now.

Morgana didn't reply to Bridget. There'd be no intelligent conversation—or even satisfying taunting—from her now.

Instead, as soon as Bridget was close enough that Morgana could feel the first touches of heat from the flames, Morgana reached behind her and raised a hand. A stream of saltwater shot forward as if launched by a super soaker and hit Bridget in the face.

The blood witch's mouth opened and closed like a fish out of water.

That gave Morgana an idea. She asked the sea for a favor, and it delivered. The second pulse of water struck Bridget in the shoulder and knocked her over with a fish.

Bridget screamed in terror and scrambled backwards.

Morgana permitted herself a small smile before bracing herself from Bridget's inevitable return volley.

Bridget's attack was expected, but the force of the magically enhanced fire hitting her shields still knocked Morgana backwards.

She stumbled and landed on her butt in the ocean. Steam rose around her, and the smell of singed hair rose into the air. The fire had penetrated her shields enough to burn her hair, and the strength of the flames was heating the seawater.

Donovan was by her side in an instant, helping her back to her feet. As soon as she was steadied, he moved out of her way again. Now that he'd lured the witch to the lighthouse, his only job was to keep an eye on things, warn Morgana and Misty if something unexpected was happening, and be the communication point between the psychics at the lighthouse and those in town.

Morgana pulled the water forward again and shot it towards Bridget in a steady stream with the force of a firehose.

Bridget countered the water with a shield of fire. Steam hissed between them, and the air grew thick and translucent.

"What's Tom doing?" Morgana yelled. She'd lost sight of Bridget's warlock, and knowing his penchant for guns, didn't want him to be sneaking around anywhere.

"Ran off when you hit her with a fish," Donovan replied. "Andy's looking for him."

That was enough to erase that worry. Morgana returned all her attention to Bridget and sent another wave of water at her. This one fell short, barely splashing the blood witch. She was putting only the bare minimum of effort into her attacks—enough to look like she was trying, but not enough to deplete her resources. This was the feint, and she needed Bridget to take the bait, no matter how irritating it was feigning weakness.

"You've lost to me twice before, and you're going to lose this time!" Bridget screamed.

Morgana didn't bother correcting her—they were at a draw currently—but she wanted to.

The steady barrage of fireballs stopped suddenly, and the mist cleared. Morgana stopped her attack but didn't let her guard down.

Bridget smiled at her. "You think you're so clever, getting me to come out here and thinking you can distract me with your psychic friend? I'll show you who's clever!"

Morgana didn't wait for whatever show and tell Bridget had planned. She picked up a baseball sized rock from a small pile of them near her feet and pitched it at the witch.

The magically enhanced rock tore through Bridget's shields and hit her in the chest. Bridget collapsed.

For a second, Morgana let the hope that a lucky shot had ended it all before they'd had to implement the second part of their plan, but when Bridget got to her feet immediately, that hope disappeared.

The last vestiges of humanity and sanity disappeared from Bridget's face. She opened her mouth and screamed.

Glass shattered, and the remains of the lighthouse windows rained down.

Morgana clamped her hands over her ears, but they didn't block the sound. Tears streamed down her face. Out of the corner of her eye, she saw Misty kneeling on the ground with her head tucked under her arms and rocking.

The scream stopped as suddenly as it had started. Her ears were ringing, and the vibrations through the silence were as nauseating as the sound.

Morgana dropped her hands and looked at Bridget. The witch was covered in blood and standing in a pile of broken glass. Almost every piece of the windows had landed on her. Paska was very good.

Bridget smiled and held up her hands.

Morgana braced herself. It was almost time.

Bridget launched herself at Morgana, throwing magic ahead of her body, and leaving herself unshielded and open.

Morgana stepped backwards, trying to steady herself on the shifting ocean sand. As soon as Bridget was within arms' reach, Morgana grabbed the witch and yelled, "Now!"

Three things happened simultaneously.

Paska dropped out of the air in front of them, whipping up a gale around him.

Morgana encased Bridget in a column of rocks and mud, then reached out to Misty.

A gun went off, and a woman screamed.

There was a blankness in Morgana's mind where Mystic Greene was supposed to be waiting to fling open the power of Oracle Bay and destroy the witch once and for all.

thirty-one

A feral snarl snapped Morgana back to the present, and a bobcat ran past Morgana and Paska.

Without the town's ancient power to rip away the patchwork of magic Bridget had woven around herself, their victory was no longer guaranteed.

"I guess we're dying in battle after all," she said to Paska. The strain of holding Bridget encased in mud was draining her magic and doing nothing to weaken the trapped witch. She couldn't even suffocate the woman; the shields she'd snapped back up when Morgana had been distracted by Misty's disappearance were too powerful.

He shrugged, and the tornado he'd created widened until it encompassed the three of them. "I never wanted to be a hero, but it looks like I don't have a choice."

Morgana let go of the column, and the water and rock ran down Bridget and splashed at their feet.

Bridget looked around, taking in Paska and the whirlwind. "Who are you?" She sounded more curious than afraid.

Morgana swallowed against the fear she couldn't dispel.

Paska grinned at Bridget, and she shrank back a little. "I'm the man who's going to kill you."

Morgana fed water into the Paska's tornado until they were inside a waterspout. She sent whips of water dancing out to slice across Bridget's shields, ripping tiny holes that Bridget was repairing as fast as Morgana could make them.

Every once in a while, Morgana would pick up another baseball-sized rock and hurl it at the witch, but now that Bridget was channeling everything she had into defense instead of offense, nothing penetrated, and the waterspout was the only thing keeping the fire from destroying them and everything around them.

Morgana was getting tired, and although Paska had more stamina than she did, he was flagging as well.

The only way they were going to get through this was to take everything they had left, drop their shields, and use their magic to tear Bridget apart. Final strike.

Morgana met Paska's eyes, and he nodded.

She reached out and took his hand. Together, they faced Bridget. She'd tilted her head and was watching them curiously and without fear.

Morgana and Paska dropped their shields and simultaneously let go of the air and water encasing them.

Delight lit Bridget's eyes, and she clapped. "Is it time, then?"

The earth rolled under their feet, and Bridget and Paska both pitched forward.

Whatever else happened, Morgana had to keep Bridget from destabilizing the Cascadia Subduction Zone and creating devastation throughout the Pacific Northwest. Morgana reached deep into the earth and funneled her power and stability to the shifting plates.

Another miniature quake rocked her on her feet. This wasn't elemental magic—at least, not that she could detect. A slight smile appeared on her face. Oracle Bay was doing its part to help.

Morgana dropped her connection with the fault zone, pulled her athame from the sheath on her thigh, and walked towards Bridget.

Paska spared her a glance, and she saw the recognition in his eyes.

Morgana raised the blade above her head, and Paska dropped his arms, ending his attack.

Bridget took a step forward, sending a continuous stream of fire into Paska, and Morgana brought the blade down into Bridget's back, slicing through fire and skin.

Paska collapsed to the ground, and Bridget whirled around before the blade had the chance to complete the path to her heart and Morgana could send the rest of her energy through the obsidian and marble.

"When will you learn?" Bridget snarled, ripping the athame from Morgana's hands and threw it towards Paska's unmoving body. "You cannot defeat me with your stupid weapons. I have so much power now, and it's older and stronger than you and your stupid knife."

Morgana reached forward, touched Bridget's face, and opened herself up completely to her goddess and the town. Without Misty to channel the power of Oracle Bay, Morgana would burn herself out in seconds, but hopefully, seconds would be enough.

Pure golden energy ripped through Morgana, filling her with ecstasy she'd forgotten was possible in the hands of the universe. The light poured through Morgana and into Bridget.

The witch's eyes widened, and she opened her mouth, but no sound came out.

Morgana didn't let go—couldn't let go. She could feel her strength waning, but she would hold on until she had nothing left.

The burn of the power blinked out, then returned at a much lower level. Morgana gasped, first in relief, then in terror. She hadn't filtered enough into Bridget to guarantee her death yet, and if Morgana couldn't hold Oracle Bay's energy, that meant she was already dying. Bridget would win.

A hand on her shoulder straightened her spine.

Donovan was behind her, and in his arms, he held Misty.

Misty was pale. Blood oozed around a makeshift bandage on her shoulder, but she was alive and had pulled the magic of earth and water through the town, through her, intensifying its power and insulating Morgana from its raw fury.

Morgana reached out her hand and clasped Misty's.

They turned towards Bridget, and Morgana let the town take its revenge on the witch who'd killed women in its borders and tried to kill its very soul.

Bridget raised her hands above her head as if it would protect her, then collapsed on the ground.

Morgana didn't stop pouring the pure, raw magical fury into Bridget until Donovan squeezed her shoulder.

"She's dead," he said.

Morgana was shaking, but she didn't stop. "How can we be sure?" She couldn't look past Bridget's prone form to see her brother's body, or she'd break down, and she couldn't do that until Bridget was dead.

"Stop," Misty said. Her voice was shaky and weak.

"I can't," Morgana said. Tears streamed down her face. She held onto the power—held on to Misty and kept her from breaking their connection.

Something rammed her right hip, and Morgana fell forward. The impact of hitting the ground severed her tenuous hold on Misty's power.

Morgana cried. "It's not enough to make her pay for everything she's done. It'll never be enough." She rolled over and tried to stand but was stopped by a cloven hoof planted squarely in the middle of her chest.

"Don't hurt her, Billie," Misty said. "She's had a rough day."

"Billie?" Morgana repeatedly stupidly. "Are you...Uni?"

The goat bleated at her, and the weight of the hoof on her chest intensified.

"If Misty says she's okay, she's fine." Joseph walked into Morgana's field of vision and took Misty out of Donovan's arms. "Save your ass-kicking for my fiancée who ran out of the house this morning to put herself in mortal danger without telling me, got shot, and doubled down on the magical warfare." The goat gave Morgana a menacingly judgmental look and backed away to stand next to Joseph.

"Fiancée?" Misty whispered.

"I had a plan." Joseph shifted and raised the arm cradling Misty's head, then pointed a finger first at Morgana, then at Misty. He wrapped his arms tighter around Misty. His voice shook with barely suppressed emotion. "There was going to be romance and roses. I have a ring and was ready to get down on one knee. But that all got thrown out the window when Drew called to tell me you'd been shot at a little, and I should head to the lighthouse. Who gets shot a little?"

Morgana didn't hear Misty's response. She crawled over to Paska's body and picked up her athame. She turned around and stabbed Bridget over and over. If she couldn't burn her out with the power of Oracle Bay, she'd destroy her body so thoroughly it could never come back.

No one said anything or tried to stop her. Finally, when she could no longer raise her arm above her head and her choking sobs had turned into silent tears, she dropped the athame on the ground.

She turned towards her brother and gathered him into her arms.

He looked up at her, the light in his eyes dimming. He coughed, and blood appeared at the corner of his mouth.

"Did I ever tell you...?" His question broke, and he started coughing again.

"Shhh." Morgana placed a finger over his lips. "Save your strength. You're going to be just fine, but you need to stop talking." She didn't look down at his ruined chest where she knew she'd see his skin missing and his internal organs laid bare and smoking.

"No. Let me." He coughed again. Blood-flecked spittle spraying out. "Did I tell you I figured out the curse?"

Morgana's eyes widened. "You didn't," she whispered.

"So. Stupid." Paska's eyes drooped.

"You're not stupid," she said, stroking his face. "It's me. I was stupid. I fell in love."

He snorted. "I'm not stupid." His voice was a little stronger than it'd been a second ago. He opened his eyes. Maybe it was her imagination, but they looked a little clearer than they had a moment ago. "The curse was stupid."

He coughed again, then turned his head to one side and spat bloody phlegm onto the ground. "I hate dying," he muttered. "It's always so uncomfortable."

"What do you mean, you hate dying?" Morgana demanded. "You will not die, not if I have anything to do with it."

"I've died more times than I can count, and you have everything to do with why it never takes," Paska said. "Help me sit up, will you?"

"I don't think you..." Morgana's voice trailed off. The color was returning to his face, and when she looked down, she could no longer see into his chest cavity. His skin was still blackened and charred, but the burned area was dissipating with visible rapidity.

Her jaw dropped.

"What?"

"Help me sit up, grab my flask, and I'll explain everything." Paska's voice sounded as strong and cantankerous as ever.

Morgana helped him sit, and Donovan handed over the flask.

Paska drained the contents in three long swallows, then sighed in relief. "I'll explain everything, but there are a few things that need doing first. We need to dispose of the witch's body."

"If you can stand, we can do that now," Misty said. She was still glowing with the radiant light that had infused her when the battle started. Her shoulder was stained with blood, but there was no wound visible.

"It's good to be the physical manifestation of a well of ancient magic," she said with a shrug. Then she winced. "Still a little sore."

Morgana and Donovan helped Paska to his feet, although it was a possibility the unsteadiness was related more to the large amount of alcohol he'd just consumed rather than any lingering effects of his not-quite-mortal wound.

Bridget's body was covered with the blood from dozens of stab wounds and barely recognizable as human.

"It was the elements, older than anything she could have stolen, that allowed us to defeat her," Morgana said. "And it is to the elements she needs to return. Her soul cannot be allowed to move on to the next life."

Misty reached out her hands on either side of her. Morgana took her left hand and Paska's right. The three of them stood over Bridget's body. Earth and water, fire and air, connected to the spirit of this place.

Bridget's body slowly broke apart and began to disintegrate.

A thread of what almost looked like nearly translucent smoke rose from where her body had been. Misty dropped Morgana's and Paska's hands, reached out, and grabbed the smoke.

Misty and the thread burned brighter and brighter until Morgana had to close her eyes. When the painful brightness no longer shone through her closed eyelids, Morgana opened them again.

Misty was no longer glowing, and the ground at their feet was covered with red and orange poppies.

"Is it done?" Morgana asked.

Misty nodded, then shuddered. "Oracle Bay shredded her soul even more than you tore up her body. There's nothing left of her to be reborn."

"Good job, girl," Paska said. He clapped a heavy hand on her shoulder. "Now, why don't you go find your farmer and his meddlesome goat and make him give you that ring? You know where we'll all be tonight when you're ready to put your clothes back on and celebrate with your friends."

Misty blushed, then grinned. "Thank you, Paska. I wouldn't have been able to do this without you."

"No, you wouldn't have," he agreed easily. "But you're a talented student. See you later."

Once Misty walked away, Morgana stepped backwards into the warmth of Donovan's body.

"What happened to Tom?" she asked.

Donovan grinned, and his brown eyes glinted gold in the afternoon sun. "I tore a chunk out of his side, then the demon flew down, ripped Tom in half, and flung him into the ocean. I think we won't be seeing him again for a while."

"Good," Paska said. "Now, let's get out of here. I need a drink, and it's time we divested ourselves of the weight of centuries of secrets."

Hazel slid a bottle of wine and a wineglass across the table to Morgana, then set down her tray and unloaded four pitchers of pale ale and a dozen pint glasses onto the table. Donovan and Drew started filling glasses and passing them around.

Morgana poured a glass of wine and leaned back into the corner. Donovan was on her right, talking animatedly to Sandy's partner Vincent about responsible real estate development. Sandy and Jezebel were oohing over Misty's giant emerald ring. Drew's fiancé Bill and Joseph were planning their next karaoke duet. Ceri was on Morgana's other side, leaning her head against Andy's shoulder and absently rubbing her abdomen.

Hazel returned with another tray, this one with water glasses, then sat on one of the open chairs. "Zeke says he'll keep an eye on stuff and that I'm fired for the night," she said, grabbing one of the pale ales.

"We'll need to expand the alcove if you psychics keep collecting weirdos," Andy groused. He accepted a glass of beer and took a long drink.

Ceri took a water, then got up, slid by Andy, and moved to a chair as far away from Morgana as was possible. "Sorry, Morgana. Elaine hates the smell of wine."

Morgana's eyes widened at hearing her daughter's name, and she blinked back the tears that formed. "There is no need to apologize. I want you to be comfortable."

"You should have said something earlier," Paska said. He grabbed the open bottle of wine and jogged out of the alcove.

"He is going to be at least as bad as Andy, isn't he?" Ceri asked, looking at Morgana.

Paska returned with a bag of ginger candy and plunked it down in front of Ceri.

Morgana raised her eyebrows at him, and he nodded. As he'd said, it was past time to stop keeping secrets.

"I suspect so. He's never had a child, but I remember how he was when I was pregnant. He was worse than my husband." A soft smile stole over Morgana's face. Gareth's face was faded in her memory, but the memory of the love they'd shared still burned strong. "He's an amazing uncle."

There were a few gasps of surprise, mostly from the mundane members of their little group—the partners of the psychics who had become her friends.

"You're siblings?" Drew asked. "How did I not see this?" He glared at Ceri. "You knew, didn't you? You knew, and you didn't tell me?"

Ceri took one of the ginger candies out of the bag and popped it into their mouth. "It wasn't my secret to tell."

"There were reasons we kept it a secret," Morgana said. "A lot of it was habit. There were centuries when we didn't want anyone to know we were related. Every person at this table, regardless of age, has a secret, and this was just one of ours. And just because we've decided to share this, doesn't mean you get to know everything. I'm not telling you our original names, but I will tell you about Elaine."

Paska took the seat Ceri had vacated and held out his hand.

Morgana took his hand and squeezed. "Elaine was my daughter, and nearly sixteen hundred years ago, when Elaine was seventeen, Vortigern, the king Paska and I worked for and Paska's best friend, did something that resulted in Elaine's death."

"I killed him," Paska said. "I greeted him as a brother and stabbed him in the back for what he'd done. And with his dying breath, he laid a curse on us. And it's that curse that kept us apart from everyone for so long."

Ceri leaned forward. "Did you figure it out? Did you get the right answers?"

Paska nodded. "I did, but it took Morgana asking Vortigern a stupid question last month for me to figure out the answer."

Vincent raised his hand. "This might be another stupid question, but if you killed him in the early fifth century, how was he answering questions last month?"

Paska favored Sandy's fiancé with a nod. "That's not a stupid question. There are no stupid questions, only stupid people."

"But you just said Morgana asked…" Jezebel's question trailed off with a sort of laughter. "God, you really are siblings, aren't you? I don't know how we didn't see it before."

Morgana grinned to herself. Paska might be committed to a new era of transparency and honesty, but he'd sidestepped Vincent's question with a smooth avoidance that'd taken centuries to master.

"As I was saying, Morgana asked a stupid question. We had the opportunity to learn how to defeat Bridget, but she wanted to know how to break the curse so she could get down and dirty with—" Paska paused and looked at Donovan.

"My boyfriend," Morgana said, putting a possessive hand on Donovan's leg.

"Everyone either saw me or read about it in the group chat," Donovan said. "I have a type of earth magic that allows me to absorb the traits of animals. It's inherited through my mother's side. But my father's family are shifters of a sort. Cat shifters."

Drew leaned forward. "Please, please tell me you can turn into an adorable kitten and come figure out what's going on with Tuppence Beresfurred or Hercule Purrot. There's something not-quite-normal about them, not least of which is they are still kittens. I've had them for over a year, and they are just as squee-inducingly cute and maddeningly evil as they were the day I found them in a box on my porch."

"I'll see what I can do," Donovan promised. "But now, before Paska steers us down another road so he doesn't actually have to tell us anything real..."

Twelve pairs of eyes turned to Paska. Morgana watched her brother puff out his chest and preen a bit under their attention. The old magician always loved to be the center of attention.

"Vortigern lay a death curse on us, and death curses are the hardest to break. For over one and a half millennia, we lived knowing that if either of us fell in love, we would die. Both of us. And neither of us wanted to be responsible for the other's death, so we stayed away from anything more than casual relationships that wouldn't result in anything more than mild fondness."

"Neither of you have been in love, like ever?" Jezebel asked, horrified awe staining her voice.

Morgana squeezed Donovan's thigh harder than she meant to, then backed off when he winced. "I was in love with my husband. He died when I was in my early thirties. Elaine died days later. I haven't stayed anywhere long enough to even have friends since then, much less fall in love."

"I was in love in my first lifetime, too," Paska said. "But he betrayed my family, caused my niece's death, and I killed him."

Before anyone could say anything intended as comforting, Morgana elbowed her brother. "Now you're trying to make everyone feel even more sorry for you than they did before you even started telling secrets. The curse, old man."

Paska looked down at her, his eyes bright with unshed tears, and stuck his tongue out. "Very right, then. The curse." He drained his glass. "I think I need to get a refill before I continue."

Four pint glasses were pushed in front of him before he even set his down.

Paska started laughing and held up his hands. "Fine. When Morgana asked Vortigern how to break the curse, he replied that we'd never figure it out in time, and that the answer 'usually comes at the beginning and not the end.' Then Morgana, bloodthirsty witch that she is, said it's a lot easier to break a curse when you can kill the one who cast it, and that it's hard to kill someone who's already dead. Then, she ditched Jezebel who was going to drive her to the airport and disappeared to Europe for a week."

"Paska, how long did it take you to figure out how to break the curse after we had tea with Ceri that morning?" Morgana asked.

"You hadn't even left London for Portugal yet." Paska grinned, unrepentant smugness on his face.

"Tell. Me. How," Morgana said through gritted teeth.

Paska pulled out the leather pouch he wore around his waist, dumped out the bones, and then reached under his chair, producing a large, black box.

"There are going to be more bones in there, aren't there?" Jezebel said.

"As long as the only bit of the dead guy's skin we have to see is that pouch, I can handle a few bones," Sandy said.

"Dead guy's skin?" Vincent asked. "And those are real bones?"

"You need to share more with your fiancé," Drew said. "And Paska definitely needs to share less with all of us."

Paska pulled out the charred pieces of the jawbone he'd shattered, placed it, along with the finger bones and the leather pouch on a stone tray he produced, and looked at it. "This is everything that's left of Vortigern. I kept these pieces because I am a terrible person who wanted to be reminded every day of how much he made me suffer, made Morgana suffer, and because I loved him so very much and needed to have something of him with me to remind me that I had once been worthy of a great love.

"When I killed him, he cursed us, but he was sloppy, and I was foolish. He said, 'I curse you and—'" Paska looked sideways at Morgana, then continued smoothly "'—Morgana to be bound to one another, undying, until the love that is between you now is broken by another. When that love is gone, all you've held on to will crumble, and your lives will move on.'"

Paska looked around the room, a smug smile on his face. Morgana stared at him. "I don't understand how that's sloppy. Once love comes between us, our lives will move on. That's happened. We're going to die."

"Ah ha!" Paska held up a finger. "The original language was even more vague and obscure than this, but we misinterpreted it from the beginning. The love that was between us wasn't *our* love. It was the love between Vortigern and me. I would have done anything for him —*did* many things I wasn't proud of for him—and I've held onto him all this time. It wasn't you falling in love with Donovan that broke the love—or rather, the lover—who was between us. It was both of us coming here, making friends, and finally letting go of the past."

"And the answer is found in the beginning and not the end?" Morgana asked. "What did that mean?"

"The Breton word for beginning is nearly the same as it is for island. He and I met on Anglesey, and that's where I fell in love with him."

"This is pretty sketchy," Ceri said. "Are you sure?"

"As sure as I've been about anything. Once I connected everything to the island, it fell into place, and the runes I cast—not using my usual bones—confirmed it. He was what was between us all this time, and now I'm ready to let him go."

"Wait!" Donovan said. "What will happen to you? Are you going to die?"

"I don't think so," Paska said.

"That does not fill me with confidence," Morgana said.

"It's more likely that our lives will move on, free of the fear he bound us with. It probably means we can die now, so more care will need to be taken." Paska grinned at her. "Trust me."

Morgana smiled back. "With my life, as always."

Paska cupped his hands over the stone covered in bones until a tiny ball of fire appeared in his palms. Then, he placed it in the tray of bones and leather. The fire flared brightly for a moment, then disappeared. The bones and leather pouch were gone, and with it, the curse bindings that had laid on them for so long.

Morgana straightened in her seat, lighter than she ever remembered feeling. "I feel almost...effervescent. Freer than I have since before my Elaine died. Thank you." She reached over and hugged Paska hard, then turned to Donovan. "I cannot wait for what comes next. I've been living in fear of feeling too much for so many years, and now I can let go."

"You've had a family this entire time," Paska pointed out.

Morgana reached behind her and put her hand over his mouth. "Shut up, Paska." Then she pulled Donovan's face down to hers and kissed him with everything she had.

She might have kept kissing him even further past the bounds of public propriety if a commotion in the main bar hadn't interrupted them.

Andy was on his feet and pushing through the group immediately. He stopped in the doorway, and his wings popped out, spilling one of the remaining pitchers of beer.

"What is it?" Ceri asked. She stood and wormed her way under his arm. "Oh my god."

Andy's wings disappeared, and he took a step forward.

Morgana leaned forward. Russell was standing in front of Andy and Ceri, but she couldn't see anything else. Then Russell took a step back, and Brandy came into view.

"Hey," she said, not quite meeting anyone's eyes. "I was wondering if I could get my job back."

· · · · ⋆ ★ ⋆ · · · ·

THANK YOU SO MUCH FOR READING! I HOPE YOU ENJOYED MORGANA'S stories. (I don't think this is the last you'll see of her!)

I'd appreciate it so much if you'd head over and review Elements of Surprise! Reviews mean so, so much to authors.

Stay tuned for news of the next Psychics of Oracle Bay novel - Dead Giveaway - and learn more about Russell's life and Brandy's afterlife.

want more amy cissell?

And why wouldn't you?

Love it, hate it, somewhere in between? Please leave a review for Belle of the Ball at Goodreads, Bookbub, or your favorite online retailer.

Links to all retails sites are at:
https://books2read.com/Elements of Surprise

Reviews are always appreciated & allow me to keep writing what you love!

Sign up for Cissell's Epistles at https://amycissell.com for new release updates, exclusive content, and a bevy of book recommendations! (You'll also get to choose a free book as a thank you for hanging out!)

Come hang out in my Facebook Reader Group - the Amyzonians can always use another shenaniganator. (It's a word. Promise.)

https://www.facebook.com/groups/amycissellauthor/

Join my patreon - https://www.patreon.com/ACissellWrites - for early access to books, free copies of my digital books, free paperbacks, and access to my entire back catalog!

* * * ★ ★ ★ ★ ★ ★ * * *

what to read next!

If this was your first dip into the Amy Cissell pool (does that sound weird?) and you're ready to dive in, there are a couple choices for you!

Midlife Magic in Eden Valley is a complete paranormal women's fiction romance series (4 novels & 4 novellas) All the protags in the novels are 40+. (And, in the case of our MC from book 4, much, much, much over 40.)

Eden Valley is an idyllic town set on the edge of a picturesque lake in the eastern Cascades of Washington State. Every summer throngs of tourists flock to the high elevation town to escape the heat, but not everyone flocks back home.

Eden Valley is not quite right, and one of the biggest tells is that no one in Eden Valley knows that anythings amiss.

Raising a Demon - the first in series - is the story of Evie & Lily. Evie is a 40-something single mom to her almost-too-precocious 10 year old. She has great friends, fantastic parents, and that aforementioned maddening but delightful child. And then... (see what I mean about those 'and thens'?) She catches her kid in the woods with a Ouija board, demon tome, and some text cribbed from Supernatural.

Next thing she knows, her world's been turned upside down when Lily's demon summoning accidentally brings Luc - Evie's summer fling from 11 years ago and Lily's dad - back to town.

In addition to the four main novels, there are also four novelitas.

Recommended reading order for Midlife Magic in Eden Valley is:

- *Raising a Demon* (novel set in ~2021)
- *Match Made in Hell* (novella set in ~2010)
- *Devil and the Deep, Blue Lake* (novel set in ~2022)
- *Fall From Grace* (novella set in early 70s)
- *Valley of Angels* (novel set in ~2022)
- *Hell's Bells* (novella set in ~2022)
- *Guardian of Eden* (novel set in ~2023)
- *Devil May Care* (novella set ~35 years later)

Midlife Magic in Eden Valley, Psychics of Oracle Bay, and **Vamps in the Vineyard** are in the same universe, and there are some crossover characters and cameos!

An Eleanor Morgan Fantasy Adventure is a 7-book series (complete) of contemporary fantasy books. Eleanor is in her mid-30s and is living a perfectly ordinary life. And then... (there's always a "and then") She finds out she was a changeling child - one left on the doorstep of a human couple by the Fae. And her quest is to reopen the gates between Earth & the Fae plane which will help bring balance back to both worlds, but maybe at the cost of destroying herself and everything she's ever known.

The Cardinal Gate is the first in this series. Eleanor definitely has a lot more swearing, violence, and explicitly naked sexy times. There are witches and vampires and zombies and dragons and werewolves. Lots of snark. Lots of adventure. And a few broken hearts along the way. Romance isn't the main theme, but there is definitely some of that going on.

I love me some Eleanor... But, if you ask some of the other people who've hung out with her, she pales in comparison to Raj, the sexy AF vampire who can't talk without flirting and Florence, Eleanor's (don't call her Ellie) bff who may or may not have had an entire secret life in the 60s & 70s...but don't ask too many questions.

You can get each of the books separately, of course, but they're also available in two box sets (alas, ebook only!).

Last but not least (except in the number of books published in the series), **Vamps in the Vineyard**.

Vamps in the Vineyard is a spinoff of **Midlife Magic in Eden Valley** set in Charlie's winery near Chelan on the eastern side of the Cascade Mountains. There's a prequel novella that takes place after the events in Hell's Bells but before Here to Slay called *Stakes and Stems* and another novella - *Slay Bells Ring* - set after the events of Here to Slay. Both novellas are currently available to newsletter subscribers only.

raising a demon

MIDLIFE MAGIC IN EDEN VALLEY #1

Raising a Demon is the first book in Midlife Magic in Eden Valley, a magical new paranormal women's fiction series. Eden Valley & Oracle Bay are in the same universe, and there are some crossover characters and cameos!

Being a single mother has its challenges, but Evie never imagined that "the talk" would involve Ouija boards and pentagrams.

Evelyn Addams is forty-three and fabulous. She has a great kid, fantastic friends, and doesn't need a man to complete her. But when she catches ten-year-old Lily summoning a demon to ask for birthday wishes—and the demon who turns up is Evie's summer fling from eleven years ago—her comfortable life is shattered.

Reuniting with an old flame is tricky enough but finding out he grows horns and a tail makes a romantic reconnection downright complicated. And when Lily is kidnapped by her newfound grandfather, the last shred of her old life is destroyed, and everything goes to hell.

Will Evie and her friends rescue Lily from hell before the lights go out and the lost souls come out to play? And can she ignore past and Luc's family complications to take a second chance on love and learn how to raise a demon's daughter? Get your copy of Raising a Demon today!

http://www.books2read.com/raisingademon

acknowledgments

Mad love to the Amyzonians—my Facebook reader group—you guys are fantastic. Thanks for liking and sharing my posts, reading and reviewing, staying engaged with me, and voting on all my weird polls.

My child, my heart, Liana. I love your "story" and listening to you grow as a story-teller; makes me feel like maybe I got at least one thing right. Being your mama is hard AF, but I can't imagine having any other child. Love you to infinity +1 and back.

Thank you to my editor Suzanne Lahna. Working with you was such an amazing experience. Thanks for caring about Morgana's story and working so hard to make it better.

Christopher—my line editor, proofreader, business partner, fellow author, and probably even more importantly, husband—thank you for giving me "permission" to step back and take a breath when I get too overwhelmed with life, the universe, and everything.

I wouldn't be the author I am now without everyone who's supported me along the way. This time, I'm stepping into the way-back machine and pulling out the people who were there for me when I was hella younger. Diane Hoines - my high school English teacher and possibly the only teacher who really liked me (or at least could pretend) at school. High school friends who never told me to dream smaller - Shanda (maybe someday we can resurrect our co-written story about Destiny and Daphne, amnesia, attempted murder, and intrigue) to great critical acclaim! Megan - remember when you were gonna be a rock star? Turns out you already are! And of course Julie - I'm so glad you came into my life and even gladder (it's a word, I'm a writer) you married my first boyfriend. For realsies.

Melodie - you stand as the best boss - almost 30 years on now. I am so pleased we've stayed in Facebook touch!

And "This is My Life" rewind would be complete without acknowledging my college besties. Steph, Sara, Marcy & I spent one memorable spring break in Winnipeg where I cemented my legend, not by writing, but by doing a little dance. You ladies are amazing AF. Thank you.

amy cissell - i spell trouble

Amy can be found on most social media channels @acissellwrites. Come visit her website at amycissell.com for blogs & books! (autographed copies, if you want!)

Amy Cissell is a USA Today Bestselling Author of urban fantasy and paranormal romance novels. She lives in Portland, OR with her husband, her haunted house-obsessed daughter, their three cats, and the murder of crows she's conspiring to turn into her vengeful army.

When she's not working or writing, she's sleeping because that's all she has time to do! There are few things Amy loves more than a well-timed pun, a good book, a glass of wine, and time at the Oregon Coast.

Although she reads anything and everything, her first love is fantasy. Eleven-year-old Amy discovered fantasy when she 'borrowed' her father's copy of The Hobbit and an enduring love affair (mostly with dragons) was born.

facebook.com/acissellwrites

instagram.com/acissellwrites

bookbub.com/authors/amy-cissell

goodreads.com/acissellwrites

tiktok.com/@acissellwrites

patreon.com/ACissellWrites

also by amy cissell

Paranormal Romance

Psychics of Oracle Bay

Not in the Cards (October 2018)

First Hand Knowledge (November 2018)

Wing and a Prayer (January 2019)

Belle of the Ball (December 2019)

Hell and High Water (June 2022)

Tempest in a Teapot (April 2023)

Elements of Surprise (April 2023)

Dead Giveaway (2024)

Bad to the Bones

Shoot for the Stars

Fun and Prophet

Box Sets (ebook only)

Seeing is Believing in Oracle Bay (Books 1-4)

Paranormal Women's Fiction

Midlife Magic in Eden Valley

(complete series)

Raising a Demon (June 2021)

Devil and the Deep, Blue Lake (September 2021)

Valley of Angels (November 2021)

Guardian of Eden (February 2022)

Eden Valley World Novellas

Match Made in Hell (June 2021)

Hell's Bells (December 2021)

Fall From Grace (January 2022)

Devil May Care (February 2022)

Box Sets

Welcome to Eden Valley (Novellas 1-4)

Vamps in the Vineyard

Here to Slay (September 2022)

Vamps in the Vineyard Novellas

(newsletter subscribers only)

Stakes and Stems (September 2023)

Slay Bells Ring (January 2023)

Contemporary/Urban Fantasy

An Eleanor Morgan Fantasy Adventure

(complete series)

The Cardinal Gate (February 2017)

The Waning Moon (June 2017)

The Ruby Blade (October 2017)

The Broken World (March 2018)

The Lost Child (June 2019)

The Iron River (May 2020)

The Dark Throne (February 2021)

Box Sets (ebook only)

Eleanor Morgan Books 1-4

Eleanor Morgan Books 5-7

* * * * * ★ ★ ★ ★ * * *

Ghosts of Valhalla

As Yet Untitled (late 2023)

* * * * * ★ ★ ★ ★ * * *

9 781949 410983